Russian Royals of Kuban

Commanding princes unlace the ladies of London!

Princes Nikolay, Illarion, Ruslan and Stepan were once the toasted royalty of Kuban, renowned for their daring exploits. Now, banished and distanced from their titles, they've arrived in London— where balls and carriage rides take precedence over swordsmanship, revolution and battle...

But in this new and unknown city, they're about to encounter women the likes of whom they've never encountered before. These ladies have resisted the rakes of London—but these princes are about to embark on the most alluring of seductions...

Read Nikolay and Klara's story in

Compromised by the Prince's Touch

Available now!

Read Illarion and Dove's story in

Innocent in the Prince's Bed

Available next month!

And look out for Ruslan's and Stepan's stories— coming soon!

Author Note

Let's play True and False: What's real in Nikolay's story?

True: Kuban is a real region in Russia—it encompasses Sochi where the Winter Olympics were held. However, there was never a "kingdom" or king like the one featured in this series.

True: The region of Kuban was indeed "settled" by Russia in the mid to late 1700s in order to provide a buffer between the Ottoman Empire and Russia and to reclaim the Crimea for Russia. These efforts were stimulated by the 1768–1774 Russo-Turkish war.

True: A large part of the population that settled the area were Cossacks from nearby regions.

True: The Cossacks were/are known for their "trick" riding abilities in battle.

True: Both rebellions cited in Nikolay's story took place. The 1825 revolt Nikolay is tempted to join did occur and was unsuccessful.

True: The rebellions were led by officers and there were connections inside the palace. The Union of Salvation was a real secret society throughout Russia.

False: There is no historic proof that Britain, private or otherwise, financed or supported the rebellion. The arms dealer subplot is my own addition. However, members of the Union had what is historically described as "British ideals" regarding government and industrialization.

True: Soho was an immigrant neighborhood in early nineteenth-century London, as were the squares where Nikolay establishes his riding academy.

I hope you enjoy Nikolay and Klara's tale set against this backdrop of the real and the imagined!

www.bronwynnscott.com

www.bronwynswriting.blogspot.com

BRONWYN SCOTT

---

*Compromised by
the Prince's Touch*

HARLEQUIN® HISTORICAL

Recycling programs
for this product may
not exist in your area.

ISBN-13: 978-1-335-52255-9

Compromised by the Prince's Touch

Copyright © 2017 by Nikki Poppen

All rights reserved. Except for use in any review, the reproduction or utilization of this work in whole or in part in any form by any electronic, mechanical or other means, now known or hereinafter invented, including xerography, photocopying and recording, or in any information storage or retrieval system, is forbidden without the written permission of the publisher, Harlequin Enterprises Limited, 225 Duncan Mill Road, Don Mills, Ontario M3B 3K9, Canada.

This is a work of fiction. Names, characters, places and incidents are either the product of the author's imagination or are used fictitiously, and any resemblance to actual persons, living or dead, business establishments, events or locales is entirely coincidental.

This edition published by arrangement with Harlequin Books S.A.

For questions and comments about the quality of this book, please contact us at CustomerService@Harlequin.com.

® and TM are trademarks of Harlequin Enterprises Limited or its corporate affiliates. Trademarks indicated with ® are registered in the United States Patent and Trademark Office, the Canadian Intellectual Property Office and in other countries.

Printed in U.S.A.

www.Harlequin.com

Bronwyn Scott is a communications instructor at Pierce College in the United States, and is the proud mother of three wonderful children—one boy and two girls. When she's not teaching or writing, she enjoys playing the piano, traveling—especially to Florence, Italy—and studying history and foreign languages. Readers can stay in touch on Bronwyn's website, bronwynnscott.com, or at her blog, bronwynswriting.blogspot.com. She loves to hear from readers.

Books by Bronwyn Scott

Harlequin Historical
and Harlequin Historical *Undone!* ebooks

Scandal at the Midsummer Ball
"The Debutante's Awakening"
Scandal at the Christmas Ball
"Dancing with the Duke's Heir"

Russian Royals of Kuban

Compromised by the Prince's Touch

Wallflowers to Wives

Unbuttoning the Innocent Miss
Awakening the Shy Miss
Claiming His Defiant Miss
Marrying the Rebellious Miss

Rakes on Tour

Rake Most Likely to Rebel
Rake Most Likely to Thrill
Rake Most Likely to Seduce
Rake Most Likely to Sin

Visit the Author Profile page
at Harlequin.com for more titles.

For Joe and Alexis and the staff at Aleron
who have all made us feel so welcome
in our daughter's horse world.

Chapter One

London—late winter, 1823

St John the Divine was entirely wrong about the end of the world. Prince Nikolay Baklanov had, in the last hour, arrived at a revelation of his own: the four horsemen of the Apocalypse weren't men armed with swords at all, but, in fact, four young ladies, armed with formidable matchmaking mamas who would give those swords a run for sharpness. He was quite convinced, as he barked at Miss Ransome for the third time to get deep into the corners on her turns, that the world as he knew it would not be done in by widespread warfare and pestilence, but by the trampling to death of his patience over the course of several Thursday afternoons as the girls sawed on their horses' mouths and disregarded his oft-repeated instructions.

'Heels down, Miss Edgars, or you'll come off your mount's back at the slightest jolt! Miss Kenmore, remember the left-shoulder rule, unless you want a collision with Miss Ransome!' He shouted orders from the centre of Fozard's arena, home to one of London's elite riding schools. But there was nothing elite about the skill of the four young misses trotting around him.

Make that three.

'Miss Calhoun, why in heaven's name have you stopped?'

'My horse stopped, not I.' The spoiled chit tossed glossy curls from beneath an expensive stovepipe hat and gave him a pout that had no doubt been practised far longer than her riding skills.

'You are the master here, Miss Calhoun.' Nikolay clung to the shreds of his patience. Surely their requisite hour was nearly up? Then just one more lesson for the day. Who would ever have imagined teaching four girls to ride was more difficult than marshalling an entire regiment?

'But…' Miss Calhoun began to whine. His temper flared.

But? She dared to argue with him? He, who was a Prince of Kuban? He, who had led and trained the Kubanian cavalry? A man who excelled on horseback? Nikolay raised his voice, overriding her excuses. 'No buts, Miss Calhoun. Set your horse in motion or I will do it for you!' The last was met with a significant amount of shocked rustling in the spectators' gallery where the girls' mothers and maids sat in vigilant attendance. He knew what they were debating in their heated whispers—the merits of questioning him for his harsh tone. Was it worth the risk of alienating him? Or did they allow him to scold Miss Calhoun in the hopes of securing his attentions?

He did not fool himself. That's what they were here for: attentions, affections. It was what all his female pupils were here for, well-bred daughters of the British peerage, angling to snare a foreign prince, even one in exile from a place most had never heard of seemed to suffice, never mind that he wouldn't be accepting any of those offers. He'd been in London for two months, since the Christmas holidays, and business at Fozard's had increased exponentially—quite a feat considering much of London society was still in the country. The rustling ceased. The jury of mamas had decided to let his tone pass.

'All right, ladies, that's enough for today. Walk your mounts and then hand them off to the grooms.' He strode towards the door, his words as rapid as his pace. If he exited fast enough, he could escape making polite small talk with the mothers before his next lesson. He headed for the private instructors' lounge and slipped inside, breathing a bit easier. It was his first piece of luck all day.

'Hoy, Nik. I see you survived the Misses Four.' Peter Crenshaw, one of the other instructors, looked up from cleaning tack.

'Barely. I've got one more and then I'm done.' Done with this day that had started badly and gone downhill from there. The morning had begun with Lady Marwood slipping a key into his pocket with a note, making it explicitly clear she was more interested in riding *him* than the lovely bay mare her besotted older husband had purchased for her last week at Tattersall's. That was how the day started and the Four Horsewomen of his personal Apocalypse had ended it. What he wouldn't give for a strapping lad who could jump something.

Peter gave him a wry look. 'You can always quit. You don't have to put up with the girls or any of it.' Nikolay didn't miss the edge of envy beneath Peter's words. Peter needed to work. Peter depended on the income. He was a half-pay officer in an army going nowhere.

Nikolay shrugged. 'What would I do with my days if I didn't come here?' He needed to work, too, but perhaps for a different reason than Peter. The income wasn't the issue. The scheduling of his days was. A year ago, he'd been a high-ranking officer in the Kubanian military. He'd spent his days out of doors on the parade grounds schooling cavalry units, leading manoeuvres. He'd spent his nights at palace revels, consorting with the loveliest women Kuban had to offer; waltzing, flirting, engaging in an *affaire* or two when the whimsy took him. Political calamity had changed that, or at least part of that. True, he still revelled at night. London, even out of the Season, wasn't much different from Kuban's glittering court and there were still women aplenty available for pleasure of the physical kind, just the way he liked it, with no strings attached. But his days had suffered. Oh, how they'd suffered.

He'd kept with his old military habit of rising early, only to discover London gentlemen rarely rose before eleven. He'd taken to walking the streets and parks, watching the town rise. He'd spent his 'mornings'—a term he used loosely since they seemed to occur briefly between eleven and two—conducting the business of resettlement: establishing accounts, garnering memberships to clubs, settling his horses. All of which was handled efficiently and quickly with little effort from him. He'd spent his afternoons sightseeing with his comrades from Kuban, the friends who had fled with him. But when that was done? When all the pieces were in place to 'begin' living the London life? How did he spend his time then?

He'd found himself at a constant loose end. No wonder English gentlemen rose so late in the day. There was nothing to do, nothing to look forward to. So, he'd come here to Fozard's, a place with horses, a place where he knew how to live—to some degree. He was painfully aware the parallel was not exact. He was a trainer of disciplined men, not spoiled girls. But it would do until he figured out who he was in this new life and what he wanted to be. It was a question which haunted him not a little these days. He'd been in England nearly a year and he still had no answer. His hopes of starting his own riding academy were still just hopes.

Nikolay picked up the file with his last client's information in it. He scanned it once and then twice, the second time more slowly, more carefully, the hairs on his neck prickling at the name: one Miss Klara Grigorieva, a diplomat's daughter. Another

'Miss', of course, because that was how his luck had run today. There was the immediate concern of her riding ability, which was probably negligible. He could only imagine how ill-suited to the saddle she would be. Diplomats' daughters knew how to host afternoon tea parties and evening dinners. They might even speak a language or two and converse on a variety of subjects. But they were not equestrians. Even so, it wasn't only that which had his neck hair prickling. It was that she was a *Russian* girl; Klara Grigorieva was the Russian ambassador's daughter, which, on the surface, made it easy to see why she'd been paired with him. What Fozard's couldn't know was the suspicion such a pairing provoked for him. Did this pairing have more sinister undertones? Had she been sent to smoke him out? Was Kuban hunting him at last? He snapped the folder shut. He wouldn't have any answers standing here. It was four o'clock. Showtime.

Only he couldn't find her. She wasn't in the waiting area. She wasn't wandering the aisles petting the horses or any of the usual places the other girls tended to be. They were going to start late at this rate, and to top it off, someone was in the arena riding when everyone knew he had one more lesson before the arena was free for instructors' personal work.

Nikolay strode to the gate of the arena, prepared to halt the intruder, and found himself halted instead. Whoever the intruder was, he was an excellent rider: solid seat, straight back, rolled shoulders, elbows in. The rider urged the horse into a canter with an imperceptible use of hands and knees. Nikolay followed the rider's trajectory to the jump in the centre of the arena—a jump that had become purely decorative. His students certainly didn't aspire to it. It was high enough to be challenging. At three feet, a rider needed to know what he was doing. The rider lifted over the horse's neck and the pair flew over the faux wall easily. The horse could go higher. Nikolay could see it in the tuck of the animal's knees over the wall. He could also see the horse wasn't one of their schooling string. This was no instructor riding early. Which begged the question—who was he?

The rider doubled back, preparing to take the jump from the other side, giving Nikolay a first glimpse of the rider's face: sharp cheekbones, the firm but fine line of jaw, almost feminine beneath the helmet, the intensity of green eyes fixed on the jump as the rider sighted the target. Nikolay couldn't be sure if the rider saw him. The horse and rider took the jump again, coming to a stop in front of him at the gate.

The rider undid the strap of the helmet and removed it, shaking loose a stream of walnut waves. *He* was a *she*. A not entirely warm smile played on *her* sensual lips. 'Nikolay Baklanov, I presume?' She tossed those glossy waves with presumption. '*You* are late.'

'*You* are riding without permission or supervision. Klara Grigorieva, *I* presume?' Nikolay countered. Best to begin as he meant to go on with this supercilious miss who clearly possessed a healthy dose of arrogance, if not common sense. Nikolay placed a booted foot on the rungs of the gate and gave his newest pupil a considering gaze from head to boot. 'You're the Russian ambassador's daughter?'

She swung off the horse. 'I am, and this is Zvezda, my mare.' She smiled broadly, eyes sparking as her boots hit the ground. 'Surprised? Not what you expected?'

'No, not at all.' She was also very tall for a woman, a fact emphasised by the male attire she wore, breeches that encased long legs and emphasised the slenderness of waist. Her hair fell to that trim waist, and she had a face that rivalled Helen of Troy, a beautiful mix of eastern exoticism in the seductive slant of those eyes arched with narrow dark brows, the sharp cheekbones of her Russian ancestors and the delicate jaw of an English rose—the perfect combination of strength and femininity.

'"No, not at all"?' she parroted. 'What does that mean? No, not at all surprised? Or no, not at all what you expected?'

Nikolay put a hand on the horse's bridle. 'You know very well you had the advantage of me.' But he would not be cowed by that surprise. Neither would he allow her to keep that advantage. Bold women were attractive up to a point. 'I think you *like* surprising people, Miss Grigorieva.' How intriguing; the ambassador's daughter had a rebellious streak. He petted the horse, looking for neutral ground before their first encounter became overly adversarial. 'Zvezda, that's Star in Russian.' He didn't miss the spark in her eyes. She hadn't known. Interesting. 'Pretty name. Pretty horse.' The mare was an excellent specimen of English horseflesh. A Russian name for an English horse, much like the daughter, apparently. Klara was a name that could bridge both worlds, where Grigorieva could not.

Nikolay watched her carefully, this Anglo-Russian creation standing before him. 'What is it that you've come to me for, Miss Grigorieva?' His eyes drifted, letting his gaze convey explicitly what his words implied. If she wanted to play with fire, he'd light the match.

'Riding lessons, of course. This *is* a riding school.' She didn't flinch.

'You already ride exceedingly well, as I am sure you know.'

'I am told you're the best. Isn't that reason enough?'

'The best at what?' It was a provocative question, hardly the sort of thing one said to an unmarried young woman. But she was not the 'usual'. One had only to note her breeches, as opposed to a riding habit, to know that much. The mischief in him wanted to knock Miss Grigorieva from her high horse. The officer in him wanted to control her, wanted to rein in the danger she might pose.

'Riding,' she answered with a cool arch of her brow that implied an innuendo of her own. She turned towards Zvezda, reaching up to grip the saddle and a bit of mane. 'A leg up, if you please?'

Touché. All the better to see her with, Nikolay

thought wryly. He cupped his hands to take her boot, keenly aware of the curve of her hip and buttock, so near to his face that he could kiss that derrière as he tossed her up. He opted for professional detachment. 'Let's try the jump again. This time, I want you to count your strides. Anyone can jump if they're brave enough,' he challenged. 'Not everyone can do it on a pace count. That's true art. Take it in five strides.' Nikolay drew a line in the dirt with his boot. 'From here.'

'I'll take it in four.' She fastened her helmet.

'I asked you to take it in five,' Nikolay responded sternly. If this had been his cavalry, he would have had a soldier whipped for such insubordination. 'If you study with me, I expect you to take direction as well as your horse, Miss Grigorieva. Can you do that?'

She wheeled the white mare around in a flashy circle but not before Nikolay caught the hint of a flush on her cheeks. Ah, so Miss Grigorieva was not used to being disciplined. He imagined not, with that haughty demeanour of hers. She was used to people doing her bidding, not the other way around. She took the fence in five strides, but it was a fight for the fifth before the mare lifted. She'd started too fast and the mare had eaten up too much ground. 'Again, Miss Grigorieva! This time with five *even* strides so it looks like you planned it that way.'

She shot him a hard look and Nikolay chuckled. The wilder the filly, the better the ride. Part of him was going to enjoy taming the diplomat's daughter and part of him was going to regret it. He just wasn't yet sure which part was going to be larger. 'Heels down, Miss Grigorieva. Let's try again.' London had just got more interesting, if not more dangerous.

Chapter Two

Heels down? Was he joking? No one had told her
that for years. She was no amateur and yet she be-
grudgingly discovered there was a bit of room in
the stirrups still for the slightest of adjustments. She
turned Zvezda around and pointed her towards the
jump. Five even strides. She'd show that arrogant
Russian prince perfection in motion. Heels down.
Hah. That would be the last time she gave him reason to find any fault with her.

They worked on counting strides for the better
part of the hour until the mare was tired, but not too
tired, not too sweaty. Sweaty horses chilled easily
in the winter. Nikolay Baklanov had a good eye, not
just for the horse, but for the rider, too. His arrogance
was well earned. His reputation did not disappoint.
Even with her experience, she'd picked up a tip or
two during their session which was something of a
surprise in part because she'd not expected to and
in part because learning something had only been
a portion of the reason she was here. The other part

was that she'd been sent on a mission of sorts to vet the young Kubanian royal. The Prince had been in London for two months; long enough to have called on the ambassador himself. Since he hadn't, her father had decided to send her to call on him. She was to meet Prince Baklanov and establish his 'quality'.

Klara dismounted to walk her horse while the mare cooled. The Prince fell into step beside her, debriefing the lesson with instructions on what to practise throughout the week. She could easily imagine him giving the same terse litany of instructions to his troops. He would be a commanding leader. Up close, he was tall, a novelty for her. She could look most men in the eye, but she reached only his shoulder, a very broad shoulder. There was no doubting he was a rider of superb calibre. He was built for it with long legs, muscled thighs evident even through the fabric of his trousers and lean through the hips. There wasn't an ounce of fat on him, only muscle: well-trained, well-hewn muscle.

This was no dandified cavalry officer whose position had been purchased by his parents and good fortune of birth. This man was a warrior, a point accentuated by the dark hair worn long at his shoulders; the firm cut of his jaw and severe, chiselled lines of his face. A woman could look at that face for hours, could lose herself in the dark depths of his eyes— eyes full of secrets. He was a man who knew how to be dangerous to both men and women—a warrior to one, a lover to the other. He did not strike her as a man who'd appreciate being manipulated.

'Do you keep a horse here?' she asked when his debrief finished. Men loved to talk about themselves, it was always safe—and useful—conversation and that's what she was here for: *useful* conversation with Prince Baklanov. Men gave hints away all the time, in their words if she was lucky, but in other subtle ways, too: the tone of their voices, the gestures they made, the way they held their bodies.

'I keep three, actually.' He smiled at the mention of his horses and the result changed his face entirely, translating the strong, stoic planes of his warrior's face into breath-taking handsomeness. Zvezda was cool and they led her out into the aisle towards a stall. 'We're passing them now.' He nodded to the left, a hand going to the pocket of his coat to retrieve a treat as they came up on the first stall. 'This is Cossack. He's a Russian Don by breed.'

'He must be your cavalry horse.' Klara ran her eyes over the muscled chestnut, taking in the horse's shiny coat. 'He's magnificent,' she complimented, but she could tell her comment, her knowledge, had surprised him.

'Yes. I brought him with me when I left Kuban.' She heard the wistfulness as his voice caressed the words. Perhaps he would rather not have left? The Prince moved on to the stall beside it. 'This is Balkan, my stallion.' He ran a hand affectionately down the long neck of a horse so dark, he was nearly black.

'Let me guess.' Klara took in the short back, the height of the withers. 'He's Kabardin, perhaps Karachay.'

'Very good!' He flashed her another handsome smile. 'You do know something of the Motherland then.'

It was her turn to be uncomfortable with his display of insight. 'I know something of horses and their breeds,' Klara replied, leading Zvezda to her stall. She grabbed the blanket hanging beside the stall and stepped inside. 'How did you know?'

The Prince lounged outside the stall door, arms crossed, eyes studying her as she tossed the blanket over Zvezda's back. 'You didn't know what Zvezda meant when I told you. You don't speak Russian and I would guess that your mother is English.' He pushed off the wall and stepped inside to work the chest fastenings of the blanket. 'I would go so far as to say you've never lived in Russia.'

'You're almost right.' Her hands stilled on the blanket straps. What would this prince think of such a woman who had no knowledge of her heritage? 'I haven't lived there since I was a little girl. It's true, I don't remember much of it. We lived in St Petersburg for three years when I was four. We spent the summers in the countryside at an estate near Peterhof. That's what I am told. What *I* remember are the grasses around the estate, how they were as tall as I was and I could hear the wind pass through them.' She loved those memories. She'd lain for hours in those grasses looking up at the sky, happy and unaware how sadly the sojourn in St Petersburg would end.

No one paid much attention to her in those days— she would only understand why much later. In the moment, she'd been pleased. She could go where she willed, do what she wanted. She'd had grand adventures. Returning to England had been the end of those adventures, except for her horses. She might have gone crazy if it hadn't been for them. England had been the start of special tutors, then special schools, the very best for a girl who was expected to grow up to marry a duke, to become a complete Englishwoman, her Russian heritage nothing more than a novel characteristic to be put on display the way one displays a parlour trick. Something interesting and entertaining, but not to be taken seriously, not even by her, although this was ground on which she and her father disagreed. She wanted to know about her Russian heritage, hungered for it, even against her father's promises to her dying mother to raise an English rose.

'St Petersburg is a long way from the Kuban Steppes,' the Prince said neutrally and she had the sense that she was the one being vetted, quite the reverse of her intentions for this meeting. It made her nervous. What had she given away? What secrets had she inadvertently revealed?

She tried for a smile and a bit of humour. 'We can't all be patriotic cavalry officers.'

The effort failed. Her remark had been meant as a compliment, but it evoked something darker. The openness of his expression shuttered. 'Who said anything about being patriotic? Come, you haven't seen my other horse, she's a Cleveland Bay. I acquired her when I arrived. I have hopes of breeding her with my Kabardin stallion.' Any chance to follow up on his comment was lost in his rambling talk of a breeding opportunity. Klara was certain it was quite purposely done. The comment about patriotism had made him edgy. She had skated close to something with that remark.

They petted the Cleveland Bay and made conversation about mares and horses in general—safe ground for them both. But she was aware the atmosphere around them remained charged with wariness. They were both on their guard now, protecting themselves, cautious of revealing too much by accident to a stranger. She didn't want him to see any more of her and her lack of 'Russianness'. It was embarrassing to her that he should see it so clearly and on such short acquaintance. Would he be as disgusted by it as she if he knew the reason—that she'd been groomed to be an expensive pawn in a dangerous game she couldn't escape? Would he even care? Disgust implied the pre-existence of caring. He was her riding instructor, nothing more. And as for the Prince—what was it he didn't want her to see? What was he protecting? Why? More importantly, why did he think a diplomat's daughter would care about his secrets? In his case, caring assumed his secrets contained something of value he was not willing to share with another. Which was precisely what her father suspected.

A stable hand came to announce the arrival of her father's carriage and Nikolay gave her a formal incline of his head. 'It is time to say *do svidaniya,*

Miss Grigorieva.' He leaned close and she smelled the scents of man and beast on him, not an unpleasing fragrance to a woman who preferred horses over the dandified fops of the *ton*. 'That means "until we meet again".'

'What makes you sure I'll come back?' She let her eyes linger on his face, her voice low. She was flirting with him as he'd flirted with her, with private words and lingering glances.

'You didn't quite get what you came for, Miss Grigorieva. You'll be back. Did you want to wait until next Thursday or perhaps you'd like to try again sooner? I have an opening on Monday.'

'Monday? That's three days away,' she answered the challenge with a bold confidence she didn't feel. This man had a way of pushing her off balance at the most unlooked for moments. What did he think she was hunting? She hardly knew herself. 'How about Saturday in the park?' she countered. 'We will ride. You can bring Balkan. Call for me at two.' She paused. 'Unless you're worried I might get the rest of what I came for.'

He grinned, a wicked warrior's smile that sent a most unladylike tremor all the way to her toes, despite her usual dislike of arrogant men. He seemed to be an exception. 'I'm not the one who should be worried, Miss Grigorieva. Two o'clock Saturday it is.'

'You should be worried, Nik. I don't like the sounds of this at all,' Stepan counselled at dinner that night. The four of them—Illarion and Ruslan,

Stepan and himself, all royal expatriates of Kuban—were pushed back from the table, enjoying vodka and sampling some of Stepan's latest *samogon*—the Russian version of an Englishman's John Barleycorn. Drinking together was their nightly ritual, an attempt to recreate something from their old life in Kuban, to create something of their own, something comfortable in this new world they were learning to navigate.

Nikolay shoved his glass forward for more. Klara Grigorieva had disturbed him on more than a political level. She disturbed him on a sensual level, too, something, he might add, which had not happened in the time since they'd left Kuban. He thought his last, nearly fatal run-in with a woman had resolved his susceptibilities to feminine charm. Apparently not. The man in him wanted to pursue her, but the warrior in him counselled caution, as Stepan did. For now, he was happy to let his friends debate the issue for him.

To his right, Illarion, always the romantic, argued leniency. 'We might just be paranoid. The girl's not Russian, for one, not really. She was raised here. Nik says she doesn't even speak the language. It's hard to believe she's invited into her father's counsels or that she has any interest, like most of these English girls.'

'Unlike most English girls—' Stepan tendered his rebuttal '—her father *is* indisputably Russian. He's an ambassador. It is his job to represent Russian interests in England.' Stepan had become their unofficial *adahop* during the months they'd been in London, the one they all turned to for advice. 'If anyone is supposed to be loyal to one's country, it's the ambassador.'

Therein lay the true concern. Perhaps the ambassador would be loyal enough to see a renegade prince, wanted for royal murder, returned home.

This had always been the risk; that Kuban would want him back and that the Kubanian Tsar would not be willing to settle for having his number-one troublemaker out of the country. Nikolay was starting to regret the group's decision to not learn more about the Russian situation in London. The four of them had decided it would be better to simply go about their lives and let the ambassador come to them if he was interested in London's four newest Russian citizens. It had been an easy choice. There had been much to do in resettling.

The strategy had worked. To date, the ambassador had been uninterested. Today, that had potentially changed. Unless Klara was only what she seemed: a riding pupil, another English girl looking for ways to fill her long, empty days until she married. But the scenario didn't suit the woman he'd seen in the riding house. In his gut Nikolay knew that wasn't a legitimate assumption. She had not 'seemed' only a riding pupil today. Whatever she'd wanted from him, she'd wanted it badly enough to swallow her pride. He'd not missed how much it galled her when he'd shouted to keep her heels down, or to check her pacing. She might be there to ride, but she was there for something else as well.

Across the table, Ruslan, always the diplomat,

seconded Stepan's advice. 'You have to admit it looks strange; the Russian ambassador's daughter, who is already an exceptional rider, shows up asking for lessons? Why? Especially given your circumstances.' Ruslan looked around the table at each of them. 'We are all awkward expatriates.'

They were indeed, especially if a condition of expatriation was 'voluntary' relocation. Nikolay wasn't convinced even a loose definition of voluntary applied to him. His choice to leave hadn't been much of a choice at all when his other option was facing imprisonment and trial for a murder that could be couched as treason, a trial he might not win. He'd argued against the traditions of the kingdom once too often. Whether the charges against him held was not the issue. The Tsar had reason to make sure that they did. There'd been plenty of occasions when he'd clashed with the traditional-minded Tsar, but this last time, blood had been spilt. When his friend, Prince Dimitri Petrovich, a man who had abdicated his title in Kuban in order to claim a bride forbidden to him under Kubanian law, had written asking him to see to his sister's safe passage to England, Nikolay had jumped at the chance as much out of the deep bonds of friendship as for his own personal benefit.

Dimitri's request had come at a time when Kuban was no longer safe for him, as it was no longer safe, in varying degrees, for the other three men who sat at the table with him. Stepan Shevchenko; who had helped him escape the Tsar's dungeons in a very literal and perhaps unforgivable sense; Illarion

Kutejnikov, whose only claim to fame *before* he'd
used his poetry to protest Kubanian marriage prac-
tices was that a cousin had been a general during
the recent wars; and Ruslan Pisarev, who might or
might not have been involved in a questionable underground operation to help people leave the country. Ruslan's knowledge in escaping Kuban without
detection certainly indicated he might be guilty as
charged. They could make no claim to Kuban now,
except for perhaps Ruslan, who might be the one
who found a way to return some day.

For now, all four of them were homeless princes
abroad in a strange land, living off Dimitri's good
graces. The first months they'd arrived in England,
they'd stayed in the country with Dimitri and his
English wife, Evie. But they did not want to over-
stay their welcome, not with Evie expecting a baby.
Their friend had a family of his own. They needed
to strike out for themselves. But even that bit of in-
dependence was a misnomer. The four of them had
come to London, thanks to the generous loan of
Dimitri's London residence, Kuban House, a loan
they were all keenly aware couldn't last no matter
how much Dimitri insisted it could. Eventually, they
would have to find homes of their own. But for now,
it was all they had, a very new concept to Princes
who had once owned palaces and summer homes
that far exceeded their need.

Former Princes, Nikolay supposed. He had to get
used to thinking of himself that way. Or perhaps
not? Could one ever be a 'former' prince? The term

'Prince' was nothing more than an honorific now. They had no palaces, no land, none of the trappings that made them princes. They'd left it all behind in the hopes Kuban would make no claim on them.

The question was whether or not Kuban had let them go. Would Kuban come after them, or was London far enough to outrun the arm of Mother Russia? That was the question he saw mirrored in the eyes of his friends as he looked around the table. Was the lovely, sharp-witted Klara Grigorieva the advance scout for a larger scheme to drag the Princes home? If so, was that net truly after all of them, or just after him? He was the only one with official charges against him. Until he knew for sure, how he chose to handle Miss Grigorieva could affect them all. For the sake of his friends, he needed to know what he was up against.

Nikolay swallowed the *samogon* and pushed back from the table. 'I'll ride with her on Saturday. If she's truly setting a trap, then cancelling the appointment will alert her to our suspicions. I can't learn about her intentions if I don't spend time with her.' That would not be a hardship. Klara Grigorieva was intriguing in her own right. He'd want to spend time with her without the need to unravel the mysteries she presented, a foreign ambassador's daughter raised to be English. He had responded to her mentally, physically, from the moment she'd taken off her helmet, shaken down all that glorious hair and chastised *him* for being late, to the moment *she'd* invited *him* for a Saturday ride. *Call for me at two.* There'd been no doubt in her mind that he would accept. A woman like that would keep a man on his feet. Klara Grigorieva wasn't for the fainthearted, but no one had ever called him a coward.

Chapter Three

Klara's finger moved south down the page of the atlas from St Petersburg, past Moscow and Kiev, to a spot between the Black Sea and the Don Steppe. *Kuban*. The home of Nikolay Baklanov; a land of mountains, steppes, grasslands and rivers.

She ran her finger over the ridges depicting the Caucasus range and along the curve of the river. A land of mild climates and severe mountains if the map was to be believed. A land of contrasts, just like the man himself. One could know much about a man if one knew where he was from. Men were products of their places. Women were, too, for that matter. She did not exclude herself from that generalisation.

The image of Nikolay's smile was imprinted in her mind. It had transformed his face completely, the smile made him approachable, made it seem possible that a woman had a chance to solve the mysteries behind those dark eyes. What might those mysteries be? What caused a man to leave his country? Not just any man, but a warrior, a man trained to fight for that country, to defend it. What caused a prince to teach riding lessons to spoiled girls?

The answers to those mysteries surely lay behind the granite-dark eyes. There were other mysteries, too, more sensual mysteries that lay behind those eyes, those lips. This was a man of deep passions. She had not been oblivious to the considerations of his gaze yesterday which had not been limited to an assessment of her riding. He had found her interesting in the way a man finds an attractive woman 'interesting'.

That made him dangerous. She drummed her fingers on the atlas page. A dispossessed Russian prince was hardly the type of man her father was saving her for, had raised her for. But obedience was not enough to stop a trill of excitement from running through her at the thought of their Saturday meeting—a chance to be with him again, a chance to trade wits, to probe beneath surfaces. Would he flirt with her? Would he look at her with those hot, dark eyes? Would he be ready with his wicked innuendos? Would he smile? Would he pursue his 'interest'? Would she let him even knowing she had to ensure the pursuit was ultimately futile? She was meant for an English peer, and soon. But knowing that couldn't stop the wondering. What would it be like to be the object of such a man's attentions? Affections?

Klara sighed, wishing she could see beyond the map. What kind of country produced such a man? Such passions? Such intensity? What did Nikolay's Kuban look like? Perhaps it was the idea of Kuban that drew her to him more than anything else. That was easier to explain than pure physical attraction. Russia was forbidden fruit. She was to be English in all ways, English like the mother who had died in St Petersburg at the end of that final summer, but that didn't stop the craving, only made it understandable.

The door to the library opened, admitting her father, and she deftly slid another book on top of the atlas. To give in to the craving would hurt him. Russia had taken his wife; he would not tolerate it taking his daughter. Her father strode towards the table, all smiles. 'At last, we have time to talk, Klara.' He was a handsome man, a tall man, in his fifties but still possessed of youthful vigour. Only the streaks of grey in his hair hinted he might not be as young as he appeared. He pulled out a chair beside her and sat. 'Tell me everything, how was your lesson with Baklanov?'

Her father was a good man, Klara reminded herself. He did care about the lesson. He'd always encouraged her riding and he was proud of her, she knew that unequivocally. But he wasn't strictly interested in only the lesson today. He wanted her assessment of the Prince. She should feel proud he trusted her input, that he allowed her to help with his work, yet she felt some guilt, as if telling her father made her a spy, a betrayer of trust. No, that was too dramatic. She was making too much out of recounting first impressions. How could she betray a man she'd met only once and knew nothing about?

Perhaps that was where she was wrong. Even after

one meeting, she did know him. She knew the caress of his wicked gaze as he flirted with her. She knew the compassion he held for his horses, had seen it in the gentle stroke of his hand on their long noses, heard it in the words of his stories. Now, she was being asked to turn those experiences over to her father. Perhaps that was the real issue. She wanted to treasure the encounter, to have it just to herself instead of giving it over to 'the game'. She had so little in her life that didn't belong to her father's game. The game had become the basis of their relationship as she grew up. Her father was waiting, patient and calm, across the table from her. Certain she'd give up whatever she'd learned for the greater good. His good.

'The Prince is very talented. We worked on pacing. Even at my level, he found ways to help me improve.'

Her father listened politely before saying, 'What of the man himself? What is his character?'

'He is intense. Committed.' She recalled hearing him shout at the unfortunate Miss Calhoun while she'd waited outside. The Prince gave his best to whatever he did and he expected the best from those around him.

'Those are useful attributes,' her father mused. That was how he assessed people and characteristics. There were only two categories as far as he was concerned: usable and unusable. Perhaps she should be grateful she fell into the former classification. Yet there were days when she wondered what her life could have been like if she'd been unusable to him and left to have a life outside the game, like she had before a summer fever and a deathbed promise had committed her to other people's dreams.

For a moment, she thought her brief insight would be enough, but he wanted more. 'Do you suppose he feels that intensity, that commitment still for his country, or is he ready to attach those feelings to a new loyalty? A man does not leave his country without provocation.'

'I couldn't say on such short acquaintance.' It was only a partial lie. She thought of the wistfulness she'd heard at the edges of his words as he'd talked of his horses. He hadn't talked of 'bringing them', but of 'not leaving them'. Such a word choice implied he did at least 'look back' occasionally, that he still thought of Kuban as home. That nostalgia might create a loyal bond difficult to break.

'Perhaps you need a longer acquaintance, then.' Her father smiled. 'We could use an intense man of commitment.' *We*. A shiver ran down her spine at the mention of that evocative pronoun. *We* meant the Union of Salvation, the covert group of officers and palace politicos like her father who plotted against Tsar Alexander back in St Petersburg. The Union had already been defeated once before, three years ago. Therein lay the danger. They were forced now to plot abroad or 'underground' in order to continue the game. That game of intrigue had become his life and she wanted to be part of his life, wanted to have his love and attention. She wanted to prove herself to him.

That was what dutiful pawns and daughters did, they obeyed and protected those they loved. She never would have played the game if her mother had lived and neither would have he. There would have been no need for it. She studied her father. Up close, one could see the first signs of ageing faint on his face, the lines about his mouth, the tiredness around his eyes; the first tolls taken in a life lived between countries. He blamed Russia's backwardness for her mother's death; a summer fever even though they summered in countryside, far from the sewage-laden Neva River of the city. Distance had not been enough and neither had the country doctor's competence. That had been in 1810. By 1817, flush from victory over Napoleon and a tour of duty beyond Russian borders, others felt as her father did: that Russia was behind the rest of Europe in all ways. Modernising Russia was her father's passion now, a way to avenge his wife's death and a way to serve his country.

'When will you see the Prince again?' her father asked, his mind already hard at work behind his intelligent eyes. Every day was a chess game and she played because she loved him.

'We are riding together on Saturday. Perhaps I can learn more.' She said nothing of the shadow that crossed Nikolay's face at her reference to patriotism. Her father would find that reference as encouraging as the nostalgia had been discouraging.

'Excellent. Ask him to stay for our dinner with the Duke of Amesbury. Prince Baklanov would be a perfect addition. General Vasilev and the others will attend. We can all take his measure then.'

She nodded, not allowing her dislike for the guest list to show. Amesbury would be there. She'd rather have the Prince to dinner without the Duke. Amesbury was a formidable man with intimidating opinions. It was no secret in their circles that the Duke was a powerful politico interested in British–Russian relations. Her father had seen to it that the settlement of boundaries in the American north-west stood to benefit the Duke's fur trade investments. She did not know what the Duke had given him in return. Something, to be sure, her father always got paid for his efforts in favours or connections. The Duke also had some very strong opinions about the backwardness of Russia. Letting the Duke expose those opinions would be the perfect test for Prince Baklanov's loyalty. Would the Prince be a traditionalist or a modernist? A twinge of guilt pricked at her. It hardly seemed fair to invite the Prince to dinner simply to ambush him. She should warn him, but it would hardly serve her father's purposes to have the Prince hide his true thoughts. Saturday would be…interesting.

Saturday arrived with blue skies and crisp air, the perfect—and rare—winter day for being out of doors. Everyone in London was taking advantage of it. Even though the Season wouldn't officially start for another three months, London was always busy. Today, Hyde Park was bursting with activity—riders and carriages with their tops down, occupants bundled against the cold in fur robes. 'I suppose the cold doesn't bother you.' She glanced at Nikolay riding beside her in greatcoat and muffler, a furred Russian *ushanka* on his head. 'Does Kuban get terribly cold during the winters?' She'd start her probing harmlessly enough. Everyone talked about the weather.

The Prince laughed. 'Cold is an understatement. Below freezing many times. There is snow, of course. We have mountains. But there is also rain, a lot of rain.' There was a hint of wistfulness in his voice. Again. Like the first time back at Fozard's. She hadn't invented it.

'I imagine British mountains are more like hills to you.' She gave a soft laugh. 'Do you miss it? Kuban and all of its ruggedness?' She would miss such a place. She'd not been many places outside of England, but she understood intuitively that the ruggedness of England was relegated to its borders. How did that compare to Kuban?

'Britain does take a bit of getting used to.' He gave her a smile, dazzling and brilliant, meant to derail. She didn't allow herself to be distracted.

'Why did you leave, then?' Perhaps the casual nature of the ride, the idea that they were surrounded by others, would cause him to drop his guard. After all, how secretive could a question be if it was asked out in the open? What could she be probing for in public?

Nikolay was too astute. His response was quick and stern, all riding master. 'Perhaps I'll tell you some day, Miss Grigorieva, but not today.'

'Klara,' she corrected. She knew full well that to ask a man to use her first name was bold indeed, that such an offer implied other liberties might be welcome, but if they were to move beyond instructor and student, she had to rid them of the formalities. 'Call me Klara, at least in private,' she added, suggesting the idea that there could be two sides to their association.

'Then you must call me Nikolay.' His eyes sparked at that. He had not missed her careful invitation. More than that, he'd *accepted* it. It indicated she'd seen his hot gaze and had understood it. Perhaps it even suggested she was willing to act on it. Was such an invitation true? *Would* she act on his flirtation? In all honesty, a very curious part of her wanted to see where such a flirtation could lead. The part that obeyed her father knew better than to engage in such useless foolishness.

'Klara,' the Prince repeated, his tone caressing her name, making it sound exotic on his tongue, a true Russian name. *Klah-rah*, with soft *a*'s, not like the harsh, long-vowel sounds she was used to hearing; *Clare-uh*. He made the ordinary sound beautiful, as if the name belonged to a seductress, a woman with the power to captivate men, to captivate *him*. 'Are there any less crowded routes in this park of yours?' Now he was being bold, all but asking to be alone with her. The possibilities inherent in such a request sent a *frisson* of excitement down her back. She was not used to men affecting her this way.

'There is a place where we can walk the horses down to the water.' She gestured towards the trees, not wanting to dwell too long on comparisons between Nikolay and the English gentlemen she'd debuted amongst. The destination she had in mind would be private, away from the other riders crowding the paths. She could try her probe again from a different angle. At the trees, they dismounted and led the horses to the water's edge. 'Sometimes the Serpentine freezes and there's skating.' She smiled coyly. 'When I was eleven, the Thames froze for a month. There was the most amazing frost fair. My father took me one day. It reminded me of the Neva River in St Petersburg. I had only been home from St Petersburg for four years, then, and still remembered it. The Neva froze every winter without fail, December through March or even April. I skated almost every day with my *nyanya*.' The Russian word for *nurse* came easily to her after all these years.

She shrugged, surprised at herself. 'I haven't thought about that for years.' It was quiet down here, the water dark and cold. Perfect for disclosures. 'I was only there once and I was very young, but I miss it,' she hinted carefully, hoping he would take the opportunity to share something of Kuban with her, a story of himself, a chance to get to know him. What did he miss about his home? Surely there must be something to have spoken of Kuban with such wistfulness in his brief remarks.

Nikolay did not take the hint. 'You will go back some day.' He was redirecting the conversation, back to her, away from him. It didn't matter. She had her opening from his own words. If he wouldn't tell her why he'd left, perhaps he'd tell her if he intended to return.

'And yourself?' she asked. 'Do you plan to go back?' There was no crowd to blame his reticence on now. Their horses stopped to drink and he faced her squarely, a glimmer of warning, in his eyes. 'I cannot go back, Miss Grigorieva.' His words were stern, a punishment for having intruded into his private realm. 'Is that the answer you are looking for?' She had gone too far. She immediately regretted the intrusion. She took an involuntary step back from his fierceness.

'I'm sorry, I had no wish—'

'To pry?' Nikolay finished sharply, advancing, not allowing her the distance. 'You had every wish. Do not deny it. It has been your intention since we met.'

Klara's chin went up in defiance. She'd been caught, but she would not give him the satisfaction of making her feel ashamed or cowed. 'If *you'd* been more forthcoming, I wouldn't have to pry.' She took another step back. This close, he was far larger than when Zvezda walked between them or when she looked down at him from Zvezda's back.

'Why pry at all? I was unaware riding instructors had to provide their pupils with detailed histories.' His advance forced her back another step. She was running out of room and becoming sharply aware that the tenor of this exchange was transforming into another sort of challenge, their awareness of each other palpable.

'Not all pupils are the daughters of foreign diplomats. Our lives are under scrutiny from two nations. We have to be careful with whom we associate.' They stood toe to toe now and she had nowhere to go, her back firmly up against a tree.

'I am a prince who cannot return to his kingdom. I, too, must be careful with whom I associate.' His voice was a caress, low and husky with caution. It was not caution for himself, but for her, a warning she realised too late.

His mouth was on hers, sealing the distance between them. He kissed like a warrior; possessive and proving, a man who would not be challenged without choosing to respond in kind.

Her mouth answered that challenge, her body thrilled to it. This was what it meant to be kissed, not like the few hasty kisses she'd experienced during her first Season out before it was clear she'd been set aside for the Duke. *That* should have told her something. Well-meaning gentlemen held their baser instincts in reserve, they didn't kiss as if the world was on fire. There was nothing altruistic about Prince Nikolay Baklanov when it came to seduction and he *wanted* her to know. As a warrior, as a lover, he took no prisoners.

Two could play that game. Her arms went about his neck, keeping him close, letting her body press against him, feeling the hard ridges and planes of him, knowing he felt the curve and softness of her. She let her tongue explore his mouth, her teeth nipped at his lip as she tasted him. There were things she wanted him to know as well. She was not one of his spoiled students. She would not be cowed by a stern look and a raised voice. She was not afraid of passion. Nor was she afraid to take what she wanted, even from him. She was good at showing people what she was not. It was easier than showing people what she *was*: a girl forced to marry, a girl who knew nothing about where she came from, a girl caught between worlds. Her hands were in his hair, dragging it free of its leather tie. She gave a little moan of satisfaction as his teeth nipped at her ear lobe.

At the sound, he swore—something in Russian she didn't need to understand to know what it meant: that their kiss had tempted him beyond comfortable boundaries. He drew back, his dark eyes obsidian-black, his voice ragged at its edges as if he'd found a certain amount of satisfaction and been reluctant to let it go. But there was only that glimpse before the words that indicated this might have only been a game played for her benefit, to show her what it meant to poke this particular dragon. 'Forgive me,' he began, 'I did not intend…'

Cold fury doused the newly stoked heat of her body. 'Yes, you did. You've had every intention of kissing me since we met.'

'*Touché.*' He gave her a short, stiff gesture, more of a nod than a bow. 'Then that makes us even.'

His audacity angered her. She wanted to lash out

in a fiery display of temper, to slap him for the advantages he'd taken, but he'd like that. It was what he expected, perhaps even what he'd been playing for—a wedge to drive between them, or even to drive her away. She had too much on the line to allow that, or anything that bore the slightest resemblance to victory. She played her trump card. 'Hardly even. My father wants you to come to dinner.' She gave him a look, part cold anger, part dare. If she'd learned anything about Nikolay Baklanov thus far it was that he wouldn't back down, especially if he believed she thought he would.

'I'll be there.'

She felt the guilt prick her again. Surely a small hint of warning would salve her conscience without betraying her father's intentions in inviting him. 'Don't you want to know why?' The words came out in a rush. She hadn't much time left with him here in this quiet grove. The horses were getting restless. They'd have to leave soon.

Nikolay gave her a frustratingly confident grin. 'Don't worry, *kotyonok moya*, I already do.'

'You've invited a potential viper to dinner,' the Duke of Amesbury postulated from the comfortable arm chair in front of Alexei Grigoriev's fire. It was hardly an original idea. Surely Grigoriev was already keenly aware of the risk he took in inviting the Russian prince to dinner. Amesbury's sharp eyes watched the ambassador as he paced the long windows of his study to the gardens beyond.

'Or,' Grigoriev drawled with considerably more optimism than Amesbury felt, 'I've invited the perfect solution. Serving Russia's better interests is always a delicate proposition, never more so than now when the country's better interests aren't shared by its ruler. I think an exiled prince would be hungry for two things: revenge and regaining his place. We can give him that.' Amesbury gave the idea a moment's attention as Grigoriev went on. 'He could be perfect. He's a military officer, a leader of men. We can send him to St Petersburg with the arms when the time is right to raise and rally the troops.'

Ah. A man to play the martyr. Amesbury could get his mind around *that*. Baklanov could be transformed into a scapegoat if anything went wrong. They knew from experience just how much might go wrong. The Union of Salvation, of which Grigoriev was a devout member, had been forced underground after the failed military revolt in 1821. They could not afford to fail again, but neither could they afford not to try again. Now, the Union plotted in secret and in safety, abroad in England and elsewhere. It was a sign of how great the discontent was that Tsar Alexander's own military was willing to consider revolutionary action. Not that Amesbury was particularly interested in the principles of the revolt, only the profit. Selling arms to the upstart revolutionaries emerging throughout Europe after Napoleon's demise had become lucrative in the extreme. Grigoriev's revolution could be the most lucrative of them all.

Grigoriev continued to proselytise from the windows. 'The military will respect the Prince and he has knowledge of courtly manoeuvres. He can handle the politics.'

'In theory,' Amesbury drawled. 'That has yet to be proven.' He liked the idea of a scapegoat if the revolt failed. He didn't like the potential, however, of Grigoriev liking this Prince more than him. He rather liked being the ambassador's right-hand man. This arms deal was a sure pipeline to profit.

'He *is* perfect.' General Vasilev, the third member of their select group, gave his moustache a thoughtful stroking from the chair opposite him. 'Have *you* thought of that, Alexei? When things are too good to be true, they probably are. Perhaps he's been sent to smoke us out.' Vasilev could always be counted to speak like a true Russian. In this case, Amesbury was quick to second him. It wouldn't do for Grigoriev to go trusting the Prince too much.

The ambassador fixed the General with a stern stare. 'If it was a trap, he'd have come forward sooner and made himself known. He can't entrap anyone from a distance.' Grigoriev grimaced. 'Besides, if we want to move forward, I don't think we have the luxury of doubt. We need someone to go to Russia with the arms...' he paused here with a dark look for each of them '...unless one of you two is willing to do it?' The last was said with an obvious dash of challenge. Neither he nor Vasilev wanted to take that risk.

Amesbury would rather talk about the Prince than

his own reticence to accompany the arms to Russia. 'Consider this for a moment,' Amesbury drawled. 'If Baklanov didn't want to be noticed, it means he's hiding something. That could be useful.' He liked sowing doubt. Grigoriev and he both assessed people through their usefulness, but where they diverged was in motives. Grigoriev used people to promote his principles. He, on the other hand, used people strictly for personal gain. His motives were selfish whereas Grigoriev's could, at times, be sacrificial. He'd prefer Grigoriev not discover he operated by a different code far more practical than the ambassador's idealism. He would allow Grigoriev to include Baklanov in their plans, as long as it didn't usurp his position until he could secure a more permanent station by the ambassador's side, one such as marriage. He'd had his eye on Klara Grigorieva for quite some time now. He didn't want new-come Princes destroying those plans.

He could feel the hint of a contemplative smile twitch at his lips at the thought of Klara Grigorieva; firm breasted and feisty. She would be an asset on his arm. Every man in any room would want to look at her. He'd turn her out in the finest of gowns, bedeck her in the most expensive of jewels. Thanks to her father, he had the money to do that and more. In public, he'd celebrate her beauty, and his triumph in winning a woman other men had failed to claim. Behind closed doors, he'd enjoy taming that long, slim-legged spitfire. He hadn't had a woman that wild in ages and Klara was the best kind of wild, the kind that would fight when cornered. He shifted slightly in his chair, crossing a leg over a knee to subdue the effects raised by such images.

He loved a good fight, especially the sort that ended up with his belt lashing out victory against round, white buttocks. He would let her run, let her fight, let her think there was the possibility of escape until she ran the length of her tether. But she would never be able to ultimately resist him. Her father had ensured that just as assuredly as her father had ensured his wealth the moment Grigoriev had invited him into this little coven of Russian rebels. Grigoriev would need his protection before this venture was through and for Klara's sake he'd give it, but, oh, how he'd make her pay for it; decadently, sinfully, naked and on her knees. Oh, yes, Alexei Grigoriev was too useful of an ally to lose to an exiled prince. But first, it seemed one more hurdle remained—ferreting out Nikolay Baklanov's secrets. If the Prince had secrets, it meant he could be blackmailed into compliance. *If* they knew what those secrets were. Everyone had their price. There were only so many reasons a prince of wealth and status fled his country.

Chapter Four

There were only so many reasons an ambassador asked an expatriate prince to dinner, but Nikolay was uncertain which one had prompted Alexei Grigoriev's invitation. He did, however, recognise an ambush when he saw one.

This one was dressed in an expensive gown of dark blue silk that gathered enticingly beneath firm breasts and sparkled with discreet diamonds in the brunette depths of her hair. Klara was to be the distraction, the forward action upfront in the hopes that he'd leave himself open to attack from behind. It was not a bad idea. The sight of her formally dressed was a stunning contrast after seeing her in breeches and a riding habit. Tonight she rivalled, even surpassed, the beauties of Kuban. 'This is classic military strategy,' he said in low tones to Klara as she circulated the room with him making introductions.

'I beg your pardon?' She moved them smoothly from the rotund, greying General Vasilev, who was in attendance with his wife and pretty daughter, to a group of young officers standing by the Italian marble fireplace.

'Are you familiar with Hannibal's ambush at the Trebia River?' Nikolay murmured, liking the sensation of having her to himself in a room full of people. She was still bristly from their encounter in the park, having not quite forgiven him for the kiss. Or perhaps it was herself she hadn't forgiven. She'd liked it well enough, had participated in it fully. Perhaps she didn't like knowing *he'd* been the one to break it off.

She gave a husky laugh as if she, too, was flirting with him. 'I know who Hannibal is, but alas, I am not a student of military tactics like yourself.'

They stopped between the two conversational groups and Nikolay took advantage of the privacy, his mouth close to her ear. 'Hannibal openly engaged the Roman corps and, while they were distracted, they were ambushed from behind by the rest of Hannibal's army.' He spoke the words as if they were endearments. As close as their heads were, the words might have been just that to the onlooker—the opening manoeuvres of a sensual game.

A coy smile crossed Klara's mouth, 'Am I the "distraction" in your theory?' Her fingers discreetly played with the diamond pendant that hung just above her breasts, highlighting her décolletage and drawing his eyes downwards. 'How am I doing?'

'No gentleman can safely answer that,' Nikolay murmured. He was in no hurry to distance himself from her. He was enjoying this far too much and they were attracting attention from the Duke of Amesbury, whom he'd met upon arrival, the only

Englishman present. That interaction had been cool, the politeness glacial. 'If I say you're doing expertly, I've implied you have loose morals. If I say you're doing poorly, I've implied you have no charms.' He chuckled softly, aware that the low rumble of his voice and the nearness of his body had the pulse at the base of her throat racing steadily. 'Either way, I end up slapped.'

'Do you get slapped often?' Klara teased wickedly.

'Worse. Sometimes I get called out.' He nodded discreetly towards Amesbury. 'Should I be worried? He's been watching us.'

Klara hesitated only slightly, but it was enough to draw his notice before she dismissed his concern over Amesbury with an airy wave of her hand he didn't quite believe. 'We are in the middle of a drawing room surrounded by guests. He can hardly be jealous of that.'

'Why would he be jealous at all?' Nikolay prompted. 'Does he have an interest in you, Klara?' He found the possibility disappointing.

'He has an interest in my father,' Klara snapped too quickly. Ah, so there was some history in that direction. The Duke's interest in Klara might not be formally acknowledged or reciprocated, but she *was* aware of him and how he thought of her. Nikolay shot a covert glance in the Duke's direction. Amesbury would be a dangerous enemy. There was a coldness around the Duke's eyes, even at a distance, that suggested one would not want to face him with pistols. Nikolay had seen that look before in the eyes of battle-hardened soldiers who didn't know the meaning of mercy. Amesbury wouldn't be the sort to delope.

The butler announced dinner and Klara tucked her arm through his, steering his thoughts away from Amesbury's firearm skills. 'You are to take me in this evening.'

'Of course I am.' Nikolay laughed, pleased but not surprised by the turn of events. 'After all, *kotyonok moya*, you are the distraction.'

Nikolay surveyed the elegant setting of the ambassador's dining room: the long, polished table set with heavy silver, multi-armed candelabra, an expensive, squat epergne filled with fruits that were hard to come by in winter and the equally rare Lomonosov porcelain made only in Russia with its distinctive cobalt and white pattern. The setting confirmed the tone. The evening was unmistakably Russian from the china place settings to the guests. The table could seat twenty-four, although tonight it had been arranged to seat an intimate twelve—Grigoriev's inner circle and their wives.

Nikolay helped Klara into her chair at the foot of the table and took his on her right, letting his gaze drift over the guests, assessing. Grigoriev would ambush him here. He would call him out surrounded by witnesses. The opening salvo would come from one of them, not Grigoriev himself. That would be too obvious, and contain no element of surprise. Would it be General Vasilev, who he'd already met? The young Count visiting from St Petersburg with his friend who had eyes for the General's pretty daughter? Perhaps the two men near his own age in uniform, protégés of the General, whom he'd not had the chance to meet officially?

It was a most intimate circle indeed, a circle that now surrounded him, a newcomer, and Alexei Grigoriev reigned over it all from one end of the table. Klara reigned from the other, dressed subtly but richly, diamonds twinkling at her ears, the blue silk of her gown nearly the shade of the dishes. There was no mistaking the Grigorievs lived handsomely in their Belgravia townhouse.

They feasted handsomely, too. Dinner began with oysters on the half-shell and caviar from the Caspian Sea, followed by a clear soup—a Russian standard—and then fish as the guests made small talk, all in English despite their ability to do otherwise. Perhaps out of deference for Klara and Amesbury? Or perhaps to illustrate another, more subtle point? By the time the roast and vegetables were on the table, however, talk had changed to sharper topics. The polite conversation of the early courses had gradually meandered into the political. The ambush was coming. They wouldn't wait until the ladies left the table.

Nikolay ran through his options once more, reassessing *why* he'd been invited. To take his measure, of course, but as to what? He didn't like where his conclusions led. An exiled prince might be angry enough to betray his country. Why would Grigoriev want to know that? To catch a traitor? Was this part of Kuban's attempt to trap him and bring him home? The timing would be right. He'd been in England almost a year; long enough for news to travel north to St Petersburg and a correspondence to take place over a course of action. Was Stepan right? Was Grigoriev to be feared? Or was there something else at work? Did the ambassador have schemes of his own?

He leaned close to Klara, aware that Amesbury was watching him and fingering his butter knife. 'Is this why you've brought me here? Your father wishes to test my political loyalties?' The ambassador might know *who* he was, but he didn't yet know *what* he was; Should he be classified as a patriot? A traitor? Or something in between, something more dangerous than either, a revolutionary—a man who loved Russia enough to want to change it.

Klara slanted him a look that would reduce a lesser man to an intellectual toddler. 'Are you always so cynical? Perhaps it is the other way around. Perhaps tonight gives you a chance to test *his*.'

Nikolay held her gaze, considering the truth of her statement. *Was* it possible? Or was it merely an attempt to disarm him? There was too much unknown to draw a solid conclusion. Did Grigoriev know what he'd done to warrant exile? Did St Petersburg care that a prince from a newly created 'kingdom' of the empire had essentially deserted? Kuban had only been firmly Russian for three generations of princes. Without knowing the answers to those questions, he could draw no definitive conclusion that this was a trap.

He let his mind pick up the thread of Klara's insinuation that her father wanted to test him for his own purposes. What might those purposes be? Treason? Rebellion? Matrimony possibly, given that there was matchmaking underway for the General's daughter based on the glances being tossed across the table. He had already contemplated compliance and treason. Why not contemplate matrimony, too?

Nikolay considered Klara; the heat of her kiss, the sharpness of her wit. Had she been trying to tempt him for nothing more than marriage? It seemed a small thing compared to entrapment for treason. Alexei Grigoriev wasn't the first ambitious ambassador looking to connect his daughter with a royal family of the empire. If Grigoriev thought there was a chance he would return to Kuban and take up his responsibilities in the military, it would be advantageous to have Klara in a position that could advance his own career. Such arrangements were made all the time in Kuban. Marriage was a political concern, romance was a personal one that was often expected to occur outside of that marriage.

It stood to reason Grigoriev would be interested in Kuban. It was an area of growing political concern. As an officer, Nikolay understood how important Kuban would be in the next several decades. The Ottomans were weakening. Their empire would fall and Russia would want its piece of the spoils, as would England. The Crimean Peninsula stood, metaphorically speaking, between England and Russia in the west, the Khyber Pass of Afghanistan stood between them in the east, Russia's gateway into British India. The time for war was not yet, but it was coming. Nikolay could feel it in his warrior's soul. There would be a time, when the country he loved would square off against the country he'd run to. It would be a time for choosing, a time for testing loyalties.

Perhaps Grigoriev knew it, too. Grigoriev wanted to be ready. But the ambassador would have to find another way into Kuban. Nikolay was not a marrying man. He allowed his gaze to slide surreptitiously over Klara's fine profile. Not even a woman as beautiful as Klara Grigorieva was going to change that. He firmly believed a career military man like himself; a man who courted danger, had no business with a wife or children. It was hardly fair when the odds were they'd be widowed and fatherless a portion of their lives.

There was the selfish factor, too; *he* wanted to live and, to do that, he didn't need the distraction of worry over what happened to him when he was leading raids and defending border forts along the river. The fastest way to be killed on a battlefield was to be distracted. The biggest distraction of all was the fear of having one's family used against one as leverage. Dimitri Petrovich was proof of that. What he'd endured for years for the sake of his father and sister was lesson enough that love—true love—was hardly worth the sacrifice.

Nikolay wiped his mouth with his napkin and sat back to let the footman take his plate. Klara smiled at him, something challenging and hot in her eyes. Oh, no, marriage was *definitely* not for him. But that didn't mean he wasn't beyond a little flirtation.

Across the table, one of the young protégés expounded to the group at large about the current situation. 'The military will support Constantine as successor when the time comes.' Somewhere between contemplating treason and matrimony, the conversation had moved on without him. He had to catch up.

'When will that be?' the Count put in. 'Tsar Alexander is healthy enough. Are we to twiddle our thumbs and wait until he dies? He's only in his forties. If he's like his grandmother, he'll live for eons. Russia cannot take two more decades of his "religious fervour".'

'Here, here.' General Vasilev, brilliant in a decorated scarlet uniform, raised his glass. 'Russia needs innovation if it's to catch up with the rest of Europe. If there's anything good to say about Napoleon, it is this: our boys went out into the world, looked around and saw their country lacking. Too long have we been a land of farmers and feudal princes.' He aimed a sharp look at Nikolay. 'Your presence excluded, Your Highness. I do not mean any offence.' He inclined his head, but his eyes never left Nikolay's. The man was waiting for him to declare himself. *This* was the ambush.

'None taken.' Nikolay met his gaze with a nod of his own, never believing for a moment those two words would be enough, but hoping he might be lucky.

Amesbury smiled, a cat anticipating cream. A wise man would know the grin was not benign. 'Does that mean you side with General Vasilev in regards to Russia's lag in the world?'

Nikolay felt Klara stiffen beside him, evidence that this was the trap that had been laid for him. A test of his loyalties confirmed. Nikolay met Amesbury's remark, confidently. 'I believe a man should be able to voice his opinion freely without fear of repercussion. The General is free to say what he will in my presence.' Even if that speech included plotting rebellion, for surely that's what lurked beneath the surface of this talk about successors and progress. How interesting. Even more interesting was the hint that they wanted him to join them. Why else would they speak of such things in front of him? To be sure, it was all very oblique, but it was there.

At the other end of the table, Alexei's eyebrows, dark like his daughter's, rose in approval. 'That is a very generous attitude, Your Highness. One that would be revolutionary in its own right in certain conservative circles.'

'We're in England, where it's hardly a remarkable courtesy,' Nikolay replied broadly and then decided some table-turning might not come amiss. He raised his glass to Grigoriev. 'My compliments, Your Excellency. What a wonderful night it has been to share a meal with countrymen like myself, men a long way from home. *Zazdarovje!*' There was a rousing chorus of *Zazdarovje* and the clinking of glasses but Nikolay was sure his message had not been missed by the ambassador or by anyone else at the table.

They could ruminate all they liked on his reference to being so far from 'home'. They could also speculate on his awareness that he knew they plotted, safe on English shores. It was hardly a unique idea. Russia was always plotting, but that made it no less dangerous. 'Just so we're clear, gentlemen, I have no desire to engage in politics. I intend to live here quietly.' Looks were exchanged, topics were changed. His remark altered the tone of the evening. By the time cheeses were set in front of him to end the meal, politics had disappeared entirely from the table. Even when Klara rose and indicated the ladies should follow her to the salon and the brandy decanters came out, politics made no reappearance, which shortened the evening, by a good two hours.

The men did not linger over brandy, and the 'musical' portion of the evening was blessedly brief. Why linger when it was time to go? He'd been here long enough to know what he needed to do, and that was disengage. There was nothing here for him but danger and trouble. He had not left Kuban to be dragged back into the mess of politics, sexual or otherwise. It didn't matter what form the politics took, it was still danger and he had no time for it, no room for it in this new life he was trying to carve out. It was a shame that Miss Grigorieva would be a casualty of that decision, but there was no other choice for it. Better to make that choice now before he might become otherwise invested or had his judgement clouded by less reliable issues than logic.

'You are something of a killjoy,' Klara murmured as she walked him to the hall, the party breaking up shortly before midnight. 'Go out often, do you?'

Nikolay laughed. 'No, not to functions like this.'

She arched a brow. 'I can see why. Are you sure you're not a politician disguised as an officer?'

'I leave the politics to my friends, Stepan and

Ruslan, when I can. But I've yet to meet a military man who doesn't have the wit to handle both on occasion.' The butler helped him with his greatcoat. Coat settled, Nikolay took Klara's hand and bent to it, lips grazing knuckles. '*Do svidaniya*, Miss Grigorieva. Thank you for such an…enlightening… evening.' Revolution was afoot in Belgravia and while his logical mind knew he should run from it, his heart was already protesting his declaration of living quietly. When had he ever lived quietly? Did he even know how? How ironic that the one thing he'd hoped to avoid in his new life was the one thing that had found him, the one thing that stirred him— if one didn't count Klara Grigorieva. She stirred him in an entirely different, but no less dangerous, way.

Chapter Five

Klara's hand was still tingling when the door shut behind the last guest, which was quite possibly what the prince intended, the arrogant man. She'd like to forget him and his seductive effect. She'd like to think he affected her no differently than any other man, but she was not in the habit of lying to herself. Her reaction to Nikolay Baklanov was going to complicate things.

'The Prince handled himself well this evening. Can he be of use to us?' Her father issued his question to the two remaining guests—his most intimate advisors, Amesbury and Vasilev. He stood in the doorway to the drawing room, inviting them to join him in consultation. 'Shall we talk it over?' She would join the men as a matter of course to work through impressions. This was the custom ever since she'd turned eighteen and had been presented to society. In this manner, her father had subtly coached her in the ways of a diplomat: how to understand people, how to read between the lines of their conversation. Such an education had only been given to her because it served a purpose. She was not the sole beneficiary of the privilege. Her father gained the advantage of his astute daughter's insights. He understood full well how unguarded men could be in the presence of a pretty young woman, especially when they assumed she was harmless to them, a female expected to be vacuous because she was beautiful.

Her father poured each of them a small glass of *viche pitia*. He toasted them, 'Another insightful evening.'

Insightful for Nikolay as well. Klara hazarded a surreptitious glance at Amesbury as she sipped. Nikolay had correctly guessed that Amesbury coveted her. She was acutely aware the Duke wanted to possess her the way a man wanted to possess a fine carriage and excellent horses. The Duke caught her gaze, his eyes hard over his glass, a cold smile hovering on his lips, cold enough to send a shiver down her spine.

Her father was speaking to Vasilev. 'What do you make of Baklanov?'

'He understood you were vetting him tonight,' Vasilev said thoughtfully. 'He was very careful with his words. He's not sure what you want him for.'

'He does now. Can he be a revolutionary?' her father queried. 'We dropped enough breadcrumbs for a smart man to follow. Will he? Klara, I defer to you on this.'

It was an honour to be addressed thusly in front of the General and the Duke, a sign of her father's esteem for her. But it was an honour that made her uncomfortable and yet she could not refuse. The words had brought Amesbury's intent gaze her direction, his pale blue eyes narrowed in speculation as he drawled, 'Yes, Klara, you know him best, it seems. You've spent more time with him than any of us.' His words carried a subtle accusatory edge to them.

She locked eyes with Amesbury. She was not afraid of him and his veiled accusation that spending time with Nikolay had been somehow inappropriate. He might intimidate others with his power and his wealth, but not her. She had those things, too. Any thought of demurring faded. She couldn't afford to. It would mean she was soft, that perhaps she harboured a burgeoning attraction to the Kubanian Prince. Amesbury had noticed their tête-à-tête in the drawing room before dinner. To confirm that impression would be disastrous. It would raise the Duke's hackles, which would not please her father, and it would prove she was indeed as vacuous as any other female whose head was turned by a handsome face. There was a certain mordancy that the best protection she could give Nikolay was through betrayal.

'As soon as he knows it's not a trap, he will follow your breadcrumbs and decide if he can afford to join you,' she said. It was a small betrayal of Nikolay to be sure, based on her intuition only. But she knew her intuition spoke the truth; the hesitation he'd shown in the park, the ferocity when he'd told her he could not go back to his country, proved her correct. Reticence was a reflex often ascribed to a man who had something to hide, a man who was wary of a trap that would seek to expose what he protected.

Her father and the General nodded. Amesbury sneered. 'Since you are playing the fortune-teller, perhaps you can tell us if your Prince *will* join us? Since you know him so well.'

'*My* prince? He is hardly that,' Klara snapped, her hand clenching around the little stem of her *viche pitia* glass. It was a struggle to keep her tone neutral. Amesbury was jealous. He had no reason to be. Nikolay Baklanov might flirt with a woman, but he was not the sort of man who allowed himself to belong to one. She did not think Nikolay's flirtation, as delightful, as sensual as it was, was an exclusive commodity. 'If you are asking about his willingness to join the Union of Salvation, I cannot say. You saw tonight that he is no newcomer to court intrigue. He will not readily reveal his secrets to anyone.'

Her father split a swift glance between the two of them and intervened. He speared Amesbury with a quelling look. 'There is no need to fight amongst ourselves. Klara was doing the job *we* assigned her. We must convince the Prince of the rightness of our cause and the importance of him taking a role in it. We need him to take the arms to St Petersburg and to help rally the troops when the time comes. He's a man others will follow.' He turned his diplomatic censure on Klara. 'However, we all risk much by taking him in too soon. We must be sure of him. The group depends on the quality of its associates. One weak link and we go from being patriots to traitors.

The line is very thin. Our next step is to discover what has brought Prince Baklanov to England and talk then.'

The glasses were empty and her father made no move to refill them, a polite signal that it was time to leave. General Vasilev rose and made his farewells, but Amesbury lingered, his thin, aristocratic mouth—proof of generations of impeccable English breeding—tight. 'Walk me to the door, Klara, I'd like a word.'

Klara obliged, for how could she refuse? On the surface, everyone would assume the Duke wanted a moment to apologise for his rudeness, that he would explain it away as a sign of his concern for her. But those assumptions would be false. The Duke apologised to no one and for nothing. Although he was similar to her father in many regards, his inability to apologise was not one of them.

The Duke was a big man with a bearing that neared military in stature. Even though she was tall, Klara had to fight the feeling of 'smallness' in his presence, for she did indeed feel small with him, unlike with Nikolay who was his equal in height. Some might call the Duke handsome with his strong facial bones and the grooves etched on either side of his mouth, reinforcing the sternness, the hardness of him. She called him cold, an iceberg personified, complete with glacial blue eyes. She walked beside him in silence, waiting for him to speak.

'I did not want to say anything in front of the others,' Amesbury began, 'However, since I have much at stake in this venture, and perhaps…' he paused here, attempting a modest demeanour that failed to convince '…a certain burgeoning relationship of a personal nature with you, I have the right to ask. How have you come by your information, Klara?'

'What are you suggesting?' She removed her hand from his arm and stood apart from him, erasing any façade of a polite couple. She had to stop those presumptions right here. If he presumed they had the foundations of a relationship, who knew what else he would presume? His arrogance would promote all nature of assumption beginning with the idea that a woman couldn't possibly find him resistible.

'I'm suggesting that you would have had to work hard to get that information. A man like Baklanov, who likely has much to protect, would not give up information easily. We saw that tonight. How is it that you've been privy to such insight? He is not immune to your charms. That was made clear tonight as well. I saw the two of you with your heads together.'

Klara did not flinch at his accusation. She crossed her arms. 'You call yourself a gentleman and yet you dare to accuse me of seducing the Prince. That's what you're implying, isn't it? That I've inappropriately enticed him? The Prince has acted far more the gentleman than you.'

He strode towards her and gripped her arm, his voice a menacing growl. 'The Prince, a gentleman? Is that what you call him? He had his damn mouth at your ear with all the presumption of a lover.' His grip hurt, hard enough to bruise. 'Forgive me my conclusions. You have never allowed *me* such liberties.'

But he was taking them anyway. The tenacity of his grip of her arm was more than a little frightening. It took all her cool *élan* not to let him see it. He had never laid hands on her in such a fashion before and this glimpse of possessive violence made her uneasy. What made him think he could do so now? It was a disturbing insight into what relationship with such a man might be like and Klara was determined to put a stop to it.

'Take your hands off me. The Prince and I rode in the park and we talked.' All true, but slightly incomplete. There was that kiss, that glorious kiss with an erotic roughness behind it that was far different than the harshness the Duke was exhibiting here in the hall. She would combat the Duke's physical boldness with a boldness of her own. 'Jealousy does not become you, nor do you have any claim to such envy.'

'Perhaps not yet. However, it cannot have escaped your notice that I aspire to have such a claim.' He removed his hand and stepped back with a curt nod, his words causing an uneasiness in her stomach that rivalled the violence of his touch. 'I'll say goodnight, then, Klara.' There had been no 'forgive me' or 'I beg your pardon'. Simply 'goodnight.' Asking for forgiveness would imply he'd done something wrong, an impossibility to Amesbury's arrogant mind.

She breathed easier when the door was shut behind him. She'd never liked Amesbury. But until recently, she'd never disliked him either. She'd merely found him blandly neutral, a shuttered, arrogant man who held himself aloof from others by nature of his birth. Now, she'd had a glimpse behind those shutters and it had been quite frightening. Klara wrapped her arms about herself. He'd laid angry hands on her in her own home. Perhaps she was reading far too much into it. Men were by nature competitive creatures and Nikolay had provoked him, perhaps *she* had provoked him. She'd known the Duke watched her. She hadn't been unaware of how she and Nikolay would have appeared to an outsider. Maybe she had even encouraged it. If one didn't poke the sleeping dog, it wouldn't bite you. Recklessness had its consequences, after all. But such reasoning didn't dispel the shiver that took her when she thought of Amesbury's hands on her. Nikolay wasn't the only one with secrets.

It came to her that perhaps her father had a secret, too. The Duke presumed a relationship between them that she felt certain she'd given him no cause to believe in. Had her father? Amid his treaties and plans of revolution, had he alluded to the potential of her hand in exchange for...something? She rapidly sorted through what she knew. Her father had increased the Duke's wealth. What was he getting in exchange? Was she somehow part of that? She'd always known her father would seek an English marriage for her. She'd been groomed for it. But to the Duke? She hoped not.

Her father strolled into the hall. 'Have they all

gone then?' he asked. 'Quite the night. You did well. Baklanov was taken with you, as he should be.' Her father smiled. 'My daughter is beautiful.' Then his gaze turned serious. 'Can you do it? Can you mine Baklanov's secrets?' He was asking her to betray Nikolay to a larger extent.

This was her opportunity to get out. She could say she wasn't up to it. But inwardly she baulked at playing the coward. It was not like her to shy away from a challenge. Still, she found herself looking for an excuse. 'How? A riding lesson is quite busy. There's not a lot of time to talk.'

'You'll find a way,' her father insisted confidently. 'Talk to him about Kuban. Talk to him about himself. Flirt a little. I've yet to meet a man who can resist the temptation to talk about himself with a pretty girl.' Her father winked affectionately.

The prospect of Tuesday's lesson came with mixed emotions. The prospect of seeing Nikolay again filled her with a breath-catching anticipation, but it required she pay her father's price—to play the game one more time. She had to consider how she felt about that, especially since those feelings came with the realisation that she was willing to protect a man she barely knew from her father's intrigues, a man who might even be dangerous to them. Why should she give him the benefit of being innocent before proven guilty when her father's precious game and her own usefulness to that game hung in the balance? She knew the disturbing answer: because Nikolay Baklanov kissed like the devil.

* * *

The devil was most definitely in the details. Nikolay stood in the darkened hall of Kuban House, wondering how he'd tell Stepan and the others about the evening without earning an 'I told you so' and without lying. He wasn't fooled by the darkness. Stepan would still be up. Stepan wouldn't sleep until he was safely home.

As if on cue, somewhere down the hall Nikolay heard a match strike, saw the shadow of its flare against the hall wall as a lamp was lit. Stepan emerged from the study and stood in the doorway. 'Come have a drink. Illarion and I are still awake.'

It was best to get it over with, Nikolay thought, taking a chair by the fire and letting Stepan pour him a glass of *samogon*. Illarion raised his glass in a silent salute and they drank.

'You've survived.' Stepan sat back easily in his chair, one leg crossed over the other; a relaxed pose unless one knew Stepan very well. Stepan never relaxed. 'Was it an ambush as you expected?'

'Was she beautiful?' Illarion asked, earning a scolding look from Stepan.

'What does that matter?' Stepan scowled.

Illarion shrugged, unbothered by the rebuke after two decades of friendship. 'Beauty always matters, but especially if one is putting himself at risk. One should always have a reward.'

Nikolay laughed, enjoying the sparring. They'd been sparring since they were children, Illarion the poet and Stepan the pragmatist. 'She *was* beautiful,

Illarion. Her gown matched the china. Lomonosov, if you must know.' He speared Stepan with a sober stare. Stepan would know the china was important. 'It was an entirely Russian evening. Clear soup, Caspian Sea caviar and all. There were twelve of us in attendance including wives, an English duke and a general's daughter.' Stepan's gaze sharpened as Nikolay had known it would. 'I believe they are planning a little palace revolt.'

Both were on alert now.

'It is easy to plot from afar.' Illarion was uncharacteristically pessimistic.

'They want you to join them,' Stepan surmised with deadly accuracy. 'Palace revolts need princes.'

'Perhaps. They wanted to test my loyalties tonight, to see if I held with traditionalists who stand against change or if I'm truly in exile because I hold more modern sentiments.' When Stepan remained sceptically silent, Nikolay hastened to add, 'There was no formal overture. They're not sure I'm what they need.'

Stepan scoffed. 'Don't be naïve, Nik. Revolutions need three things to succeed: military support, financial backing and leadership in high places. An English duke isn't the same as having a Russian prince for a Russian revolution. You know what a palace revolt means.' He knew very well what it meant. A change in leadership from the top down. Revolutions were serious business—business that didn't end well if the rebels failed. 'They'll make you an offer as soon as they're sure of you.' That had been his assessment as well.

Stepan kept his gaze even, his voice firmly quiet. 'Don't let them be sure of you. Cut all ties with the ambassador *now*. He'll understand what that means.' That he wanted no part of the revolt regardless of his sympathies. That had been his knee-jerk reaction, too, once he'd realised where the dinner conversation had been headed. His initial reaction had been one of horrified fascination. A revolt in many ways was something he'd longed for, been willing to participate in, should the situation ever arise when he'd been in Kuban. He'd realised over three years ago that, left to its own devices, Kuban would never change, regardless of the need to advance. That realisation had soured him. Three years ago, Nikolay would have been the ambassador's man. He'd left those ambitions behind when he fled Kuban. They'd been put aside in exchange for his life the night a woman had come at him with a knife. How ironic that those ambitions had found him now when he could not be of use.

'We came to England to avoid such contretemps.' Stepan's voice was steely with warning. Were his thoughts so transparent? He was losing his touch if Stepan could read his mind so easily, or did Stepan guess at the temptation? The temptation was definitely there, increasing the longer he thought about it. Nikolay could leave his home behind, his *things* behind, but principles and beliefs were as portable as the man himself. Kuban needed to change, Russia needed to change, not just because he wanted it, but because the people the nation served *needed* it. The old ways were, well, *old*, tired and worn out, unable to serve the needs of the people in a modern world.

'Such contretemps nearly saw you killed,' Stepan reminded him.

Yes, and now here he was, living a half-life in London, a life that had him teaching spoiled rich girls how to ride horses, a life that was waiting to start. Frankly, he was bored—or he had been until Klara had come along with her breeches and long legs, her smart mouth and challenging eyes and his blood had thrilled in the old ways, despite the promises he'd made himself to be more careful with women. One night with any woman, that was all. No long-term attachments.

'I'll decline future invitations,'. Nikolay said. There could be no association with Grigoriev. There was no other choice. If he felt let down by that decision, it was simply because he was restless. He needed to move forward. The sooner he got his riding stable started the better. He would have something to do, something to distract him from temptation.

'And the lovely Klara?' Illarion asked. 'Will you decline her invitations, too?' Nikolay shot Illarion a disapproving look. He could have done without the mention of Klara. Apparently, his thoughts weren't the only ones that had gone straight to her. The man in him toyed with the idea of keeping Klara as a riding student. But the realist in him recognised the impossibility of that. She was Grigoriev's link to him. She could never be neutral. His initial instincts had been right. He had to let Klara go. It would be far easier to break things off when there was nothing to truly break off, just a baiting kiss in the park and bantering words. It would be for the best. He knew already just how dangerous association with the wrong woman could be.

Chapter Six

Nikolay had barely stepped out of the arena from his Tuesday lesson when the words assaulted him. Klara Grigorieva blocked his way, dressed in breeches, hands on hips. 'You had me reassigned.'

'Captain Crenshaw is an excellent instructor.' He moved to the right to go around her. So did she.

'I don't want Captain Crenshaw.' He should have known she wouldn't go without a fight—perhaps that in itself was a reason he had to hold firm to his decision. If she was willing to fight for this, there must be something to fight for, proof that Stepan had been right in his concern.

'What exactly is the problem with Captain Crenshaw? Doesn't he let you wear breeches?' He stepped left.

She matched him. 'He could let me ride naked and it still wouldn't matter.' Well, now, there was an image to keep a man up all night. Klara's eyes blazed with a green fire. 'He's not you.' Of course not. Crenshaw couldn't help promote rebellion, further proof

that she had ulterior motives to come back for more
than a kiss.

He kept his tone polite, aloof, treating her as if
she were any other student. 'I think it's best that he
isn't.' What couldn't be gone around had to be gone
through, a primary lesson of the cavalry. Nikolay
stepped forward, forcing her to step back. This had
worked once before with her, in the park. But then
the outcome had been very different to the one he
intended today. He stepped forward again and again,
driving her back towards Cossack's stall. He meant
to ride tonight and there was no reason to change
those plans, certainly not a reason with long legs
and breeches.

'For the best?' She spoke fast, as if she realised
she was giving up ground too quickly. 'Who is it best
for? Me or you?' She was one step away from Cossack's stall when she fired her next salvo. 'You're
afraid of me, Nikolay Baklanov.' Her eyes glinted,
narrowing like a cat who's playing with a mouse,
her gaze somewhere between seduction and challenge. Her tongue flicked across her lips. 'I didn't
think you a coward.'

He bristled at the accusation even though he knew
she was poking at him, wanting to get a rise of temper. 'I am no coward. Simply because fire is good
for cooking doesn't mean a man should run into a
blazing inferno with his steak on a stick. A smart
man knows the difference.' And a *wise* man would
act accordingly. Nikolay knew what he should do. He
understood the situation perfectly in theory. It was
being wise in practice that was difficult, especially

with Klara Grigorieva standing eighteen inches from him, eyes flashing, breasts heaving beneath the folds of her man's shirt.

'Blizok iokotok da ne ukusish,' he muttered, reaching around her for the latch to Cossack's door.

'Don't do that.' She pressed back against the stall door, preventing him from opening it, her voice fierce. Did he imagine it or did her nostrils flare? Behind her, Cossack nudged her with his head. 'Don't say things I can't understand.'

Nikolay blew out a frustrated breath. 'I will remove you bodily from here if I have to.' The image of such an action hung between them, far too potent to be the deterrent he intended. The last thing his body needed was the temptation of hauling Klara over his shoulder, that delectable, round derrière of hers against his cheek, his arm wrapped across her thighs. The only reason he hadn't done it yet was that he was sure she'd hit him for it. He could already feel those fists pummelling his back.

'Tell me what you said and I'll step aside.' She crossed her arms.

'Fine. I said, trouble never comes alone.'

'Is that what I am? Trouble?' She stepped aside, allowing him to lead Cossack out to the cross ties.

'So much trouble in so many ways, if I may be blunt.' Nikolay opened the trunk beside the stall and took out a grooming kit and began to brush the horse.

'Please, do be blunt.' Klara picked up a brush and started on Cossack's other side.

'Aren't you leaving?'

'I only promised to step aside. I didn't promise

anything else. Where's your curry brush? He's got some mud dried here.'

'Just dig. It's at the bottom of the box.'

She flashed him a smile and he realised too late what he'd done: he'd given her permission to stay. He'd be saddled with her unless he took drastic action. Except that he already had taken drastic action by English standards. He'd walked through her, he'd insulted her with his directness, he'd kissed her. These were all brash behaviours that would have sent a typical English miss running for the protection of her mother and perhaps a pistol-wielding brother. But those efforts had only served to urge Klara on.

Nikolay set aside his brush and patted Cossack's side. This would only take a minute. He ducked under the cross tie, taking the curry brush from her. 'I need you to leave and it is not up for discussion. The stable is closed for the evening. It is not appropriate for you to be here with me, or any instructor, unchaperoned.' He hoped calling out the obvious consideration of her reputation would be enough, but it only encouraged the minx.

A smile teased her lips. 'Are you afraid I'll compromise you?' She slid her arms about his neck, her body flush against his without the protection of skirts, he might add. By Jove, she was bold and, heaven help him, he liked it, liked it enough to want to forget the decisions he'd made, the rules he needed to keep for his own safety and the safety of his friends.

He unwrapped her arms. 'Klara, this is unseemly.' Lucifer's balls, he sounded like a prude. Unseemly had never stopped him before. He'd done plenty of unseemly things, some of them in alcoves, shielded from hundreds of guests by only a curtain. But none of them seemed as dangerous as this, this game that was not only about the crackling, emergent attraction between a man and a woman, but also between a diplomat's daughter, perhaps even a spymaster's daughter, and a prince who might yet prove politically useful. Only the naïve would pretend this was a game that involved personal feelings alone.

She leaned in, the spicy scent of her, vanilla with a note of woody amber, teasing his nostrils. 'Perhaps I can put your mind at ease. I am not trying to compromise you, nor am I looking to be compromised.' Then she pricked at his ego. 'I thought you'd have more imagination than that.' He had plenty of imagination, all right. Any prince who lived long enough at court did. It was that imagination that allowed him to see all the layers.

'Next you'll be telling me you just want to be friends.'

She scoffed. 'Why would that be so hard to believe?

'I don't think dinner was about becoming friends.'

'That's my father's business and yours, should you choose to pursue it. That doesn't have to be about us.' The edge of her softened. 'Is it so hard to believe that someone would want to be friends with a prince?'

'No, that's quite easy to believe.' He made his cynicism evident. He didn't want her pity, just her awareness. He was not a simple Englishman overcome by her beauty, a man who could be toyed with.

He moved away, grabbing Cossack's tack. He'd do best to stay busy and not invite any more wandering hands, arms, bodies, thoughts. There was an attraction between them, but it could not be acted on. Not for the first time, he was aware that she was fishing for something, something that went beyond his initial concern over political gain. She wanted something from him on a personal level. If she could be believed, that 'something' didn't involve matrimony, which left his imagination a bit empty as to precisely what it was she was after. 'Everyone wants to be friends with a prince. Everyone wants something. Why don't you tell me? What is it you want from me?'

What did she want from him? More hard, rough kisses in the park, more barking orders at her in the arena, more matching of wits, more everything. Just being in a room with him was exciting, the anticipation of watching him the way she had at dinner, or wondering what he'd do next. He'd not been afraid of the Duke's questions. Klara watched him throw a saddle pad over Cossack's withers, considering how best to name her desire, how best to get him back. Training with Crenshaw would serve no one's purpose, not hers or her father's. She'd been furious when she'd shown up to the stable and discovered she'd been reassigned.

She opted for boldness. He liked her bold even if he'd convinced himself he couldn't acquiesce to it. 'I want *you*.' This was met with a querying look over the horse's back. He started to give her a look full of assumption.

'I thought we'd established *that* was not on the table.'

Klara smirked. She would enjoy taking a little wind out of him. 'You can stow your male arrogance. It's not that kind of want.' She drew a breath and prepared to dissemble. 'I want you to teach me Russian. I want you to teach me about Kubanian culture, Russian culture.' The idea had come to her as she'd thought about how to engage him, how to uncover the secrets her father wanted. Nikolay seemed at his most vulnerable when he spoke of Kuban. But now, saying the words out loud made it more than a play for information. It was something she wanted, just for herself; to know, at last, that piece of her heritage.

His eyes were on her, considering the statement. Weighing its truth. 'Your father can teach you that,' he said slowly.

She shook her head. 'He hasn't, you know that, and he won't.' She paused. She had to give Nikolay more, allay his suspicions. How ironic that he was suspicious when this was something she truly wanted for herself. 'I'm meant to be English. He expects me to marry an Englishman of rank at some point.' That point was starting to panic her, however, since the dinner party. Had her father meant the Duke all along, or was that a contretemps entirely of the Duke's making? But her admission wasn't enough for Nikolay. She had to give him something more than compelling. 'My mother died in Russia.' She lowered her gaze, dissembling. 'It's why I've never been back. He has never forgiven the country for that.' There was a long silence. She began to worry. *Please don't let him deny me.* If this did not convince him, she wasn't sure what would. This was something she wanted; not for her father, although she should want that, but just for her.

'I deduce that your father would be displeased,' he argued wryly, but he hadn't said no. He *was* thinking about it, she could tell by the way he tightened Cossack's girth with a certain determination. She had her answers ready.

'My father doesn't have to find out. How would he know anyway? And if he did find out, it would be too late. What could he do? He can't take the knowledge from me.'

'What did I tell you?' he grumbled to Cossack, leading the horse towards the arena. *'Blizok iokotok da ne ukusish.'* But a little smile pulled at his stoic mouth. Klara tamped down a trill of pre-emptory victory, not wanting to be thwarted at the last because she'd got cocky too early.

Inside the arena, he swung up on the horse's back. 'Tell Fozard's to schedule you for three lessons a week at the end of the day.' He'd want that, of course, she'd be less conspicuous. No one would be here waiting for a lesson to follow hers.

She grinned, but Nikolay merely shook his head and kicked Cossack into a canter, dismissing her for now. She let him go. She'd got her victory for the day.

That victory buoyed her through a tedious evening of cards with the General's wife's friends. Russian lessons would start tomorrow. She'd got what she wanted. She would get to learn about her heritage. Of course, her father had got what he wanted, too: an entrée into Nikolay's personal life. She hoped Nikolay wasn't hiding anything. She hoped there might not be anything to report, that Nikolay was exactly what he claimed to be: a prince teaching riding lessons with no ambitions.

As she claimed another trick in piquet, Klara knew that even such a simple truth couldn't save Nikolay from her father's net. Nikolay had already lost simply by coming into her father's notice; if he was 'friendly' her father would want him for the Union of Salvation. If he refused to participate, her father would want to see him deported or dead. For Nikolay, there was no scenario where his life and his choices were any longer solely his.

Guilt pricked at her, harder and stronger now that the die had been cast. No matter what happened next, no matter what she discovered, or what she revealed, she was involved now, completely. She had to take ownership of the fact that everything had changed for Nikolay the moment she'd walked into the riding stable.

Chapter Seven

'You don't really believe it will stop there, do you? What do you suppose she's *really* after with her Russian lessons?' Stepan eyed him over afternoon brandy at the club, scepticism rife in his gaze. It made Nikolay regret bringing the subject up and yet he needed Stepan's counsel.

Late afternoon was usually Nikolay's favourite time here—not so today with Stepan's censuring eyes on him. White's enjoyed a brief lull before the evening crowd; gentlemen grabbing cognac and commiseration before heading out to hours of dancing and debutantes. 'This place makes me think of our club in Kuban.' Nikolay swirled his brandy, trying a rather obviously evasive manoeuvre. He was eager to talk about something other than Klara Grigorieva. 'I hear during the Season it's almost impossible to get a seat.' White's was an exclusive club. Their membership had been secured with the presumption of their titles. London was fascinated with foreign princes, apparently, even exiled ones.

'Then enjoy it while it lasts.' Stepan's voice held a tinge of cynicism. 'I wonder how long we'll be allowed when London realises our limitations? That there are no thrones to inherit, not even any land or palaces, or coronets. None of the things that define a prince.'

'We are not precisely paupers,' Nikolay argued, willing to engage in the debate for the sake of drawing attention away from the issue of Klara.

'No, but if money were all that mattered, merchants would be clamouring for entrance.' Stepan's comment reminded him their titles alone hadn't been their only recommendation for White's. While they'd given up considerable wealth in terms of palaces and possessions, there was other wealth that was convertible, more transportable for their flight. That wealth was now securely housed at Coutts and Company on the Strand, where it waited for each of them to decide what to do. For now, they'd limited themselves to living off a portion of the interest and reinvesting the rest. That had been Stepan's idea.

Stepan shrugged. 'Wealth is finite unless you do something with it. If not, it *will* run out.' Like time. Time and money had a lot in common and Nikolay felt as if he were running out of both.

Nikolay signalled a waiter to refill their glasses. 'How long do we wait?' Stepan would know what he meant. How long did they wait before they invested in their new lives? How much longer did they live in limbo, wondering if Kuban would come after them, if there would be repercussions for their departure? It was time to start living their English lives.

'We promised ourselves a year,' Stepan reminded him.

'That year is up in March,' Nikolay pressed. When they'd arrived, they'd spent time in the country with Dimitri, then come to London after the Christmas holidays. That year was almost done. There'd been no pursuit. They'd nearly been safe. It was a damnable time for Klara Grigorieva to show up and cast doubt on that safety.

'We are all eager,' Stepan said, reading his impatience. 'Perhaps we should wait until after the Season before we do anything.' In other words, they should give Klara Grigorieva plenty of time to show her colours. But it would mean another year lost before he could set up his own riding academy in town. Another year before he could breed the Cleveland Bay. He wanted a January-February foal, which meant a March or April mating. If Stepan had his way, Klara had put those hopes at risk.

'I know you're anxious, but waiting is prudent,' Stepan cautioned. 'This wouldn't be the first time a woman has played you. The last time was nearly deadly.'

Nikolay grimaced at the reminder, feeling the old stab of pain when he thought about the night that had changed his life. 'Klara Grigorieva is not Helena.'

'So you *think*.' Stepan was a severe sceptic when it came to women in general. Helena had not helped his viewpoint.

'You'll end up a monk with an attitude like that,' Nikolay replied drily.

'I will never get stabbed in my own bedroom either,' Stepan shot back with the sharp remark. 'If I were you, I wouldn't be so cavalier.'

'I am not being cavalier,' Nikolay argued. 'What happened with Helena will never happen again. I made mistakes with her I don't intend to repeat.' Namely sharing too much, feeling too much and believing that level of emotional investment was reciprocated. 'I have my rules now: don't let them get too close. Keep it physical, keep it short.' He shifted in his seat, restless and a little angry over being taken to task. 'You are not my father.'

'No, I am not. I am your friend.' Stepan took a swallow of his brandy with a sense of finality that signalled this part of the conversation was over.

The front door opened, admitting a trio of gentlemen. The club was growing busier as the shadows lengthened. The quiet time was ending. It was time to wrap up the conversation about Klara and move on to other things. Nikolay might not be as sceptical as Stepan, but there was no reason to speak of private things where they could be overheard. One never knew who was listening. 'I've found a few places with potential for the riding academy.' Nikolay moved the conversation onwards.

Stepan was all caution again. 'I'd wait a few months before I put money down.'

'*You* would. I wouldn't. I don't want to miss out. If I wait until everyone comes to town for the Season,

I may lose my opportunity.' Nikolay sighed, frustrated with Stepan's reticence, yet his friend's caution was why he'd sought Stepan out. His caution was the perfect balance to Nikolay's own tendencies towards recklessness. Still, there was a limit to how much caution was warranted. 'We never said we'd be invisible, Stepan. We never said we'd let fear drive us into hiding, otherwise what's the point of having left?' That was more of a theoretical argument. Living was the point of having left—more so in a quantitative sense for him. He'd risked death by staying. The others had their own reasons.

'We also never planned on falling for an ambassador's daughter,' Stepan countered. 'It seems plans change.'

'I am not falling for her,' Nikolay argued, only to be met with a look of question from Stepan. His friend was being ridiculous. He wasn't falling for Klara. He merely found her interesting and fresh, a woman who stood out from the rest. Besides, he'd promised himself he wouldn't fall for anyone ever again. He blew out a breath. 'Aren't you tired of waiting, Stepan?' He was restless by nature, but in London he'd become more so. 'These English gentlemen do nothing all day.' He wanted to ask more, too—*Don't you miss Kuban? Do you think about home?* What would Stepan say if he told him the reason he'd accepted Klara's request was because it gave him a way to remember the home he'd given up.

'It's your money,' Stepan assented without answering the question. He leaned close. 'Promise me you won't seduce her. Not yet. I don't know if we can save you a second time.' Nikolay saw the care-driven concern in his friend's gaze. Stepan had been the one who'd had him released from the Tsar's jail, the one who had spearheaded the getaway. Stepan had risked much for him. The Tsar was not likely to forgive Stepan easily, if ever, for that. He owed Stepan his loyalty and more.

'I'll be good. It will be a long time before I let a woman get close.' Maybe not ever, Nikolay thought. He had his own scepticisms, too, when it came to the fairer sex, he just wasn't going to be a monk about it. No more than a single night with any woman would serve in the place of celibacy. 'Thank you.' He gripped Stepan's arm in gratitude. Beneath the warning, he understood the magnitude of what Stepan had given him; They would begin their English lives as planned. He could get that riding school as soon as he decided on a location.

Nikolay raised the remainder of his glass in a toast, a sense of excitement surging through him. He could proceed with his riding academy. '*Za vashee zda-ró-vye*. To our health and to new beginnings.' The ache of purposelessness was starting to recede, the temptation to be part of Alexei Grigoriev's revolt was ebbing, to somehow manufacture a return to his country. He just needed something to do.

'To new beginnings,' Stepan echoed. 'Let's hope our health doesn't need it.' Then he raised an arched brow and added wryly, 'And to being good.'

* * *

Nikolay *did* mean to be good. It shouldn't have been hard. He had a scar low on his hip to remind him of the high price of not being good and there was no mistaking the Grigorievs had a daring political agenda, the kind he was forbidden by common sense to embrace. That alone made Klara off limits. The very nature of her duality made it impossible to know what was real and what was artifice, and there was artifice aplenty. He knew already she'd sought him out for a purpose, she'd invited him to dinner to be vetted by important Russian nobles, making it clear that purpose was not based in an honest flirtation. But when he'd kissed her in the park, when she'd raged at him for changing her lesson, *that* had been real.

There had been no artifice in her anger. That had intrigued him. She should have been angry because of the obstacle he'd placed in her path. She could no longer continue to vet him for her father if they were not together. Yet, that had not been the entire source of her anger. She'd been angry for herself. She'd been angry because he'd denied her time with him. Just her. She'd wanted him for herself, or rather she'd wanted his knowledge just for her.

He'd seen it not only in the flash of her eyes, but in the nature of her request. She wanted him to teach her about Russia, about Kuban. That was not a request her father would have her make if he had kept her Russian heritage from her. The last thing Grigoriev would want was someone ruining the English upbringing he'd spent a lifetime cultivating.

The woman she'd been in those moments challenged him, stirred his body and his curiosity to the point of *wanting* to set aside his distrust of desire for just a while, to set aside what he knew of the agenda Klara had been sent to promote. He wanted to explore the possibilities of Klara Grigorieva's passion, to explore Klara the person, instead of Klara the pawn. That was why he'd accepted the request, why he found himself sitting across from her in the tackroom-cum-classroom three nights a week, trying to resist temptation while tasting just a little of the pleasure of her company. He was hoping the taste would appease his curiosity's appetites, hoping his fascination would wane as it so often did with pretty women after a while.

It was the devil's own bargain, one that could so easily lead him down a slippery slope of deception. That brief dose of honest chagrin made her all the more dangerous. Her honesty made it difficult to separate the real emotions from the game. He should leave her alone. He tried to, he really did. He kept himself remote, focusing on the grammar and the alphabet instead of the culture. He ignored the brilliance and passion that was Kuban. There would only be trouble showing her that path. She would fall in love with Kuban, with its wild landscapes and rivers, the heroism of the Cossack Tsars, the rugged generation of new Princes, the exotic mysticism his country shared with the Ottomans even while repelling them. Such lessons would only torture them both.

Instead of opening up a new world to her, he kept

the lessons dry, doing his best to model every tutor he'd ever hated in the hopes that she would be disappointed and leave. He taught her the alphabet, the numbers and basic conversation; *My name is Klara, how are you? I am well, thank you.* And it didn't work at all. It was, in fact, making things worse. The more boring the lesson, the more flirtation she engaged in, as if she were doing it on purpose.

By the beginning of the third week, he was certain she was goading him with the toss of her hair, the leggy confidence of her stride, the lingering gazes across the table that lasted just long enough to make a man think, the sway of breeched hips as she marched down the stable aisles with a hint of feminine swagger. Never enough to call her on it, but always enough to make a man wonder, to make a man ache alone in his bed at night. By the end of the third week, he was certain: she was teasing him. Where his game of boredom had failed miserably, her flirtation had succeeded: he was a primed powder keg. It would take only the slightest provocation for him to go off.

Nikolay shifted in his seat at the tackroom table, trying to make himself comfortable, a deuced difficult task when Klara seemed intent on making sure he was quite the opposite. The damn table had shrunk, it seemed. Everything was too small tonight: the room, the table, his trousers. Klara twisted a long curl around her finger, her eyes drifting slowly over his mouth, not unlike the gesture he'd used on her at the park, as he tried to explain that the Russian language didn't use articles.

'Let me get this straight, there is no *a*, *an* or *the*.' Klara's voice was low and seductive, a bedroom tone to be sure. No one spoke like that at the dinner table. Her eyes were back on his mouth, tracing his lips with her gaze. That girl was a quick study. 'As in everything is interchangeable parts. There is no difference between *a* kiss and *the* kiss. *A* lover and *the* lover. That must have its conveniences.'

Her tongue wet her lips and Nikolay snapped. 'What the hell do you think you are doing?'

'Learning Russian. What do you think I am doing?' She was all surprised innocence now, so innocent, in fact, he wondered for a moment if he hadn't misjudged her game. But, no, he knew he was right. Klara was toying with him, because she knew, dammit, that he was toying with her.

'Exacting revenge is the response I was going for,' Nikolay growled. It was high time for a different sort of lesson. He rose from his bench, gratified to see her gaze turn wary. As it should be. When young misses lit powder kegs, they had to be prepared for explosions.

'Why ever would I do that?' Her words might proclaim innocent unawareness, but she knew what she'd done and perhaps worry came to her for the first time. Klara rose, using her height to meet his.

They stood close now, his eyes boring into her sharp green ones, his voice a quiet, firm bass. 'You know why, Klara.'

She did drop the façade then. The pulse at her neck beat fast. She narrowed her eyes, grabbing on to anger because she didn't want to be roused by this quarrel, by this exposure, by him. Good. That made two of them. He didn't want to be roused by her, but he was. 'You mean the horrid lessons? Yes, I want revenge for these awful lessons I've had to sit through where you treat me like a child, teaching me the most basic of facts in the most basic of ways.' Klara fumed. 'This is not what I bargained for.'

'Not what you bargained for? What about me? I didn't bargain for you to come sashaying into the stables with your father's political agenda as a calling card.' He was starting to catch fire now, the fuse of his temper in full spark. 'Well, I don't want to play.' Not entirely true. He did want to play and he wanted to play rough. He had her backed to the wall before he could reconsider. It was time she learned the sort of man she was dealing with. He had her arms pinned over her head, his mouth on hers with ravishing authority, but Klara wasn't done fighting.

'This,' she gasped between kisses, 'is not about my father. It's about us, about our agreement.' Her teeth took a nip out of his bottom lip. 'I came to you wanting to learn about Kuban and you gave me your word. But you haven't shown me anything.' Her hips came up hard against his. She would find more than she was looking for there if she wasn't careful. Then again, he'd come to realise Klara Grigorieva wasn't the careful sort.

'You cannot walk through these stables swinging

your hair and swaying your hips in those breeches and not expect a man to notice,' Nikolay growled, taking a retaliatory bite of her earlobe and watching her suck in her breath.

'You lied to me. You had to pay,' Klara said fiercely, her hand sliding down to the hardness of him between them.

He covered her hand, staying her motion with a shake of his head. 'No.' Arguably the hardest word he'd spoken in a while, but this wasn't going to end with an angry rut on the tackroom table for many reasons. 'You've called my honour into question. I cannot let that pass. You want to see Russia? Come with me. I'll show you Russia. Get changed. We leave in ten minutes.' He drew back, freeing her body. 'Unless you're afraid?' She was going to get what she asked for. He would take her to Soho, where the Russian immigrants lived. He would take her as close to home as he could get in London.

'Afraid to experience Russia or afraid to be with you?' She gave a haughty toss of her head. 'The answer is neither.' She grabbed her satchel from the floor and slipped around a corner in the tackroom where the grooms changed. She flung a white shirt over the dressing screen, conjuring up images of what she was *not* wearing. 'I'm not afraid of you, Nikolay Baklanov.' The light from the table casting her silhouette in relief behind the thin fabric screen, the curve of her high breast, the slimness of her waist as she put on a blouse and buttoned up a form-fitting jacket.

It was he who should be afraid of her. He'd over-played his hand this time. He hadn't scared her off with his dry lessons, with his bold kisses or daring suggestions. Instead, his efforts had drawn her closer, leading her to call his bluff. Stepan would have a fit if he knew what he meant to do—taking a genteel unmarried girl out into public without a chaperon.

Klara stepped around the screen, twisting her hair into a bun at her neck. 'Will I do?' Nikolay took in the blue wool habit, plain but well fitted, not too ostentatious for Soho. She would do, but Klara was the sort of woman who would attract attention wherever she went, even if she were dressed in beggar's rags. The magnitude of that was starting to settle on him in full. If they weren't careful, if she were recognised, if word got back to her father… Well, suffice it to say, all those scenarios ended in matrimony.

'No one will miss me,' she offered, as if reading his thoughts, or perhaps merely trying to convince herself this madness could escape undetected. 'My father has a dinner in Richmond tonight at our house there. Men only. He won't be back until tomorrow,' she added. Nikolay detected some nerves. Good. She should be scared just a little. Not of him certainly, but of the situation.

The stakes were indeed high. But the point of no return had been reached. He had offered. She had accepted and both of them were too stubborn to back down. Nikolay crooked his arm for her. That simple gesture changed everything and she knew it. Despite her bravado, he caught the slightest of hesitations before she slid her hand through the crook of his elbow. He drew a deep breath and reached over to settle his hand atop hers in acknowledgement. There could be no going back now. They were no longer antagonists, no longer teacher and student. Perhaps they were not even Miss Klara Grigorieva, ambassador's daughter, and Prince Nikolay Baklanov, exiled royal, but something simpler—co-conspirators in a secret dash across town. In doing so, each of them would be exposed to the other in a way they hadn't been before. Such vulnerability raised a provocative question: what might happen if plain Klara and Nikolay went to Soho without their titles to protect them?

Chapter Eight

This was true freedom! There was no one to answer to except herself, no expectations except the ones she made. Stepping into the cab had been like stepping into a new skin and leaving the old one behind. Klara settled into the musty interior, realising the enormity of what she'd done. She'd left behind the civilised world for an adventure with a man she barely knew; a man, she might add, who had, less than a half-hour ago, pushed her up against a wall and kissed her like sin itself and to whom she had responded in kind a *second* time. In retrospect, her boldness left her burning with a heat not entirely generated by embarrassment. It was easy to be bold with Nikolay.

The cab jerked into motion, entering the traffic. She stole a glance at Nikolay seated across from her, his jaw set stoically as if he, too, needed a moment to let the realisation set in. What was running through his mind? Regret? Worry over being caught? No one would catch them, of course. Her circles didn't frequent Soho. 'Why did you stop me, back there in the stables?'

He didn't need further clarification. He knew precisely what she meant. 'Because we were angry with one another. We were competing and that's not what I would want for your first time,' Nikolay answered bluntly, bringing a blush to her cheeks with his frankness.

'How do you know that?' she said defensively, suddenly ashamed of her virginity, as if it was no match for Nikolay's superior quantity of experience.

'If you've been raised in privileged English style, you'll be a virgin on your wedding day.' How different he was compared to the English gentlemen she knew. She would never talk to them like this, never behave with them as she did with Nikolay.

Nikolay gave her a warm smile devoid of condescension. 'Feminine virginity is nothing to be ashamed of, Klara, any more than a woman should be ashamed of her naturally passionate nature.' He was absolving her, even approving of her boldness. Yet he had halted for the sake of whose honour? His or hers? Competition implied a winner and a loser. Had he feared losing? Had he halted her because *she'd* gained the upper hand? To a man like Nikolay, control was everything; on horseback, at the dinner table, or in the bedroom, he'd want control in all aspects of his life. She remembered the feel of his grip shackling her wrists, the pressure of his mouth, a rough but not unpleasant exposition of that control, so unlike the control exhibited by Amesbury in their last conversation after dinner. Then, she'd felt vulnerable, threatened. But although Nikolay had been more physical, she had not felt afraid once.

'How is it that you know so much about virginity?' Klara asked with a coy smile.

'That's a fairly leading question,' Nikolay answered her with a grin of his own. He crossed a leg over his knee, starting to relax. It was a question she feared he would laugh off with a drawing-room response. He did not. Perhaps he sensed her need for a deeper truth. 'Kuban is not much different than England in that regard. Our noble women are prized in marriage for their extreme purity.'

She heard the tension beneath his answer. 'You don't approve?' She furrowed her brow, his undertones at odds with his earlier remarks.

His dark eyes held hers, 'I don't approve of stealing choices from people. Self-imposed virginity is fine, self-selected marriage is fine. I have nothing against either institution. However...' He paused and her breath caught, her intuition signalling she was on the brink of a secret. Understanding this was elemental to understanding him.

'When young girls are locked up in convents that are more like prisons and denied the right to look upon a male until they're brought to court or pledged in marriage to men they've never met until the altar, that's a crime against the individual. I cannot support such behaviour. Nor can I support the marriage regulations placed on noble-born men. Those regulations are different, certainly, but no less paralysing. Kuban requires all noble men to take their place at court by the age of thirty. That place is usually accompanied by a prearranged, politically beneficial marriage.' He fell silent, the full force of his gaze on her. 'Have I shocked you, Klara? Was that not the type of thing you wished to learn about Kuban?'

He had been truthful with her and she would respond in kind. She was careful not to look away. 'No, it is not what I expected to learn about your Tsardom. But, no, I am not shocked.' She ventured the hypothesis that had been forming as he spoke. 'Is that why you left? Because you would not allow yourself to be sold in marriage?'

Nikolay gave wry, harsh laugh. 'I'm a soldier. I'm not a marrying man. I did not fear such a marriage for myself. However, that's no reason for me not to fight against such injustices for others. A man cannot limit his sense of justice to only the causes he champions for himself. That would be the ultimate hypocrisy.'

Her immediate thought was that he'd all but called Amesbury a hypocrite. What he had defined as justice was the opposite of all the Duke stood for. Her next thought was that here sat a man of principle, a man who would fight for those who could not fight for themselves. If her father knew what Nikolay had just revealed, he would never let Nikolay go. This passionate devotion was what her father was looking for. He'd want to harness that passion to his own cause. She pushed the thought away. Tonight was not about the game. It was about her and Nikolay. Just the two of them. The cab pulled to a stop and Nikolay looked out the dingy window. 'We're here. Ready?'

More than ready. Klara stepped out into the misty Soho evening. Whatever was said and done here would matter not at all to the real world. It was the unspoken rule of the evening, the reason they had come. Nikolay held the door to a small eatery open for her and she stepped inside the warm space, immediately overwhelmed by the smell of hot food cooking and the loud sounds of a crowded room eating dinner.

'Nikolay!' A robust man with a dark beard and wearing a large white apron hurried over to them. He said something in Russian, too fast and too far beyond her repertoire of words. Nikolay seemed to protest, modest in the wake of the man's effusiveness, but in the end, he let the man lead them to a table for two by the fire. There were no menus, but shortly after they sat the man bustled back with two steaming bowls of rich-smelling stew and a loaf of black bread.

'It's *solyanka*,' Nikolay explained after the man had gone. 'It's a sweet and sour stew.' Nikolay cut them each a slice of bread. 'This is peasant food,' he warned. 'This is not food from the Tsar's table.'

'It's delicious, is what it is.' Klara took a bite of the stew, catching a potato with her spoon. 'I like it.' He was testing her, wanting to know how badly she wanted to engage her Russian heritage. She had not forgotten what had started this venture into Soho.

'If you're trying to scare me off, you've gone about it the absolutely wrong way. I'll want to come here every night.' She nodded in the direction of the man who'd seated them. 'What did the man say to you? I couldn't keep up.'

'He was just glad to see me.' Nikolay dismissed the comment, but she was certain it was more than that.

'He knew you from before. Do you come here often?' She would if she had such freedom. She'd never felt trapped until she'd met Nikolay. True, she had the privilege of her birth, but that privilege was also a prison. She was suddenly jealous of men, for being able to go where they wanted, when they wanted.

'A penny for your thoughts.' Nikolay leaned across the table with a grin. 'Where did you go just now, Klara?'

'I was thinking of the women you told me about in the cab, how my life isn't so different from theirs,' Klara said quietly. 'I don't live in a convent, of course. I don't mean to make light of that repression, but I never understood until I met you how illusory my freedom was.' The words came out slowly, each one chosen carefully, so new was the thought. Perhaps she had not even realised it until this very minute.

'You wear riding breeches, Klara,' Nikolay pointed out, but he wasn't debating her assumptions. He was probing, almost as if he wanted her to come to certain realisations.

'I do. I suppose to many people I look free on the outside. I know there are men like Amesbury who think I run wild, but I'm on a leash, just a rather long one. At some point that leash will run out and yank me back. I ride my horses. I wear breeches. I have any thing I want. But there is a price for that. That price will be marriage to a man of my father's choosing, at my father's time.' Why hadn't she seen it before? She shrugged, trying to hide how much the realisation shook her. 'All the more reason to enjoy tonight, I suppose.' She reached for her mug. 'Teach me a Russian toast.'

Nikolay favoured her with another smile. 'We might say *budem zdorovy*...to your health.'

'*Budem zdorovy*, then.' She smiled, clinking her mug against his. When they had taken a drink, she fixed him with a look. 'Tell me, why do you come here?'

'I come here when I miss home,' Nikolay said sincerely.

'Is that often?' she asked softly. Intimacy settled about them, the noisy room receding into the background as she waited for him to say more. This revelation was different than what they'd talked about in the carriage; it was entirely personal, entirely private.

'More often than I thought it would be.' Nikolay reached for the pitcher and poured for them. 'Here I'm not alone.' Klara nodded. All around them people spoke Russian, ate Russian food. They might all be from different parts of Russia, but in this tiny café they all had a few vital things in common and that was enough to recreate home.

'You are very brave. I think it must take a strong person to leave their home, their family, in order to make a new life.' The enormity of what Nikolay had done was overwhelming. He tried to hide it, of course, behind the flirtation, behind the swagger and the bold words. 'You are a prince who's become a riding instructor.' The thought emerged in halting sentences as she put the idea together. She gave the room a furtive scan. 'I wonder how many other such men are gathered here?' How many men had traded the status and wealth of one life to start another in the hopes of more? Had they found it? How did they measure it?

Nikolay directed her attention to two men deep in conversation by the door. 'They used to be officers in the palace guard in St Petersburg. They were caught up in the 1821 revolt. Do you know it?'

She stopped eating, the *solyanka* now heavy in her stomach. 'Yes.' It was a revolt like the one her father planned.

'They come in and drink and talk about the old days. They relive the revolt, over and over.' He nodded to another group of men in the corner. 'They came to England because they suffered persecution. They refused to bow to the Tsar's laws.' These men were older, all of them in their fifties. 'They've been in England for twenty years. They've got older, but their memories haven't. So, yes, there are men here who will not rise to the status they once had.'

Klara saw the pity, the anger in his gaze, maybe even contempt for those men trapped in the past, unable to move past their choices. She heard the fear that he was not that different, that he would become them in time. 'That will not be you,' she offered. He was too alive, too vibrant of a man. But put in the context he presented, it provoked the old question: what caused a man to leave all he had, both material and immaterial, for a land that would not allow him to rise? Where he would be limited by language and a hundred other barriers?

'Why did you come, Nikolay, if you did not come to escape an unwanted marriage?' she asked, letting her hand rest on his on the table.

'I came for the same reasons they came. I had no choice.' He gave a snort. 'It's ironic, all these men are here because they wanted things to change and now *they* are the ones who cannot change.'

She could read a revolution in that statement as she formed other hypotheses. Had Nikolay, too, wanted change? She thought of the men by the door, the former officers. Perhaps men like Nikolay. Had he attempted to create change and then been forced to flee? *Forced* was the right word here. One did not simply leave one's whole life behind because they merely wanted something. The man in the apron was back before she could pursue that line of thought further. He cleared away their bowls.

'Will you stay for the dancing? And the vodka?' he asked in broken English, his accent heavy. Around them, people were already pushing tables to the sides and stacking chairs. An accordion and a guitar materialised. Nikolay looked at her, raising his eyebrows in challenge. He was daring her, again. She would answer that challenge.

'*Da*, we'll stay.' She was not ready to go home, her discoveries were too new. She might never pass this way again. There was no way she was leaving now. She flashed Nikolay a look. 'And we'll dance.'

Chapter Nine

She'd never danced like this—quite literally. Klara laughed out loud as Nikolay spun her across the floor in a fast polka. She was sweaty and hot, and happy. They'd danced two hours straight. The dancing had been full of new experiences. There had been ring dances, *khorovods*, and line dances with people touching. These were not the staid dances of Mayfair ballrooms with the polite, metred steps of the English aristocracy. This was dancing as it was meant to be; flying without leaving the ground. For all her sophistication, it was shocking to note how small her world was. Miniscule indeed, considering all the 'nevers' she had crossed off her list tonight and just a few streets from home. Soho was surprisingly close to Mayfair when one considered the distance. Streets away, worlds apart. The dance ended and the band took a break. Thank goodness. She hadn't wanted to stop dancing, but she was breathless.

'Thirsty?' Nikolay offered. His hand hadn't left her back the entire evening since the dancing started.

That was another plus to dancing here. There was no two-dance limit. She'd danced with him all night. She felt alive, here in this nameless café, whirling to a two-man band in Nikolay's arms. Nikolay handed her a small glass of clear liquid. 'Vodka,' he warned. 'Drink it down in a single shot.'

'I am familiar with vodka.' She laughed, watching him toss his head back, the strong muscles of his neck exposed as he swallowed. His coat had come off, his jacket, too. He danced in his shirt, his sleeves rolled up. He might be any man in this room, a working man instead of a gentleman. Her coat, too, had been discarded. She might be any woman in the room, in a plain blue skirt with a white blouse. How tempting it would be to be Nikolay and Klara, to have no secrets between them. Some of those walls had come down tonight, while making her more acutely aware than ever of the walls that remained. The temptation had been replaced by a nascent fantasy born of her realisations tonight: what would it be like to have a different life? A life outside her gilded cage? A life filled with nights in this café instead of London ballrooms? A life with Nikolay the riding instructor? Fantasy indeed if she was imagining her future with a man she'd only met a few weeks ago. It was dangerous to think of falling in love with Nikolay Baklanov. He was by his own admission not a marrying man. Better to think of the vodka.

'Budem zdorovy.' She lifted her glass and swallowed. The vodka went down smoothly. She was used to it in *viche pitia*, but it tasted extraordinarily

delicious tonight. 'Another, please.' She was thirstier than she realised.

Nikolay laughed. The band was starting up again, lively strains getting a cheer from the crowd as the cry went up, *'Hopak!'*

'Nikolay, you must dance with us!' The aproned man and another, younger, version of him tugged Nikolay out on to the floor where the men gathered. Klara grabbed another glass of vodka and found herself tugged into the circle of women on the perimeter.

'The men will dance for us now,' a young woman told her as the music began. The dance started traditionally enough, involving deep squats, and leaps in some organised fashion. As the tempo sped up, the dancing kept pace, the leaps becoming higher. One man turned a back somersault, earning applause. That was the key the dancing had become something more, a competition. Many of the men bowed out, but three remained. Nikolay and two others took over the centre of the room, each taking turns to display their skill. Nikolay went last, leaping into the centre with a front handspring and landing on his feet. He kicked high and leapt, and repeated it, leaping higher each time until the third leap where he did a mid-air split and touched his toes. He concluded with a series of backhand springs that had the crowd roaring their approval.

'Nikolay is always the best,' the woman beside her whispered. 'He is a real Russian man, so strong, so virile. Every woman in here wants him, even the married ones.' She giggled.

Everyone wanted him, but tonight he was hers. She was bursting with pride as he strode towards her, sweaty and dishevelled, his hair falling loose from his leather tie, his shirt out of his waistband. No gentleman would ever dare to appear like this in public, but this was no gentleman. This was a Cossack warrior, a product of his heritage, and it merely added to Nikolay's appeal, to the fantasy that somehow her life could be different. Klara felt her heart starting to pound at his approach. His steps were purposeful, his eyes on fire. He was on a mission and that mission was her. She was about to be claimed. Nikolay drew her to him and kissed her hard on the mouth, while the crowd around him took up the cry, *'Za zda-ró-vye!'*

There was more vodka, more dancing. The evening was growing late and Klara began to fear leaving. She didn't want this to end, but even the band was winding down. They played a slow *mazurka* and she and Nikolay were one of the few couples left on the floor dancing. He held her against him, murmuring something about this being a Russian waltz. She didn't care, she only cared that he held her obscenely close, that she could feel his body move against hers. Intuitively, she knew this would be the last dance and she wanted to linger in it with him; her arms wrapped about his neck, her head against his shoulder. She doubted this was even the appropriate format for the mazurka. At some point form had ceased to matter.

'We have to go,' Nikolay whispered, sounding

as reluctant as she as the music ended. He helped her into her jacket and shrugged into his own garments with far more dexterity than she possessed. She could not master her buttons. 'We'll get a cab,' Nikolay whispered. Thank goodness. She could dance, but she doubted she could walk, although cold air would do her a world of good. Her head had been deliciously foggy the past hour, focused only on Nikolay and the music. Nikolay kept his arm tight around her as they said their goodbyes and exited into the night. Nikolay found them a cab and settled her inside.

'I do think you're foxed, Klara.' He didn't bother to sit on the other side of the carriage. He sat beside her, his body warm and inviting.

'I am not. I've drunk vodka before,' she insisted, but she was starting to wonder if maybe she was a teensy bit hummed.

'Not that much at once, I'd wager.' Nikolay laughed easily. 'You'll have a dragon of a head on you tomorrow. Are you sure you will want to ride?'

'I'll be fine by then.' Klara yawned. 'That's hours away.' She laid her head against his shoulder. 'Tonight was wonderful,' she said dreamily. This was nice, being with him without challenging one another, without constantly matching wits. She'd been to the other side of the mountain, she'd seen things, done things, thought things that had changed her. How could she possibly go back now? How could she be Klara Grigorieva again? 'Nikolay, how do you do it? How do you leave it?' It would be easier for him, of course, he had the promise of going back whenever he liked. She might not get another chance. Tomorrow, they'd be Miss Grigorieva and Prince Baklanov again, student and instructor again, their roles would be in place and their behaviours would be, too. The game would be there, too. 'What happens next between us?' They had shared a lover-like intimacy tonight, his hand always on her back, and that kiss, Lord, that kiss! That was not all. They'd also shared themselves, a few tentative peeks into each other's souls that had left her changed.

'We tell ourselves tonight existed out of time, a break with reality,' Nikolay murmured. It was what she had told herself hours ago, a lifetime ago, stepping down from the cab.

'Hmm. I thought you might say that.' She was not so drunk she didn't know what she was doing. If there was only to be tonight, she'd make it last as long as she could, drink from it all that she could. Klara settled herself on his lap, straddling his thighs.

'What are you doing, Klara?' His eyes were dark with desire, with dancing and vodka.

'You said a woman should not shrink from a passionate nature,' she whispered her words against his mouth as she took his lips. 'You claimed me with a kiss in front of everyone. Now, I think it's my turn to claim you.' If this was to be a night out of time, so be it. She kissed him slowly, her mouth lingering on his lips, her tongue tasting him, aware that his mouth tasted her in return, that his mouth was devouring her in lingering bites; her earlobe, the curve of her jaw, the column of her throat. His hands were at her breasts, kneading them beneath the wool of her jacket. She moaned and moved her hips into him, feeling the hardness of him against his trousers as the want between them fired and burned in the dark of the cab. She had his face in her hands, kissing his mouth, his jaw, but it was his hand that slipped between them, his hand that pushed up her skirts and pressed against her mound until she wanted to scream.

'Let me give you pleasure, Klara, just a little, just enough.' His voice was hoarse with the need to do this for her.

'Yes,' she said, her own voice hardly any better. She'd consent to anything to be touched by him, to be relieved of this ubiquitous sensation flooding her body, firing her veins. His fingers touched her then, finding the source of pleasure hidden in her secret folds. 'More, Nikolay, more!' She moved against him in her urgency. Dear Lord, no matter how much he touched her, stroked her, the pressure built, it wasn't enough, until suddenly it was and she broke against him, positively shattered against his hand, her mouth muffled against his shoulder.

The cab came to a halt. The short ride was over and she gave a groan of desperate frustration. It was time to go home. No, not now. Not now when she could barely think, let alone walk. Tonight had been a beginning, but the beginning of what? What would she do with all she learned about herself, about him?

Perhaps she'd been wrong earlier. Wanting *was*

enough. Maybe she'd just never wanted anything bad enough. Until tonight. She wanted more freedom, more *solyanka*, more vodka kisses, more Nikolay hot from the *hopak*. She wanted those things enough to think the unthinkable—she had to protect Nikolay from her father. If her father knew what she knew he would never let Nikolay go. Nikolay would not like that, would not like having choice stripped from him.

Nikolay helped her out of the cab and she drew him close for one last kiss, fired by determination. It was doubly important now that no one ever know about tonight. Nikolay's freedom depended on it.

Damn that bitch, making free with her favours past midnight in Mayfair with that Kubanian prince. Amesbury threw his opera classes on to the carriage seat. The so-called Prince didn't even have the decency to debauch her in his own vehicle, but a rented public hack at that. Disgusting. From the looks of it they'd been out who knew where.

He kicked at the plush seat opposite him and swore every vile curse he could think of. She was his! Grigoriev's plans to sniff out the Prince's politics could go to hell. He was sure Grigoriev didn't intend for Klara's efforts to stoop to whoring. Baklanov wasn't even a real prince as far as he was concerned. Not any more. When a man ran away from his own country, he forfeited any right to call himself a prince. His anger started to simmer to a more controllable level. He pulled a knife from his ever-present sheath inside his boot and fingered the blade, the motion bringing calm. He wondered what Klara would think of her handsome prince if Baklanov sported a scar across his face? The bastard would have nothing then, not even his looks. He'd like to cut off the man's balls while he was at it, too. Then he would not only not be a prince, but he wouldn't be a man either, just a useless nothing.

He watched Klara slip into the townhouse. As for her, she would not escape punishment for her infidelity, for making him wait outside in his carriage for hours after his men had told him she hadn't come home from riding lessons. Hadn't he made himself clear the other night? Hadn't he hinted politely at what he wanted from her? Perhaps he'd been too polite. Apparently, Klara liked a bit of rough, preferring to hole up in rented cabs with Baklanov instead of the pristine elegance his wealth offered. Amesbury chuckled. Well, he could certainly oblige on the rough part. No knife for her, but a riding crop could work wonders. Not too soon though, not before the wedding night. He'd begin with her as he meant to go on, though. No sense in doing otherwise. Klara Grigorieva needed a stronger hand than he'd anticipated. But he was up to the challenge. He shifted on the seat and undid his trousers. He put a hand on himself and stroked hard. Oh, yes, he was up to the challenge in all ways.

Chapter Ten

He'd brought Klara Grigorieva to climax in a rented cab, her cries sobbed against his shoulder. It was the most erotic thing he'd done in some time if the lingering effects were any indicator. Such wicked behaviour was not well done of him and he was paying for it in a long sleepless night. Nikolay got out of bed and dressed, giving up entirely on sleep. He'd broken his word to Stepan. But that was not the least of what he'd done. He'd told her things about himself that he hadn't told anyone since coming here, things only his closest friends knew about him. To be sure, he hadn't told her the darkest part of his story regarding what had actually driven him to England. Even so, he'd said too much, exposed too much of himself when he knew better than to get too close to her.

She had shared with him, too. He'd seen the shock of realisation on her face when she'd talked of being a prisoner to privilege, to her gender. But it wasn't the same for her. She had nothing to lose. He could not hurt her with that information. *Could* she hurt him? *Would* she? They had determined it was to be a night out of time. Would she tell her father or would she honour their unspoken rule?

Nikolay shoved his feet into his boots and palmed a small dagger. A good walk would soothe him. He was used to being up early with the workers, but a man didn't go out into the London dark unarmed. He crept down the staircase, careful not to wake the others. Stepan would want to go with him and right now he wanted no company other than his own thoughts.

Outside, the dawn was cold, precisely what his body needed to cool his thoughts. Despite his worries over what Klara might expose in the light of day, his mind persisted in lingering over the night as he walked, how Klara had been in his arms: the light in her eyes, the laughter as they danced, the wide smile on her mouth tossing back the vodka. He could still smell the vanilla-amber scent of her on his clothes where their bodies had pressed together, the way she'd shattered against him at the end.

He'd been reckless last night. He chalked it up to cabin fever. That was the easiest answer. He'd obviously been too long without a woman, or perhaps he'd merely been too long without a project that claimed the attentions of his body and mind. In Kuban, his *affaires* had been a sort of entertainment, something he did after long days in the saddle with his men. Now, no matter how many hours he spent at the stable, he still had too much time on his hands—all the more reason he was eager to move forward with his ambitions. It was time to stop dithering and decide on a property. Which was why he was up early, walking in spite of the late night. It might also be because he couldn't shake the memory of Klara, but it was harder to admit to that because it meant admitting to a host of other feelings as well—feelings he'd promised himself to avoid, feelings that had seen him betrayed before.

The hair on his neck prickled. Nikolay halted, his hand slowly reaching for the knife inside his coat. He was being followed. His fingers closed around the hilt and he drew a deep breath. Let them watch, whoever they were. Let them come. The warrior in him was alert and ready. It could be nothing more than a common footpad, but, based on the events of the last week, it could be more than that. It could be Grigoriev's men—if so, there was nothing to fear. Grigoriev would just be watching, studying. It could be Amesbury, though. His hand flexed around the hilt. Amesbury would be dangerous. Amesbury saw him as a threat.

He started walking again. If he wanted to draw them close, it was best not to let on that he knew. Nikolay forced his thoughts to focus on his riding academy as he retraced the route back to Soho. A riding school would need a unique property, one that had mews and a riding house. He turned left towards one of his oft-walked routes through Soho Square, trying not to be paranoid. He altered his direction, taking a more circuitous route. No one going to Soho Square would find this route efficient in the least. The feeling persisted, yet when he turned around to scan the area, he could see no one out of the ordinary for this time of day, only workers and vendors hurrying into place before the city awoke fully. It was likely nothing more than Stepan's worries carrying over to him.

He reached the square. Whoever was following was still there, but further back. He quartered the area with his gaze, trying to pick a figure from the shadows. Whoever it was, they were good. He saw no one. Nikolay pressed on, pausing before a property. His mind sifted through the information almost by rote: Leighton House, Number Four Leicester Square, a large townhouse with impressive Georgian windows, an enormous rear space containing mews for horses, a riding house large enough for jumping and a small *manège* suitable for outdoor work.

As a bonus, the adjacent mews were also for sale, that home's owner no longer interested in keeping extensive stables in the city. Twenty stalls in all. He could expand. Once he considered boarders and the space his own schooling string would need, twenty stalls filled up quickly.

The house and property were everything he could hope for in a city where land and space were at a premium. The newer homes deep in Mayfair and out by Regent's Park were smaller. The gardens were too tiny to accommodate something as magnificent as a riding house. Only the older era homes still maintained some of those luxurious outbuilding features. But the problem with older homes was their locations.

The hairs on his neck relaxed. His stalker was gone. Whatever he'd come to learn, he'd learned it.

Nikolay let his thoughts loose, they were free to wander now and Klara was the first place they went. What would Klara think of the property? Would she come here to study? The thought was most unlooked for, not because it was about Klara—he'd been thinking about her plenty—but because it implied a desire for permanence, a desire to continue his association with her for an undetermined length of time. Maybe he was reading too much into the thought. After last night, she was simply on his mind. Likely, she would wear off like the others. He just had to give it time. No woman had been able to hold his attention for long. No one except for the deadly Helena, a perfect validation for no long-term attachments, especially those that commanded a modicum of his emotions.

Nikolay shoved his gloved hands into the deep pockets of his greatcoat to ward off the morning chill. Even the cold was different in London. He wondered if he'd ever get used to it. In Kuban, the cold was crisp, sharp and could be warded off with mufflers and fur hats. But London cold had a dampness to it that could find a man beneath his coats. He looked about and spied what he wanted—a *salop* vendor still out after a long night. A hot drink was exactly what he needed. Nikolay fished a coin out of his pocket and gave it to the woman, who handed him a small, steaming bowl in exchange.

He breathed in the aroma, enjoying the smell of the drink and the warmth of the bowl as much as the taste on his tongue. He thanked the woman and stepped back from her stall to contemplate the house and her other early-morning customers, men and women going to work in the great houses that remained in this part of the West End, or to the small businesses that had sprung up. These customers spoke a variety of languages, greeting one another in French, Greek, German and his beloved Russian. The woman would work for another hour or two and then go home. *Salop* was a drink for the dark, cold hours between midnight and eight.

Her customers would not be his customers. A riding academy did not cater to a working class of artisans and craftsmen. The families of physicians and bankers perhaps, but he needed the patronage of the wealthy. Therein lay the rub, the one thing holding him back from purchasing Leighton House. Leicester Square, like its neighbouring squares, Soho and Golden, had been fashionable once, sporting the residences of princes. But no longer. London's elite had moved west to Mayfair, leaving their houses behind. This was now the neighbourhood of immigrants, at least those with the means to rent or buy. Would purchasing here be a deterrent to his potential clients? And yet where would he find another property so ready for him?

Nikolay finished his *salop* and returned his bowl, standing at the woman's stall long enough to indulge himself in speaking Russian with his fellow customers. It was nothing more than an exchange about the weather, but it was manna to his ears. Lord, he missed the sound of his native language. Did Stepan and the others miss it, too? They never mentioned it. Did they, too, have secret rituals, private things they did when they went out into the city that assuaged their need for home?

There was still no sensation of the stalker. Nikolay started to walk. If he didn't keep moving, he'd become maudlin. There were other properties to revisit and consider yet again. It was far better, he knew, to look forward to the future than behind to the past. Wasn't that the reason he'd crossed words too many times with the Tsar in Kuban? Hadn't he argued that looking back was Kuban's problem, Russia's problem? And here he was, walking the streets of one of the world's most modern cities, doing exactly that. What did he have to be maudlin about? It was true, he could never go home again, *but* he had money in the bank and a future he could direct entirely.

'What do we know of his daily behaviours? Is he ready to commit?' Alexei Grigoriev leaned back in his desk chair, facing Amesbury, waiting for the morning report. It had been so easy to talk Grigoriev into having one of the General's men follow Baklanov. Amesbury had argued it was to check the Prince's associations when, in reality, Amesbury had rather personal motives. The sooner Baklanov could be eliminated one way or another the better.

'I think he spoke true when he said he had no interest in politics,' Amesbury offered. The fastest way to eliminate Baklanov would be for Grigoriev to lose interest in him. 'Here's what we know and it all supports that conclusion.' Amesbury pushed a sheet of paper forward to Grigoriev and Vasilev, and gave them a moment to study it. 'His schedule is very regimented. It's almost as if he has tried to recreate a military-style routine for himself. He walks the city early in the mornings.' He nodded towards the General. 'Your men have seen him leave his townhouse regularly at the same time and return at the same time before going to Fozard's.' There were morning walks before reporting to the riding school, days filled with giving lessons, afternoon drinks with Baklanov's Russian friends at White's, evenings spent in typical gentlemanly pursuits: clubs, gaming, an occasional musical evening. Nothing extraordinary, nothing that indicated he had political interests. Grigoriev would soon tire of Baklanov at this rate and that suited the Duke just fine.

Grigoriev shrugged, unconcerned. 'Maybe he's not interested *today*. But every man's mind can be changed. The tougher part is knowing what will change it and the most opportune time to strike. To know the answers to those questions, one has to know the man in question. Klara is working on that.'

Amesbury shifted and leaned forward. 'About that. I'm not sure that's wise. Baklanov is a hot-blooded Cossack and he may not be careful with her honour. Baklanov is a prince, but there is some roughness to him, his nature is unrefined.'

Vasilev nodded in considered agreement. 'There may be some merit in what Amesbury says. Your daughter's virtue may not be safe with him. He went to Soho today. He goes to Soho often. It is not a gentleman's destination.'

Amesbury grimaced. Vasilev was not helping his cause. While the General's revelation might convince Grigoriev to take Klara off the scent, mentioning the bohemian West End would intrigue Grigoriev and keep him interested in Baklanov. Revolutions came from the bottom up as much as they came from the top down, perhaps even more so in the world outside Russia. Russia, it seemed, was backwards in all ways, even with revolutions that started with high-placed army officers and court nobles. Soho these days teemed with disgruntled Russians, not all of them useless peasants. Military men had fled after the failed 1821 uprising. Those who had not been captured had sought refuge wherever they could find it. London had taken some of them in. Those were the men Grigoriev would want to harness, men who might be compelled to try again when the time came. Men the Prince, it seemed, was acquainted with. If Baklanov could deliver those men, he might be very useful. Which was quite useless to Amesbury.

Vasilev went on. 'My man says Baklanov spoke in Russian to two men at a *salop* stall shortly before half past six. The interaction was congenial but short. We didn't hear what was said.'

'It's a start, General,' Grigoriev commended him. 'We will win the Prince over, just wait.' Hardly the endorsement Amesbury was looking for. Time to try another angle. If he couldn't remove Baklanov from the equation, perhaps he could put Klara beyond Baklanov's reach.

'Again, I must beg you to take Klara out of this. She is spending a considerable amount of time with him.' Amesbury paced his words with delicate hesitation. 'It is not seemly for a girl about to become a duchess.' He let the import sink in and managed to feign manly modesty. 'I have long wanted to ask for her. I dare not wait any longer, Your Excellency. With things as they are, I think it is time to make my offer official.'

Grigoriev beamed with fatherly pride, as Amesbury knew he would. He was quite a catch. Matchmaking mamas angled for him year after year. He could have married the daughter of a duke or a marquess. That he'd chosen the daughter of a foreign ambassador, whose only tie to England was a dead wife who'd been the daughter of an earl, was certainly a feather in Grigoriev's cap, a tribute to Klara's beauty and upbringing. She had succeeded where so many had failed.

He knew, too, that with an alliance sealed through the permanence of matrimony, Grigoriev would count on him for protection if the revolt failed. It was a good trade for them both. Grigoriev would have protection from treasonous charges if need be. In exchange, he would have Klara and an ambassador in his pocket.

Grigoriev rose and offered him his hand. 'I would be honoured. You may speak with her once we've settled the paperwork.'

Chapter Eleven

The errand boy slipped the paper into Nikolay's hand at the end of Klara's lesson. Nikolay ran his hand over the thin, ragged scrap. He already knew the message he'd find inside; a horse was in trouble. This was how the cries for help came, scrawled on torn pieces of whatever was handy. He watched Klara take Zvezda flawlessly over a double oxer at the end of practice. Apparently the vodka hadn't affected her as badly as he'd anticipated. He'd been impressed when she'd shown up on time. Even more impressed when she'd swung up on Zvezda without wincing.

'Try the jump again, Klara, from the left this time. Zvezda needs to be stronger from that direction. Then we'll call it a day.' She had ridden beautifully, but he was glad the lesson was over. They were back to instructor and pupil again on the outside. But there had been a *frisson* of tension underlying their interaction, the memory of last night too fresh to ignore, and they were trying too hard to pretend last night had not happened. Nikolay saw her over the jump before opening the note.

His jaw tightened as he read. He'd been expecting this; a friend of Peter Crenshaw's had landed in River Tick, everything had been taken, even the prized bay thoroughbred who'd been the cause of Crenshaw's friend's demise. Unfortunately, the bay had not found its way to Tattersall's, but to a less savoury auction in Smithfield by the abattoirs. A butcher would pay good money for prime horseflesh. The kill pen sales were tomorrow. The plea was always the same. *Please, go and save the horse.* It wasn't the first time, or even the second, such messages had found him. He was acquiring quite the reputation with the 'horse underground', as he called it. It was how he'd 'acquired' his Cleveland Bay mare. He'd seen the horse Peter's friend referenced in the note, a magnificent creature. There was no question of not going. He would take Stepan.

'Not bad news, I hope?' Klara walked Zvezda beside him as he folded the scrap up and put it in his pocket. There was an edge to her voice, her face paler than usual. Maybe the vodka had taken a toll after all. Maybe *she* was expecting some news to be delivered? It had been a week since the dinner party. Did he dare hope the ambassador had simply let him go after his comments? Had she given her father reason to follow up? Had she told her father all she'd learned last night? The night was behind them. They were back to the game. He was back to second-guessing her and reading between the lines. His safety and that of his friends depended on it.

'Nothing I didn't expect,' Nikolay replied, realising too late how cryptic that would sound to her. Last night had been open and honest. They had simply talked. And danced. And kissed. And climaxed. They had not been concerned with hidden agendas. He *liked* that. It had been refreshing. In many ways it had been the kind of evening he'd come to England to find, a chance to live a straightforward life outside court and politics. But he was learning, too, that such a choice had its price. It left his life a little emptier, a little more rudderless. He'd served at court because he'd believed his country was worth fighting for. In the absence of that, what else would he find worth fighting for?

'Unexpected news doesn't mean it wasn't bad news,' Klara prompted. 'It was bad, wasn't it? I can see it in your eyes.'

He opted to relieve her worry. 'It's about a horse. A friend has asked me to attempt to acquire the animal when it goes to auction tomorrow.' That was as neutral as an explanation could get.

Immediate concern washed over her face. 'I'm sorry to hear it. I can't imagine losing Zvezda.' Klara shook down her hair and ran a hand through it. It was meant to be an efficient gesture, not a sensual one, but Nikolay's mind was finding it hard to separate the two. His imagination wanted to swap out the dust of the arena for the candlelight of a boudoir, breeches for a white satin nightgown.

'Will you be able to redeem the horse?' she asked.

'I hope so.' That was the risk. The kill pens were always full and he had to *find* the thoroughbred first; one horse among hundreds. It was always a race against time.

'I'll come with you,' Klara offered matter of factly. It wasn't a question, but a statement. 'Surely, two of us working together is better than one working alone.' He knew she was thinking of how to manage the bidding. In her mind, this was a trip to the gentlemen's world of Tattersall's, while he was worried about searching the pens and finding the bay before the butchers did.

'An auction is no place for a lady.' Even if it had been Tattersall's, she was not an appropriate guest.

She had a ready answer for everything. 'I'll go in disguise. I'll wear my breeches.' Nikolay gave her a dubious look. No one would believe she was a boy on close scrutiny. But he could sense she was going to prove intractable. Perhaps the truth would get her to rethink her offer.

Nikolay stopped and faced her squarely so she could see his face. 'I don't *want* you along. My business may be unpleasant.' In fact, he was sure it would be. In this case, honesty was not the best policy. It only caused Klara to entrench.

She narrowed her gaze. 'Where, *exactly*, are you going?' A look of disbelief crossed her face. He could almost hear the words before she said them. 'You're not *stealing* him, are you?'

'I hope not.' But Nikolay would if it came to that.

The response silenced her. She said nothing more about the outing as they brushed Zvezda and settled her for the evening. He walked her out to her father's waiting carriage. '*Do svidaniya*, Miss Grigorieva.'

She paused before getting in. 'There's something you don't know about me. I am very good with a pistol. An American diplomat took me out shooting a few years ago. I was a natural.'

Nikolay inclined his head in acknowledgement. 'I am sure you were.' Klara was the type of person who was good at everything she tried, dancing and vodka included. Despite all the reasons he should keep her at arm's length, it was hard not to like her, hard not to want her. Worst of all, hard not to trust her.

She gave him a tight smile. 'Just as *I* am sure you will need a "second" tomorrow, someone to watch your back. How early are you going? What time shall I be here? Or shall I just come at dawn and wait you out?'

'Is that a threat?'

'I hope not,' she replied wryly, borrowing his words. 'I no more mean to threaten you than you mean to steal that horse tomorrow.'

So be it. Klara Grigorieva was a mule in breeches, stubborn as she was. Sometimes the best remedy for stubbornness was to let it have what it wanted and live with the consequences. It worked quite well on green recruits in the cavalry. They seldom questioned their superiors again. 'I leave at half past four. That's in the morning, not the afternoon.' If she wanted to come, he would let her. She could sit in the carriage and wait once she realised what she'd got herself into.

Her stubbornness was being sorely tested and it was only five o'clock, a half-hour into the adventure. Klara had seen London at five in the morning, but only in sleepy glimpses out the windows of comfortable carriages on the way home from a ball. She'd never seen it on foot and that made all the difference—a cold, chilly, damp difference. In the last three days, she'd seen more of her city than she had in fifteen years. There was some irony in seeing it through the eyes of man who'd only been here six months.

Nikolay laughed when she told him. 'I walk the city in the early mornings. Call it reconnaissance. I am very good at that. Are you cold?'

She and Nikolay had left the carriage four streets behind them. She was already freezing although she'd dressed warmly in attire she borrowed from a boy who worked at the house. It wasn't just the weather that had her teeth chattering, but the excitement of the outing. No, not excitement, if she was honest. Anxiety would be more apt. She was nervous, although she wouldn't admit that to Nikolay. He'd have her back in the carriage with Stepan. 'Tell me again why we couldn't bring the carriage this far?' she muttered.

'We don't want to look too prosperous. We won't get a good deal if people think we're rich.' Nikolay's accent was heavier than usual this morning, his *r*'s rolling thickly, sounding more like *d*'s. The sound of him, the look of him, was the least English she'd seen him. Gone was the immaculate riding attire, the tailored breeches, the polished boots, replaced by scuffed workman's boots, rough homespun garments and a frayed cuffed greatcoat that had seen generations of wear. His hair was loose about his shoulders. He looked rough and dangerous, like a man willing to fight, *wanting* to fight. Most of all, he looked as if he fit in.

Around them, the foggy streets of London teemed with working life. People emerged, wraithlike from the mists in equally ragged clothing, equally grim stares on their faces. Some passed them on their way to their own destinations, others fell into step with them, headed for the same place, wherever that was. Nikolay had not disclosed the location, but she had her guesses now. They'd gone north-west of central London, towards Smithfield. While this part of London and these people, had been known to her only in theory until this morning, she knew what went on here. Smithfield was London's meat market. The great abattoirs were here. Her stomach tightened at the implication. The horse Nikolay wanted was destined for the slaughterhouse.

They stopped briefly at a vendor's stall and Nikolay thrust a warm bowl in her hands. 'Drink this, it will help chase away the chill. It's *salop*.' She had never heard of it, but it tasted delicious and hot and that was all that mattered. Klara began to wonder, not for the first time, how often he did this. The clothes, the accent, the confident knowledge of dark streets could come only from experience.

She sipped, grateful for the warmth, but she didn't dare complain. He'd already tried once to convince her to stay in the carriage. He went over the horse's description again. 'The horse is a bay with a white star on his forehead and a white sock on his back right leg. He should look fairly healthy and well cared for.'

'Why is he here, then?'

'He was a mediocre racehorse and his owner went bankrupt.' Nikolay's gaze stayed on guard, watching everyone moving around them. She was acutely aware of the gold watch she carried in her pocket and the filigreed cross on a thin gold chain beneath her shirt, two items she put on daily without thought, even today. Either item would feed a family of four for several months in this end of London.

Nikolay drew a breath. He was going to try to dissuade her, but there was no way she wanted to be here without him near. 'It won't be pleasant, Klara. Any horse not sold today before the bell will be slaughtered. Even some of the horses purchased don't escape that fate. Butchers are there to buy the finest for their shops. Some of the horses are beyond saving. Others are here for reasons beyond their control: farmers losing their land, farmers who have moved to the city to work in factories and can't afford to keep a horse with no field to plough, gentlemen who have overextended themselves.' He shook his head. 'Keep your face forward, keep your mind on your mission to save the bay, and remember, you can't save them all, you can only do what you've been sent to do. If you can do that, you will have made a difference for at least one more horse.' She could imagine him giving a similar speech to soldiers before battle, helping them prepare their minds, their consciences for what came next and then what came beyond that—living with the failures and the successes if they were lucky. It was an insightful glimpse into the officer he must have been. He was the sort of man other men followed.

There was a general surge ahead of them. 'They've opened the gates. Let's go,' Nikolay whispered. 'We have an hour to find him.'

Chapter Twelve

Klara smelled the kill pen before she saw it, the scent of fear and faeces, all preparation for the sight that met her eyes; horses of all shapes, sizes, colours and breeds crammed into holding pens. Nikolay shot her an encouraging look, lending her strength with his gaze. This was what he'd warned her against, but he was too much the soldier to say *I told you so*. Whether or not she should have come was irrelevant now. It was too late to turn back. And yet, for all of his strength and all of his stoicism as they pushed into grounds with the others, he was not unaffected. 'Find the bay, Klara,' he murmured, perhaps as much for himself as for her, a reminder of what they *could* do.

The words were not encouraging. How would they find one horse among so many? At the first pen, a dark bay mare ran along the fence, leggy and thin, perhaps once a beauty. She whickered and tossed her head as if she were beautiful still and the sight tore at Klara's heart. Some horses would get out alive today—those who could still pull a cart and not cost too much to feed, those who were hearty enough to be useful to a cabbie or dray driver. The mare would not be one of them. No one would look at her and see that potential. A thoroughbred, Klara thought, an animal bred for beauty and speed, a luxury and not much else. Instinctively, Klara reached a hand out to the mare, petting her muzzle.

'Don't torture yourself.' Nikolay's voice was grim and low. 'He's not in this one, let's go.' He urged her on, but the mare followed, trotting along the fence until she ran out of room. She gave a last wicker. 'Don't look back,' Nikolay ordered in a voice that would have kept men on the front line of battle.

The bay wasn't in the next pen, or the next. Klara felt the minutes ticking by, she felt Nikolay's nerves draw tighter. Already, people were walking out with horses they'd bought for discount rates and a new fear took her. What if they were simply too late? What if someone else got to the horse first? If Nikolay felt the same panic, he kept it well hidden, his eyes methodically going through each pen, assessing and discarding the potentials. It didn't help that nearly every horse seemed to be a bay. By the fourth pen, Klara knew one thing with certainty: she never wanted to come here again. The people were coarse, the animals abused, the whole transaction process demeaning. She felt uncomfortable to the point of fear. She did not know this rough world. She didn't want to leave Nikolay's side, but she knew what she had to offer if they were going to find the bay in time.

'We need to split up.' If the bay was in a pen at the back, they'd never make it before the bell.

'Are you sure?'

'I'm not helpless, but your horse is.' It took too much to force those words past the tightness of her throat. She would cry when she got home, she promised herself. But she couldn't break down now, not when Nikolay needed her strong, not when there was a horse out there who needed her. If there was anything good about the morning, it was that they were Nikolay and Klara again, as they'd been in Soho.

Nikolay halted, terse excitement in his voice. 'Klara, over here, I think that's him, I think we found him.' He moved hurriedly towards a pen, already signalling the pen manager to bring the bay forward, but a whinny in the distance claimed Klara's attention. The whinny of a horse came again, cutting above the noise followed by a commotion that drew the eye. A chestnut stallion reared up, hooves striking out, a fighter among the desperate and downtrodden. Handlers struck at him with heavy, knotted ropes and still he fought. A whip cut across his back, and cries of 'Bring him down!' broke out. It was a battle between man and beast now and the beast was going to lose if someone didn't do something fast. Klara forgot her own fear. Without hesitation, she dived into the crowd.

He had the horse! Nikolay gestured to the man working the pen and then turned back to Klara, only to find her gone. Panic took him. He scanned the crowd. Where was Klara? He could do nothing now until he had the bay. He searched the crowded pens, the crowded aisles, his gaze looking for trouble, knowing instinctively that was where he'd find her. Only serious trouble would have routed her from his side. She was brave, but this place, the whole morning, had been a shock to her. In a far pen a stallion reared, striking out with his hooves against men holding him with ropes, striking him with whips. That was going to end poorly, he thought. Then he saw her, a slim figure climbing the pen rails. Fear clenched at him. Good God, she was going in there!

Nikolay grabbed one of the urchins hovering around looking for odd jobs. He thrust some coins in the boy's grubby hand. 'Take this horse to the entrance and wait for me. I've more coin when I come to get him.' Anger and worry surged through him. Lucifer's stones, this was exactly why he hadn't wanted to bring her! It wasn't that he'd thought she *wasn't* courageous enough to face the horrors of the kill pen, but that she *was*. She'd see the atrocities, the illogic of it, the pathos of it and she *wouldn't* run from it. She'd throw herself *into* it. She'd try to save them all.

Nikolay plunged into the crowd. Had she even thought about what she'd do when she reached the horse? How was she going to pay for that horse? How was he going to pay for it? He had enough money for the bay. A kill pen was a place that expected payment upon sale, but that didn't mean a man walked into such a place with a fortune on him unless he wanted to be robbed.

Klara and the stallion had drawn quite a crowd by the time he'd shouldered his way to the pen. Miraculously, she had the stallion under control, her hat had come off and her hair was down, her disguise destroyed as she stood between the sweating horse and the crowd. Ruined disguises were the least of Nikolay's concerns. Perhaps the ruined disguise had worked in her favour. The men weren't sure what to make of a woman in breeches, let alone one who wielded a gun as if she knew how to use it. Now, it was her and the horse against the crowd.

'That's a dangerous horse, miss, you'd best step away and let us do our work,' one man attempted to coax her into surrendering, although there was no logic to the attempt. They'd already failed in their work. She'd been the one to calm the beast and her gun said she and the men were not on the same side. Even so, Nikolay could see she was out of tricks. How long did she think she could hold them off? Her eyes flicked towards him and he saw her relief. But the glance had cost her some of her attention.

Nikolay vaulted the fence in a single fluid motion. 'Don't even think about it. You touch her and I'll touch you.'

The man, a beefy, big-shouldered fellow, refocused his attention. 'And who might you be?' He spat a brown stream into the ground.

'I am the man you'll have to go through if you don't let us leave here peacefully with that horse.'

His coat was already back, revealing a sheath. He had his knife. Klara wasn't the only one who'd come armed.

'Nikolay, there's a foal. He was fighting for the foal.' Klara spoke low and fast, her eyes flicking towards a brown ball on the ground near the stallion. He followed her gaze. Oh, dear, sweet heavens. A foal. A sickly, weak foal, who looked to be no more than three months old. Nikolay felt his heart sink. The odds of getting out of here safely had just grown slimmer, although they'd been pretty slim to start. The stallion was already nudging the baby with his nose. The foal struggled to its feet, confirming his worst fears. This foal wouldn't make it. How could it, with no mother?

'Be ready to move,' Nikolay murmured. He stepped between the man and Klara. 'We'll be leaving now.'

'Not with those horses. They ain't free, mister.'

'I will send payment,' Nikolay tried, making direct, intimidating eye contact with a man not used to backing down. He loosened the knife in its sheath.

'We deal with cash only, straight up,' the man growled.

'My pin should do.' Klara pushed forward with a piece of jewellery fished from her pocket. 'Take it.'

The man grabbed it, hefting the delicate piece in his big hand. 'What else you got? That's pretty small for such a big horse. The butcher will give me—'

Nikolay brought the tip of his knife up beneath the man's chin. 'It's not what he'll give you that should matter right now, but what I'll give you. I don't think this wild boy is worth getting cut over, do you? Quite above your pay, I'd say. The pin is expensive, well worth your inconvenience. I suggest you take it.' He yelled over to a boy at the fence, flipping a coin towards him, 'Open the gate.' A voice with authority could work all sorts of miracles, which was good because he was running out of coins. He had one left for the boy who held his bay.

He let Klara go first, leading the sorry-looking foal, the stallion urging the baby ahead with his nose. He wished they'd move faster before the intimidation wore off. 'To the entrance, Klara, as fast as you can.' He would scold her later for her impetuosity. For now, he wanted her and the horses safe. He was ready to protect them, spoiling for it, his emotions high, his blood racing. He wouldn't mind a fight at this point. The pens were thinning out, a sure sign the bell was about to ring. The sun was coming up, slowly, the grisly work of the morning was nearly done. Only decent business was done in daylight and there was nothing decent about this place.

They passed the first pen when the peal came. The mare was still there. The mare saw Klara and ran the length of the fence, calling out with a shrill whinny. 'Klara, keep walking,' Nikolay warned. 'You have the foal.' But if his own heart was racing and he'd had the benefit of being prepared for the morning, he could only imagine what state Klara was in. He wouldn't easily put aside the picture of her in that pen, hair loose, her eyes on fire, a gun in her hand, ready to shoot the first man who tried to take it or the horse from her.

Klara stopped, letting go of the foal as she reached her hands behind her neck to pull something over her head, something she'd worn beneath her shirt. 'I want the mare, Nikolay.' She pressed something gold and warm into his hand. He looked down at the filigreed cross and chain and looked up to see the desperation in Klara's eyes. She was close to breaking, close to asking for the impossible, or worse, trying it on her own.

'All right.' He handed her the stallion's rope, a mad plan coming to him. 'But I need you to do something for me. You must follow my instructions exactly to the letter. I have to be able to trust you.' He pressed his last coin into her hand. 'This is for the boy outside. Take these two and the bay and walk to the carriage.' He held her eyes. 'Klara, no matter what you see, what you hear or what you think is going on, do not look back for any reason. Tell Stepan to go and I'll meet you at Fozard's. You have to trust me and I have to trust you. Your mare depends on it.'

He saw her safely through the gate before he started slipping the bolts on the pens. One, two, three pens open. It was survival of the fastest, the smartest now. He could do no more. When Klara's mare nudged the gate open and started running, he was ready. This was easy. How many times had he run this manoeuvre on the training grounds of Kuban? Nikolay ran alongside, knowing he'd have no more than three or four steps before the mare's long stride would outpace him.

He leaped, grabbing fistfuls of mane as he swung up on the mare's back, his legs gripping her thin sides. Other horses were starting to realise their gates were open, a small stampede beginning as horses poured into the narrow aisles queuing towards the entrance, Nikolay and the mare in their midst, herding them towards the exit the best he good. A man called out, 'Hey, you have to pay for that horse!'

Nikolay tossed Klara's cross. 'Keep the difference!' He charged through the gate, the pressure of his legs keeping the mare from panicking wildly in the streets as horses spilled out into the narrow lanes of London. He guided her towards the direction of the carriage, the vehicle already in motion ahead of them, the horses tied behind, Klara on the box next to Stepan. Nikolay drew the mare alongside, flashing Klara a wicked grin as they flew past. 'Race you home!'

The mare was sweaty and spent by the time he reached Fozard's. She was a game one, but her energy was gone, her thin form shaking as he rubbed her down with a handful of hay. The carriage pulled in ten minutes later. Klara barely waited for it to stop before she climbed down, her leggy stride eating up the ground between them.

'What have you done!' It was evident emotions were riding her hard. She was part-exhilaration, part-disbelief, part-anger. Her eyes sparked as she challenged him.

'You couldn't save them all,' he said simply, 'but I could save some.'

'You crazy, crazy Cossack!' She was in his arms then, her arms about his neck, laughing, crying, overcome by the emotions of the morning as words bubbled out of her. 'I could hear the commotion behind me, I could hear men yelling and I heard hooves. I didn't look back, I promise. Then you flew by, grinning as if it was all child's play. How? What did you do?'

'I slipped the latches. I opened the gates.' He'd do it again to feel like this, to feel like a god, to have her against him, his blood singing the way it did after battle and having emerged alive. He hadn't felt like this, like his old self, in ages. He kissed her on the mouth then, drawing her hard against him, caught up in the moment of victory. He shouldn't have done it. He'd promised himself he wouldn't. But a warrior's soul was a complex thing. It did not answer to the dictates of reason or the parameters of self-proclaimed promises.

He had her against the wall, her hands were in his hair, her mouth answering his in equal measure, driving them both to take this far further than it should go. Stepan coughed behind them.

'Ahem, what shall I do with the horses?'

Nikolay released her and reluctantly stepped back, realising too late how public his display was, the only thing saving them being the early hour. The other instructors hadn't arrived yet to begin their day. 'Fozard's has let me use some vacant stalls in the old mews.' Nikolay moved to take the chestnut stallion. 'Follow me.'

* * *

The exhilaration had worn off by the time the horses were established in their new homes. Reality set in as Nikolay surveyed the horses. Only the bay and the chestnut stallion showed any real promise. The bay, in fact, far exceeded Nikolay's expectations. 'We'll let him have a day or two to get comfortable and then we'll see what he can do.' Nikolay gave the bay a final pat before moving on to the chestnut. 'This boy is a diamond in the rough.' He hoped. That was the optimistic outlook. Klara's chestnut was something of an enigma. His coat was healthy but shaggy as if he'd lived the cold months out of doors and he had some ground manners. He'd been no trouble to Klara walking through the streets, but other than that, it was hard to see what his training and background might be or his potential. He was a leader, though, a fighter. He knew how to protect a herd, that much was clear. It spoke of time in the wild and yet he had time among humans, too.

Nikolay moved to the mare's stall. She was quiet and eating her hay, a good sign. 'She needs some weight on her.'

'We'll feed her,' Klara answered, reaching out a hand to rub the mare's head. She'd raised it as soon as she heard Klara's voice. 'She's a jumper, a steeplechaser, with legs like that.' The waver in her voice only emphasised what they were both ignoring. The bay would be fine. Captivity and deprivation had only been his lot for a very short time. The stallion was hearty, the mare could be nurtured back to health if not into Klara's jumper. But the foal?

He was in the last stall, curled in a ball, his hay untouched. The trek from Smithfield to Fozard's, tied to the back of the carriage, had sapped him entirely. 'He needs his mother, Klara,' Nikolay began gently. She'd been through so much this morning but he could not shield her from this. 'He needs milk.' Nikolay could only guess what else he needed. Had there been a chance to gradually wean him before he'd ended up in the kill pens? He was clearly starving and yet so weak he couldn't help himself to the food nearby. If they were in Kuban, he'd feed the poor foal camel's milk, but he had no idea where to find a reliable source of camel's milk in London.

'I can get cow's milk,' Klara said resolutely.

'Cow's milk causes diarrhoea.' Nikolay ran through options in his head. 'It's higher in fat and lower in sugar.' He ran a hand through his hair. 'I've used goat's milk before.' He'd have to send to the countryside for it. He'd need to fashion a bottle for the foal, as if he had time for this on top of lessons, finding a property and wondering what move Klara's father would make next and the extent of Klara's complicity. 'He might not make it through the night, Klara. We have to prepare ourselves for that.'

'I will not accept it,' Klara said, but her voice wobbled.

'I think it's time to get you home.' Nikolay turned to Stepan. 'Will you see her home?' He'd prefer to, but the foal needed him now.

'I want to stay,' Klara began to argue.

'You need to get home, Klara. It's nearly eight o'clock.' He shook his head. He'd already risked too much bringing her along, the consequences of which were now filling up three stalls in his borrowed barn. He put a hand at Klara's back and began forcefully ushering her to where the carriage waited. 'You can see them all tomorrow when you come for your lesson.' There were a lot of reasons he wanted her away and she would deny every one of them. She was pale, the thrill of adventure wearing off. He knew too well what happened next: the horrors would set in. He wanted her somewhere safe when that happened, somewhere she could be alone. Instinctively, he knew Klara wouldn't want anyone to see her in a moment of weakness. There was self-preservation to think about, too. There'd be hell to pay if anyone guessed what she'd been up to, alone, with him in the dark. Their antics went beyond compromising.

'Are you sure you won't be caught?' he asked, holding the door for her.

'You can only be caught if you're sneaking. I left a note for my maid in case she came in. I told her there was an emergency with Zvezda.' Klara shrugged, unconcerned. 'I never rise before ten. She doesn't check on me until eleven.'

He shut the door, exchanging a look Stepan. 'You're right about one thing,' Stepan said from the driver's box. 'She is trouble.'

Chapter Thirteen

The trouble with adventures was that they ended and, when they did, they deposited you back into the real world. It had happened twice now. Klara stood in the centre of her bedroom, reluctant to embrace the morning. Was it really just half past eight? Had it only been four hours since she'd left? Four hours; the span of a formal dinner, *less* time than it took for a ball. And yet so much had happened.

She'd roamed through London's early-morning streets, seen the faces of those who went to work before the sun rose. That alone was shock enough. She was not naïve. She knew that she lived differently, that she was a child of privilege because of her father's position. She did charity work with the wives of her father's acquaintances, visited the orphanages, but those visits were sanitised to say the least, the children turned out in their best, a dutiful few called forward to show off a new poem they'd memorised. But to see the working class up close, to be part of it, was something else, much like it had been something else to join with the immigrants at the café.

That had only been the beginning. Then there had been the pens... She shuddered, her mind less successful now in keeping the images at bay. It was easier to push those images aside when she'd had action to keep her thoughts moving forward. But now her mind wanted to rivet itself on them; each long face with soulful eyes, some desperate, some frightened, some resigned. *Focus on what you are here to do.* Nikolay's words played through her mind, her only armour against being entirely overwhelmed, both then and now.

Nikolay. If she hadn't been intrigued with him already, she was fascinated with the mystique of him now. He'd played the poor immigrant carter to the hilt today in his shabby clothes and heavy accent, but she was hard pressed to think anyone was fooled for long by the disguise. He wore his power, his self-confidence, like a second skin, something that couldn't be shed or hidden. She'd felt safe with him, amid the teeming masses of rough men, safe enough to challenge the brutes holding the stallion. She'd had no plan when she'd climbed over that fence except to save that horse, but part of her had been sure that Nikolay would be there when she needed him. And he had been. Among the images she'd always carry with her from today, was the sight of him coming over the fence, fierce and feral, ready to fight for her; there was the image of him crouched low over the neck of the mare, riding neck or nothing through the twisting, narrow streets of London, his hair flying. What possessed a man to free kill pen animals and set them loose in London? It was an interesting proposition, especially when she held that same mirror up to herself.

What possessed a woman to do what *she* had done? She'd left her home, alone, dressed as a boy, to traipse around darkest London with a man she barely knew. The risk was extreme and yet there'd been no risk at all. She'd never once felt in danger. She'd *trusted* him and that scared her very much. The danger that came from Nikolay was an entirely different peril. What had started as part of her father's game was quickly becoming something much more personal.

Until now, it was easy to tell herself the intrigue was in the actions; she was in love with the adventure, the risk, the world he opened up to her. After this morning, she could no longer avoid the reality: she wasn't only in love with the adventure. She was falling in love with *him*, the man he was beyond the powerful physicality of his body. Today, she'd seen his compassion, his tenacity, his protectiveness, not only of the animals, but of her. She'd been wilful, stubborn, disobedient even. She'd forced her company on him and still he'd protected her; still, he'd been willing to fight for her. She wasn't fool enough to believe in some misguided notion that he'd done it because he'd fallen in love with her. He was not a man who allowed himself to love easily. He'd done it because his moral code demanded it and that had given her another glimpse inside his soul.

Mere glimpses would not be enough. The more she knew of him, the less satisfied she was. Was this how an addict felt? Always craving? What would it take to satisfy those cravings? Admittedly, they were becoming less about the adventures and more about the man. She wanted more of him, more of his body, more of his mind, even though each touch, each glimpse put her at greater risk, forced her to hide even more from her father because exposure risked them both now.

The warning came to her again: *If your father knew the principles that lie in Nikolay's heart, the hunger for change, he'd never let him go.* A new warning added itself: *If your father knew you wanted him he'd put an end to your association.* Or would he? It would be a terrible dilemma for her father— to save her for the English marriage he'd promised her mother, at the expense of letting his revolutionary prince slip away. It provoked a deeper question that had begun to plague her since Soho. What was her worth to her father? Was she truly a daughter or merely a pawn? She had allowed herself to admit she played the game to earn her father's attentions, but never had she allowed herself to think that was the whole sum of her value to him. That was a bold question indeed, just one more way in which Nikolay was changing the way she viewed her world and herself.

Klara sniffed, catching the scent of herself for the first time. The only thing bold about her at the moment was the odour. She needed to wash and change. Her nightgown was still on the floor, validation that no one had missed her. All she needed to do was put it on and climb into bed, and it would be done—the great adventure over. Perhaps that was why it was so difficult to slip off her shirt and take off her muddied trousers. Removing them would be like removing the experience, packing it up to store away.

Klara yawned and slowly, very slowly, she began to strip off her clothes, never dreaming she'd lie down to sleep only to be awakened by a nightmare.

'Miss, your father wants you downstairs right away!' Her maid flew about the room, pushing curtains wide and flinging open her wardrobe. Klara squinted through one eye, taking in the clock on her bedside table. Eleven, already. An hour past the time she usually rose. It seemed like she'd just lain down.

'Can't it wait?' Klara groaned and fell back on her pillows.

'No, miss. The Duke is with him.' The maid was in earnest, tugging at her covers. 'You have to get down there right away.'

Amesbury, here? She registered the maid's anxiety. The maids didn't like Amesbury. Klara threw back the covers. 'What's going on, Mary?'

Mary shook her head. 'I don't know, miss. I only know that I am to have you downstairs.' She opened the wardrobe and pulled out two dresses. 'What shall it be? The teal with the satin stripe or the violet and grey plaid?'

'Neither. I want the royal blue, the one with the white lace, and I'll want my mother's strand of pearls.' She always felt in control in that gown and this morning she was going to need all the control she could get. She was already burning with resentment and anger at the summons. If Amesbury had threatened her maid, she'd skewer him. Somehow. She'd faced down three men for the sake of a stallion this morning, surely she could face down Amesbury.

Mary had her ready in record time, sending her on her way with a meekly whispered, 'They're in your father's study.'

Klara paused outside her father's door, fingers resting on the handle as she drew a deep breath to calm her nerves. Secrets were terrible things. One spent an inordinate amount of time worrying over them. Was Amesbury here because he knew what she'd been up to? Who was in danger here? Herself or Nikolay? Both? Those questions wouldn't get answered standing in the hall. Klara pushed the door open and went in, letting all her attention focus on her father, and deliberately ignoring the Duke. 'Father, you wanted to see me?' Her father could summon her. Amesbury could not.

Her father was seated behind his desk as usual, but today there was a tension to him. The sight of him sobered her. His jaw was tight, his face hard and unreadable. This was the Alexei Grigoriev who struck fear into diplomats who crossed him on negotiations. 'The Duke of Amesbury has brought me disturbing news, Klara.' He gestured across the room, forcing her to acknowledge Amesbury's presence.

Amesbury stood by the window, straight-backed and tall, his face set in its impassive lines. 'There's been rumours this morning that wild horses were set free in Smithfield. *Some* reports put Baklanov at the heart of the mischief.' His cold eyes lingered on her, watching for a reaction as he dropped his next piece of information. 'Rumours also say he had an accomplice.'

She kept her features neutral, no mean feat considering the shock that was running through her. How could he know? 'Freeing horses from kill pens sounds rather noble to me.'

'Noble?' The Duke's narrow brows arched in supercilious argument. 'I have other words for it, but your father and I disagree. What I call thievery, your father calls bravery. He thinks it bodes well for bringing our prince into the fold for the revolt.'

Her father shot the Duke a scathing, impatient look. 'The point of you being part of this conversation, Klara, is that the Duke and I both agree you're not to see him again.'

'Not see Amesbury?' Klara knew the deliberate obfuscation would needle the Duke.

'Not me,' Amesbury interrupted, frustrated. 'The Prince. You shall not see the Prince again outside of polite company. There will be no more riding lessons.'

'That is ridiculous. He is the finest instructor in the city.' Klara's temper flared. 'You do not have the ordering of me.' She turned towards her father to plead her case. 'I am helping you with the Prince.'

'Not any more, Klara. Amesbury is right. The revolution can tolerate, even use, the Prince's recklessness, but I cannot risk you. A woman's reputation is everything.' He pushed a hand through his hair with a tired sigh. 'This is where I've failed you, Klara. I should not have allowed you to associate with him without knowing him better. Your mother would have known...' Oh, she was furious now. She saw Amesbury's signature all over this. He had talked her father into this, brought the memory of her mother into this, knowing full well the pathos that held for her father. She glanced Amesbury's way and he smirked in confirmation.

'I appreciate your time, Grigoriev. If you'll excuse me, I have other appointments this morning.' Amesbury made his farewell. 'Klara can see me out.'

She walked him to the hall, but she did not touch him, would not take his arm. 'You are upset with me, Klara,' he said in tones that hinted at amusement, boot heels clicking on the marble of the hall. 'It will pass. What you feel for your Cossack Prince is girlish infatuation. You will get over it.' He gave a dry laugh. 'Are you surprised I know? You owe me, really. I could have told your father you've been sneaking out with him.'

Klara stopped cold, her insides churning. He could only know that if... 'You had me followed.' The words spilled out, an extension of her thoughts.

'Not far enough, I'm afraid. I have no idea where

you went the night he brought you home in a rented hack. But I saw the kiss you gave him and I know you were with him this morning in Smithfield. You disgrace yourself with such behaviour. You never know who is watching.' Klara swallowed hard, anger and loathing rising in her. *He'd* been watching. He knew. 'On second thought, infatuation might not be strong enough. Have you gone beyond that, Klara? Do you fancy you're in love with him?'

His eyes narrowed to icy flints. 'At first, I wondered what he could possibly have to offer you that would make you lower yourself to such an indiscretion. Then I realised what it was. You have a fancy for some Russian cock.' His face was close to hers now, a sneer on his mouth.

'You have a filthy mind.' Klara held his gaze. She would not beg him, she would not argue with him. He would like that too much. He liked to strip people of power, render them weak and reliant.

'On the contrary, am I not generous? Am I not mercy itself? You should thank me that I'm not running to your father with your little perfidy. Stay away from Baklanov, Klara, or you will both be sorry. One knife in the dark and Baklanov's body ends up in a Soho alley. One misplaced bullet during a palace revolt will do the same trick.'

She stepped back from him in horror. 'He won't join you. He has no interest in your rebellions.' But that wasn't entirely true. She wasn't sure he *wouldn't* join them.

'You're so naïve, Klara. Of course he'll join us.

While I was waiting for you this morning, I shared a little finding of mine with your father. I think we are reasonably assured that Prince Baklanov will join us one way or another.' Amesbury shrugged. 'He'll be receiving an invitation to your father's Maslenitsa gathering. It will be the perfect opportunity to get to know him a bit better.' That was the Duke's euphemism for blackmail. 'I think the Prince will discover new depths of patriotism for his former country.'

'Are you threatening Nikolay?' The horrors wouldn't stop. What had she put in motion? A jealous man with a political agenda was a hydra indeed.

'I'm hardly threatening him, my dear. I'm just using him as collateral against your obedience and his.'

That was when she decided to run, the first chance she got, and she knew exactly who she was running to. She had to warn Nikolay. Obedience be damned.

Nikolay heard her before he saw her; the quiet rush of slipper-clad steps on stone, the susurration of silk skirts coming down the aisle, followed by the disbelieving gasp when those silk skirts came to an abrupt stop at the foal's stall and found it empty. 'No!' There were layers upon layers of despair in the anguished hush of that single word.

'Klara, we're in here. All of us,' he called softly, struggling to his feet. It was no easy feat to dislodge a sleeping foal from one's lap.

Her skirts were on the move again as she came to the door of the mare's stall, the lantern hanging outside caught the relief on her face as she spotted the foal. 'He's all right,' she let out a breath. 'When I saw the empty stall, I thought...'

Nikolay shook his head, not letting her finish. 'It's bad luck to say such things out loud.' The foal would need all the luck he could get. 'He was too cold to sleep alone. I thought the mare might take him in and she has. Your darling girl has quite the maternal streak.' Nikolay smiled, holding up the empty improvised bottle. 'I've been feeding him as often as he likes. But I could have told you all of that tomorrow.' What was she doing here? She was clearly dressed for somewhere else. She was also clearly agitated about something more than the horses. Something had happened to upset her. Had someone found out about this morning?

'It will be tomorrow in a few minutes. Then you'll be right on time.' Klara paced the aisle, a moon goddess come to life in a ballgown of starlight silver, her hair tricked out to match with brilliants that winked in its dark depths. She looked pristine next to his unkempt appearance, a reminder that he'd been up for eighteen nonstop hours. She also looked out of place.

'Silk has no place in a stable, Klara,' Nikolay observed. Neither did unmarried daughters of ambassadors.

'I wanted to see the horses. I couldn't wait until tomorrow. I've done nothing but think about them all day.' He heard other unspoken words in those sentences. *I wanted to see you. I've done nothing but think about you all day.* At the last her gaze dropped almost shyly to her hands, a disposition he did not readily attribute to her, this bold wonder of a woman.

'They are doing well.' Nikolay stepped out of the stall, glancing up and down the aisle. 'Are you alone?'

Klara shrugged as if it were of no concern. 'I told my father I was going home with a friend to spend the night.' Her eyes glittered with mischief and something else that hovered between desperation and desire, a very potent combination. 'We have all night. Let me help you with the foal tonight. You're exhausted.'

'In that dress?' He should send her home. Stepan was right. Klara was trouble and not just political trouble. That seemed to be the least of his worries right now. She was the kind of trouble that saw a man marched up to an altar and legs-hackled for life before he could come to his senses.

'I can change. Surely there are some clothes about that I can borrow.' Holy St John the Divine, the last thing he needed was to undress her in the tackroom and pretend he was oblivious to her charms. The night was cold, but it wasn't that cold, and he wasn't a man used to pretending he was a eunuch.

'That dress won't come off by itself, Klara,' he warned.

'Would you like to bet on that?' She shrugged an elegant shoulder and moonlight began to slide.

Lucifer's stones. Klara Grigorieva stood before him naked, managing to look more stunning out of her clothes than she did in them. Every part of him was in rampant agreement. Nikolay's gaze swept the exquisite, sculpted length of her. She was all feminine angles and curves from the defiant point of her chin, to the high, firm breasts—two small, perfect globes with dusky rose centres, pointed and pouting, ripe for a man's mouth to suckle them. Further down, her narrow waist gave way to the delicate flare of hips and a dark triangulation of thatched shadow between them, wet and silky even at a distance. And those legs, by God those legs! They could wrap around a man, hold him close and tight in passion's vice. He should refuse. He should take off his jacket and throw it around her. There was a plethora of reasons he should not take her up on her offer, but at the moment, he couldn't remember a single one.

'Klara, what is this?' But he knew what it was before she spoke.

She raised her hands to her diamond-studded hair and began to pull out the pins one by one, her breasts thrust into high relief. 'This is your seduction.'

There were so many questions he should ask. What had prompted this? Did she understand the consequences? Was she here for herself or for the larger game? He should remind her of the consequences, mainly that there would be *no* consequences. He could not be her lover. He could not be her father's political plaything. Whatever happened in the next few minutes could not be exchanged for those things. But the only word he could formulate was, 'Why?'

She moved towards him, against him, the open

palm of her hand pressing his length, hot and hard behind the confines of his breeches. 'Because I want you and you want me. That is reason enough.' Her mouth toyed with his ear, whispering illogical temptation. 'Nikolay, trust me. All I want is pleasure.' But her tenacity already proved the words a lie. She wanted more than pleasure although he was damned if he knew what that was.

Still, he could do pleasure. Already, his mouth was answering her, pressing kisses along the line of her jaw even as his mind argued he shouldn't. Pleasure was never simple. Experience had taught him it was never without consequence no matter how much one reasoned it could be. But those were considerations for another time when everyone had their clothes on. And she was wrong; this wasn't his seduction, it was *hers*. He cupped her breast in one hand, his thumb running over the tender peak of nipple, feeling it go rigid with wanting. He bent his mouth to it, sucking hard as she gasped. Call him old-fashioned, but a woman deserved a man who could lead in the bedroom as well as the ballroom. He knelt and kissed her navel, his hands bracketing her hips, and his mouth moved lower. A woman who was bold enough to ask for pleasure was entitled to receive it.

Chapter Fourteen

Klara's fingers dug into the rough wood of the stall wall, her body seeking purchase against the onslaught of Nikolay's mouth at her breast, at her navel, at her core. When had she lost control of this seduction? Had she ever *had* control? Perhaps she was humouring herself that a man like Nikolay ever allowed himself to be led. And yet, wasn't this what she'd come for? To find pleasure? To know something of the mysteries of passion? To know something of him—a man who could deliver on those mysteries. That was too simplistic. She'd come for more than that. His fingers skimmed the wet, sensitive folds guarding her core, teasing them apart for his tongue as it flicked over the nub hidden inside.

'Ohhh…' Her gasp was a barely veiled moan of the most primal sort. She could feel his thumbs pressing hard into the flesh of her hips, holding her steady for his feast of tongue and tastes. She was a ball of contradictions. She wanted to urge him to hurry. Wherever they were going, she was desperate to get there and yet she wanted to beg him to linger, to torment her further.

When she'd imagined tonight and what she meant to do when she got here, she had not possessed the *imagination* for this, for what it meant to be laid bare in both flesh and feeling. Her only consolation was that she wasn't alone. He nuzzled her, a groan escaping him as he lapped at her folds, licking and lingering, teasing her towards *something*, an unknown but instinctive summation of this torturous pleasure. Nikolay would not be rushed. He was in control and he was intent on putting off satisfaction for them both as long as possible. Gratification delayed, the ultimate dilettante's delight.

He murmured Russian love words, maybe dirty words that she didn't understand, against her core, his breath coming in jagged rasps, his hands hard at her hips. She'd have bruises there in the morning. She wouldn't mind those marks. They would be reminders of what had passed between them in the night, proof it wasn't all a hot dream.

He did something wicked with his tongue, sending an intense thrill through her and she was nearly there. She gripped the barn wall, starting to thrash. A final sob, more cry than moan, escaped her and she let herself shatter, exhausted, replete, the emotions of the day held at bay for a while, as pleasure swept her cares away into forgetfulness. In this dark pleasure there was no more horror of the kill pen, no more thought of the horses she couldn't save, no more political agendas that tested her loyalties, no more ballrooms and sordid proposals that bordered on blackmail from a man who saw her as an alliance to be made, wealth to secure, a trophy to carry on his arm.

As horrifying as the kill pen had been, the day had held other horrors: Amesbury's threat, his demand that she not see Nikolay for lessons. That was why she had come. She might not get another chance. She pushed away thoughts of Amesbury's cruelty away. There would be time to talk later. She wanted only Nikolay in her mind, now. His breathing came as hard as hers, his arms wrapped about her hips, his dark head pressed into her belly, as they waited for the world to settle.

Nikolay rose first, shrugging out of his coat and draping it over her shoulders. 'You'll be cold.' His voice was still rough around the edges. What had transpired between them had taken a toll on him as well, a reminder that while there had been perhaps an emotional, mental pleasure for him, there had not been any physical release. A chance then to take back the seduction.

She put her hand on him. 'Let me see to you.' Perhaps it was bold. English girls hardly knew what a man's member looked like, let alone how to handle it. But a curious woman raised around horses could hardly claim such naivety. 'You nearly brought me to my knees,' she whispered, her hand working the flap of his trousers open. 'Now it's my turn. Against the wall, Your Highness. You'll need it before I'm through.' She found him hot and hard and long, oh, so long, and ready, a veritable stallion. She would please him, if he would let her.

He groaned in appreciation as the first pass of her hand stroked his length, his body tensing, and she hoped this time he would allow her to drive the encounter. Then, his mouth took hers, one hand at the nape of her neck, the other at her breast, and she was no longer in charge. He intended to make this reciprocal, to match her caress for caress, touch for touch; her thumb at his wet, tender head, his thumb at the peak of her breast, until her hand gave way to her hips grinding against him, his length thrusting at her thigh, thrusting against her, teasing her swollen bud from its rest.

'This was supposed to be about you,' she panted. Dear Lord, she was going to shatter again, but this time so was he. She was determined it would be so.

'It is, *lyubov moya*.' His own words were hard in coming. 'Take me in your hand.' Even nearing the throes of release, he could command. She closed her hand over him, feeling him pulse and tense as completion neared. One stroke, two strokes, and he was there at the edge of his pleasure, his member coming hard in her hand, the intensity that so often marked his features absent for just a precious moment—a moment when his guard was down, a moment when the warrior was satiated.

Beyond them in the stall, hay rustled. The foal was stirring. Nikolay's eyes shut and he drew a resigned breath as if he, too, was savouring these moments, knowing they wouldn't last. The world had its demands. 'He'll be hungry,' Nikolay murmured.

She sat on a hay bale in the stall, wrapped in Nikolay's coat, surrounded by warm straw and the scent of horses, while Nikolay bottle fed the foal, the thin mare watching protectively but calmly. Watching him with the foal was nearly as intoxicating as kissing him, being touched by him. It was not a large leap in a woman's maternal mind to imagine him with a baby in those arms. The rough warrior would make a good father. But that's not what she'd come here for.

'Perhaps he'll be able to drink from a bucket tomorrow and take some hay,' Klara suggested softly. A three-month-old foal needed more nourishment than what could be fed in a bottle. To do so would be a full-time job, one Nikolay didn't have time for.

Nikolay nodded, his eyes intent on the foal. She'd not been ready for his next question. 'Did you find what you were looking for tonight, Klara?'

'I beg your pardon?'

He glanced over at her. 'We don't need to pretend you only came to see the horses, not when that's been reduced to a fairly flimsy fiction at this point.' He set aside the empty bottle and settled the foal against the mare's side. 'Whatever you found or think you found, it doesn't change anything. I am your riding instructor, nothing more.'

'You have never been a mere riding instructor,' Klara dismissed the warning in his words. She held his gaze, forcing him to look at her, knowing full well the coat didn't cover everything. She crossed a long leg over the other, slim and bare, watching him follow the movement with his eyes. 'Is that why you do it? Always taking control? Don't think I haven't noticed. You won't even let me kiss you without needing the upper hand.'

'Be careful you don't ask too much, *lyubov*,' Nikolay warned. It was as good as an admission. She was right. He *did* do it for control.

Klara held his eyes. 'You're a mystery, Nikolay. You can't say that and not expect me to wonder why you need that control, or what you fear by letting it go.'

Nikolay gave a short bark. 'You're too obvious, Klara. You should start with the easy questions, not the hard ones. You've got to sneak up on a man, catch him unawares if you want to figure him out.'

'All right, we'll do it your way.' Klara cocked her head, considering him. 'What do you mean to make of yourself here in England?' Her heart hammered. For a moment she thought he would deny her yet again, then a small smile crept across his kissable mouth. It was not entirely a warm one. Klara braced herself for the cut that was surely to come.

'I am looking to establish a riding academy. I've been searching for a property and for horses to act as a schooling string.' He shrugged. 'See, I am just a riding instructor, after all. That will disappoint your father.' There was the bite. Even after intimacy, even after laying herself bare before him, he was still wary of her, still saw her as the ambassador's daughter.

'You still can't see beyond *him*, can you?' Her prince was a hard cynic. 'After all I've risked, after all we've done together, you still don't see *me*.' Her throat thickened. The emotions of the day threatened to overwhelm her: the kill pen, Amesbury, now this. Nikolay's insinuations would not let her forget who she was.

Nikolay's voice was stern steel. 'Did he send you tonight to convince me up to join the revolution? Should I be expecting it? Does he have reason to believe I changed my mind?'

Her body tensed as if slapped, the intimacy of the moment slipping away along with the other reason she'd come. 'Do *not* turn tonight into negotiating chips. How dare you imply I'd play the whore in exchange for information?' He was protecting himself, she knew that, but it didn't make his words any more palatable.

'*Is* that what you've done? Have you given him hope to think I might relent?' Nikolay stood up, brushing straw from his trousers. He ran his hands through his hair, tying it back with a leather thong. His voice was a hoarse whisper. 'Was I wrong to trust you? Did you tell him about me?'

'I did not tell him.' She stood, too, her voice shaking. She knew what he meant. He had shown her more than Soho that night in the café. He'd shown her a piece of his soul. 'I have not betrayed you.' She risked going to him, placing her hands against his chest. 'Can you believe that?'

'I shouldn't.' Nikolay's hands covered hers, his

grip tight, his breathing hard. 'You're the daughter of an ambassador from my former country, a country that may wish I be returned to it in some undesirable manner. Since I've met you, I've been invited to a tense dinner that had extremely political overtones. A coincidence? A man has to wonder what it is you're not telling him.'

'A woman has to wonder what you're not telling her.' But she thought she knew. Intimacy was his Achilles heel, the one flaw in this warrior's armour. Whoever had hurt him had done a masterful job. Klara kissed the knuckles of his hands. The walls between them were high indeed if they could not trust each other. 'We trusted each other today. Klara and Nikolay trust each other.'

'But the ambassador's daughter and the Prince keep secrets,' he argued, 'out of necessity.'

The olive branch had to come from her. 'I came tonight because I needed to warn you. Amesbury knows about Soho and the kill pens. He's had us followed.' Her fingers gripped the folds of his loose shirt. 'If you want proof that I am here of my own volition, know this: he has forbidden me to continue my lessons. He means to harm you in order to keep me in line. He means to blackmail you into compliance with the revolution and my father will allow it because his cause needs you.'

Harm him? The Duke would have his work cut out for him then. He'd proven hard to kill before. But one look at Klara's sombre face told him he could not shrug this off with a soldier's nonchalance. Klara had risked much in coming here tonight and it was Klara, the woman who danced with him in Soho and drank vodka, who had stood with him today in the kill pens, who was pleading with him now to take the warning seriously. For her sake, he could not brush this warning off.

The hard shell of him began to seethe and crack. Anger began to bubble. He should have been outraged over the blackmail. He could imagine what that would consist of. But his immediate anger was over Klara instead. How dare the Duke threaten her! And yet, her own fear had been overruled by her fear for him, just as her fear had been set aside for the stallion and the foal today. His Klara was a saviour. *His Klara.* Not the ambassador's Klara. *His.* 'I can manage the Duke. Thank you for the warning.' He covered her hands with his, feeling how cold they were. 'Shall I challenge him to a duel?' He could protect himself, but who would protect her if he didn't?

'No!' Klara was aghast. 'The last thing I want is men fighting over me.'

'The last thing *I* want is for you to be hurt on my account.' He kissed her knuckles, his breathing shaky. He meant every word. He would duel the Duke, and more, to keep her safe. The intensity of that response surprised him, shocked him. How was it that this woman had slipped beneath his armour even when he'd been on guard? When he'd forbidden himself to feel anything beyond the physical? And now the woman he was willing to duel a duke over was the woman he should most avoid.

The irony was not lost on him and it posed the dangerous question: was this Helena all over again? His gut twisted at the thought that Klara's beautiful, upturned face with those worried eyes was a façade for betrayal. But that's what he had to think, wasn't it? He had a scar on his hip that demanded he *always* think the worst. If he didn't, the only option left was to trust—the one thing, for all his wealth stored safely in a bank, he could not afford.

'Nikolay, promise me…' Klara began. Nikolay pressed a finger to her lips.

'Do not ask me for promises, Klara.' He needed her to go. He was tired and not thinking clearly. It was a recipe for mistakes if she stayed longer. He reached for her gown hanging on a hook and helped her into it, letting his fingers drift over her skin as he worked the fastenings, allowing himself this one tenderness before he let her go. 'You were brave to come here tonight. You must not risk such a thing again, not for my sake, but for yours. I am not afraid of Amesbury.'

'I am not afraid of him either.' Klara turned in his arms. 'This is not goodbye, Nikolay. Amesbury does not have the ordering of me.'

Her stubbornness would be the death of her. He set her away from him, finding the will to be strong. 'Go home, Klara, there is nothing for you here, nothing worth the risks you are willing to take.' Certainly not him. He would only disappoint her in the end with his warrior code and his walls of distrust. Klara would want all of a man and he could not give her that. He could give no woman all of him.

Klara's eyes flared. 'I don't believe you. Tonight—'

'Was a moment out of time,' Nikolay said firmly. 'like all the other moments between us: beautiful and rare and entirely outside the realm of reality.' It could be no other way, but even now he was already testing the limits of that possibility with two of the most powerful words he knew: *what if*.

Chapter Fifteen

'What if it's a trap?' Stepan was an early-morning cynic. The ill-fated invitation Klara had warned him about lay between them on the breakfast table.

Nikolay chuckled. 'My, my, since when has my mail held such fascination for you?' He made a show of unfolding his napkin and settling it on his lap.

'Since it comes from the Russian ambassador. Since I saw the way you've managed to "stay away" from Klara Grigorieva in the stables yesterday,' Stepan huffed. 'You were devouring her and she you, and it didn't appear to be the first time such a "feast" had happened.' Stepan pounded his fist on the table in abject frustration. 'You promised me, Nikolay!'

Nikolay's eyes went straight to the bottom of the page where the signature was boldly written: Alexei Grigoriev. The thought of celebrating Maslenitsa generated warm memories for him. He'd always loved Maslenitsa in Kuban, the celebration that marked the beginning of spring and the last of the festivities before Lent. It would be different here, of course. There was no snow for sleigh rides. 'How can it be a trap when I know what I'm walking into? How can *she* be a trap when she was the one who warned me? She told me point-blank not to come.'

Stepan's eyebrow notched a new level of cynicism. 'What if that's exactly why she told you? She knows you'll do the reverse. She told you to stay away because she knew it would make you want to come all the more.' His friend sounded more than cynical. He sounded…fearful. 'Maybe this one time you don't have to run towards danger and a beautiful woman, Nikolay.'

Nikolay set down the invitation. There was more at work here. 'What is really bothering you, Stepan?'

'You're leaving and I won't be able to protect you.' Stepan's face was naked with stark emotion. There was nothing left to hide and the depths of that exposure rocked Nikolay. Stepan was always so steady, so sure of himself. 'Nik, you forget that I was the one who saw you with that wound, in that cell. Everyone was talking treason and murder while you bled. No one cared if you died while they argued.'

It would have been convenient for the Tsar if he had managed to expire. He couldn't say Stepan's reasoning was wrong. 'You made them care,' Nikolay answered quietly. He didn't remember much in those pain-dazed hours, but he remembered that. 'You came.' Miraculously someone had got news to Stepan. 'You came bursting into the dungeon with five men behind you, waving a torch and a sword and demanding I be seen by a doctor.' A doctor Stepan had brought, a man who could be trusted to stitch him up, not finish him off. Stepan had seen him safely to his father's house and his father had taken things from there. Without Stepan and his father, he would have died one way or another. 'You saved me that night.'

'Of course I saved you. You have been my friend since childhood,' Stepan said sincerely. 'I would save you again if I could. But you don't want to be saved. You are running headlong into trouble with this woman, as if Helena's dagger in your side wasn't caution enough.' Stepan paused. 'And you are thinking about joining them.'

'Yes.' He would not lie to Stepan. 'Grigoriev sees the need for change as do I.'

'You do not have to be that change,' Stepan argued. 'Let someone else lead that fight. Perhaps there is a way to foment change from here. You know what will happen to you if you go back to Russia and are caught.'

'Stepan, when I left Kuban I never meant to leave my principles behind. I'm lost without them, I'm lost without a cause to fight for,' Nikolay tried to explain.

'It's not that I don't understand. It's that I worry.' Stepan sighed. 'You are all leaving me. Illarion will go next. He can hardly wait for the Season to begin. Already, his evenings are filled with English nonsense.'

'You will always be our *adahop*, Stepan. You always have been. Even in Kuban you were our leader,' Nikolay consoled. Usually it was Stepan who did the consoling. Nikolay picked up the invitation. 'If

I don't go, I look like a coward,' Nikolay said simply. There was no question of refusing the invitation. 'If I don't go to them, they might very well come to me. I don't want to bring them here.' He rose from the table. He didn't want this to become an argument with Stepan.

Stepan gripped his arm as he passed. 'Just be honest about your reasons. Going because you mean to protect us is one thing. Going because you mean to risk an *affaire* is another. One reason I can accept. The other, I cannot. I don't want to patch you up again. Please, Nikolay, I don't want to be right about this.'

Was Stepan right? Nikolay called to the valet and began issuing instructions. The effort of packing focused his thoughts, boiling them down to one: was Klara a part of this? Was he thinking of joining Grigoriev because of her? Was he going the house party because of her? Or would he be going anyway because his conscience demanded it? If she was a part of it, if befriending him was part of reeling him in, then he'd been betrayed once more. He'd been right not to trust her last night, not to give her the real pleasure she'd come wanting. Last night had been hands and mouths, an imitation of true consummation, a consummation that could have bound him to her in more permanent ways.

It also meant that what he'd experienced with her had been an illusion, which called in to question everything she'd told him, shown him. He didn't want the Klara Grigorieva he knew to be a lie. That was a woman he could fall for, if he could separate that woman from her father's politics. There was no question she was her father's pawn. The real question was whether she had realised it and wittingly capitulated. On the other hand, if the woman he'd seen last night, the woman who had risked herself to warn him, was the real Klara, he could not let her be manipulated by her father or Amesbury. That woman would need him and he had yet to leave a damsel in distress. Stepan was not entirely wrong. He *was* going for Klara, to determine once and for all if he could trust her. He would put both himself and her to the ultimate test.

'Is there anything particular I should pack beyond the usual?' the valet asked.

Nikolay glanced at the emptying wardrobe. Only his military gear remained. 'Pack my uniform and my sabres.' Then he added, 'And my lance.' The lance was a Cossack's specialty.

'And your cavalry pistols?'

'Why not? Throw them in as well.' Politics and passion when they involved a prince made for a volatile *ménage à trois* indeed.

It was hard to imagine anything bad could happen in Richmond, so bucolic was the setting, Nikolay thought as he approached the long drive leading to Grigoriev's country estate. The day had turned out to be fine weather for a ride; the air was crisp with winter but the sky was blue overhead, he was warm and Cossack was in fine spirits. He'd sent his trunk and the valet down the Thames to meet them.

The house came into view, red bricked and majestic, the front lawns acres of green. He knew, without seeing, that the back lawns would terrace down to the river where a ferry could dock—the benefits of having married a rich Englishwoman. Grigoriev had been lucky in that regard. Such an alliance allowed him wealth and a foot in both camps. Such alliances were not unheard of in Kuban where a prince might be 'encouraged' to marry the daughter of a Turkish border pasha in order to keep the peace where military strength could not. Perhaps that rationale explained why Grigoriev was intent on Klara marrying an Englishman, to keep his options open.

A groom met Nikolay at the top of the drive to take his horse. Nikolay took a moment to survey the house with its white columns framing the wide front door and the fan window overhead. Windows everywhere, really. Beautiful long windows with white shutters flanked each wing of the house.

At the door, a footman escorted him across the blue-veined marbled hall to the drawing room where guests were gathered for an arrival tea, done in the best Russian fashion, silver samovar and all. Grigoriev himself crossed the room to greet him, not with a handshake but with a customary Russian embrace and three kisses, two on the right cheek and one on the left, signifying great affection. 'You rode the entire way!' Grigoriev exclaimed. 'We must get you some tea.'

Grigoriev led him to the table where the food was laid out: plates of small, silly English sandwiches and silver bowls of caviar were amid the delicacies of Russian sweets. Nikolay's mouth watered at the sight of them. Perhaps his eyes did, too. There were slices of *medovik*, a layered honey cake, and the traditional round Russian tea cakes made of shortbread and rolled in confectioner's sugar. There were thin blinis swaddling berries in their delicate crêpe-like folds.

'Eto ideal'no,' Nikolay murmured appreciatively, taking a cup of strong, black tea from a lace-aproned maid.

'Come, there are people I want you to meet.' Grigoriev had him by the elbow, guiding him about the room. 'You will know the General already, of course.' He nodded to Vasilev and kept moving. 'We are eager to know you better since our dinner party.' Nikolay kept half an ear tuned to Grigoriev's talk. He knew the path Grigoriev's rhetoric travelled. He was safe enough for now. His eyes were busy. There was only one person Nikolay was interested in seeing and he found her by the long windows looking out over the terraced lawns.

Klara was silhouetted between the heavy, impressive floor-length portières, dressed in a deep indigo afternoon gown, her hair pulled back into a proper twist at the nape of her neck. Everything about her was sleek and smooth, immaculate and elegant, a pristine juxtaposition to the woman who had slipped her gown from her shoulders and stood naked before him in the mews. Immaculate Klara was not alone. Amesbury stood with her.

Grigoriev caught his gaze and directed their path towards the windows as if Nikolay and Amesbury were not polite antagonists at best. 'I'm sure you'll want to renew acquaintances with the Duke and say hello to Klara, too.' If Grigoriev knew what had transpired between he and Klara, the man covered it beautifully.

Amesbury was not so diplomatic. The Duke gave a small bow at their approach, his eyes cold. 'Baklanov, it is good to see you again.' Nikolay hardly spared the man a glance. His gaze was on Klara, watching surprise and disapproval flare in her green eyes.

Grigoriev stepped in with a hand at Nikolay's shoulder to redirect the conversation. Nikolay had the fleeting impression he didn't want Amesbury saying too much just yet. 'Our festivities this weekend include a martial riding display. The General has some of his captains with him. I do hope you'll consider taking part.'

'Gladly.' Nikolay nodded. 'Will you be joining us in the display, Your Grace?'

'I'm a pistol man, myself,' the Duke offered with feigned modesty, but the challenge was unmistakable.

Nikolay grinned. 'I find guns to be impersonal weapons. One doesn't have to think too much about whom one is mowing down with a pistol, not like a blade. Blades are a real man's weapon.' He felt

Klara's slipper press down on his boot in warning. She didn't like him antagonising the Duke.

Klara cleared her throat. 'We are so pleased you could join us this weekend, Prince Baklanov. Have you had a chance to taste the *medovik*? We had it made especially for you. The General's wife has a lovely recipe.' He jumped at the chance to steal Klara away from the Duke.

'No, perhaps you could show me?' He offered Klara his arm, while casting Amesbury a look of veiled victory.

'Go on, Klara.' The Duke smiled tightly, unable to challenge him publicly without appearing boorish. 'I have things to discuss with your father. It would only bore you.'

Klara scolded him the moment they were out of earshot. 'I told you not to come.'

'All the more reason. I wondered later if that was what you intended; to ensure my attendance by warning me off?' At the tea table he helped himself to a slice of the layered cake. He held her gaze; his latent cynicism had put her on alert.

'You don't trust me, even now after the kill pens, after going into Soho with you? Would I have risked so much without a personal reason? You still think this is about my father's game.' There was naked hurt in those words. His accusation had cut her and he regretted it. How did he tell her that he wanted to believe her, wanted to believe in her trust? He simply couldn't. That belief was too expensive. Her green eyes mirrored her disappointment in him. When had he ever disappointed a woman? When had a woman ever wanted more from him than he could give? He could give pleasure, he could give flirtation and intrigue, a merry game of pursuit, but not trust. Trust was too close to love.

Her hand closed secretly over his, out of sight where no one could see. 'For a moment, when I saw you walk into the drawing room, all magnificence in your greatcoat, your hair blown by the wind, I thought you might have come for me. Just for me.' The disappointment was still in her eyes. 'I see now such hope was for the impossible.' She glanced past his shoulder. 'My father is coming to take you away to meet other guests.' She let go of his hand. 'Be careful. This is a dangerous party.'

Oh, she did not play fair! Was she dissembling now for the sake of deepening the game or was this genuine concern? It was damned inconvenient that he simply couldn't tell. What if she was sincere? What if she had risen above the game? Did that change anything? Nikolay let her father lead him about the room. He bowed here, nodded there, smiled when appropriate, murmured a few necessary words, but his mind wasn't on the conversation. It was on her, as was his gaze when he could spare it.

The Duke had reclaimed his spot at her side. By force or had she allowed it? Wanted it? If faced with a choice between him and the Duke, who would she choose? Why did he care? Perhaps believing the worst of her was easiest. It meant he had an excuse not to engage any emotions. Believing the worst was the safe road. Believing she had genuine feelings for him was more complicated. That meant he had to answer for his feelings as well and, to be honest, he did have them.

He'd felt a rather strong surge of competition just now upon seeing her in the window bay with Amesbury. He wanted her with him, not Amesbury. Couple that with the stab of fear at the kill pens when he'd realised she was gone from his side, the panic at seeing her in the stallion's pen, the intense rush of desire when they were alone together, the feel of her in his arms as they danced at Mikhail's bistro. All of it suggested Stepan was right. He was falling for her. The realisation nearly stopped him in his tracks. He couldn't remember the last thing Grigoriev had said. It was quite the revelation to have in the midst of a drawing room where his thoughts should have been focused on his own survival. Perhaps Klara hadn't been wrong. Maybe he had come for *her*, after all.

By dinner, it was clear Klara had told the truth about the invitation. He was indeed being wooed overtly for the revolution. In classic diplomatic fashion, Grigoriev was trying to sweeten the pot in hopes of not needing to sour it. His methods were quite effective in spite of being obvious. The Maslenitsa house party was designed to conjure up the best of Russian folk culture. The tea, the cakes, had all been delicious, followed by a beautifully executed traditional Russian dinner.

It was more than delicious, Nikolay thought as he

fingered his glass of *medovhuka* after dinner. Around him, the men switched to Russian. The ladies had left and taken the English with them apparently, a signal that it was time to get down to business. He let the words flow over him along with nostalgia. To hear the words, to taste the food, to let the sweet honey-mead liquor linger on his tongue, was to recall potent images of home. No, not home any longer, but a land denied to him except for glimpses like these.

'We have business partners who are willing to sell us arms,' General Vasilev was saying with a nod towards Amesbury. 'His Grace's connections have proven true. We will be able to give our troops the latest in weapons, weapons they didn't have the last time.' Nikolay's attention sharpened. Weapons were a serious step that bridged the gap from dinner table talk to reality.

The Duke began to speak. 'Cabot Roan has been able to assemble a very generous coterie of ammunition and gun manufacturers who can provide us arms at an affordable rate.' So that was the Duke's role in all of this. His Grace was acquainted with an arms dealer, and not just any arms dealer, but one who'd been tried for treason a year ago and been let off. How 'enterprising' of Amesbury. It made Nikolay wonder just how Roan had got off, and if it had anything to do with Amesbury's deep pockets and deeper connections. The commission on this arrangement must be hefty indeed if Amesbury was willing to bend the straight path of justice.

'We may not need the arms,' came another opinion from one of the young captains Nikolay had met previously. 'If Constantine is named the heir, there will be a peaceful transition of power. The military is pledged to him and his ideas already.' Nikolay slid a glance towards the Duke to see how Amesbury was taking the idea of no arms. Not well if the frown on his face was an indication, but the General was willing to argue on his behalf.

'But if not—' Vasilev's bulky form leaned forward to make the case '—we must be prepared to strike hard and fast. Constantine's ascendancy is not ironclad.'

'When, though?' another guest challenged. 'Must we wait that long?'

'That's the question, isn't it?' It was Grigoriev's turn to speak. The ambassador eyed the table, looking at each man in turn. 'If we wait for the natural course of events to run itself out, we may be waiting for years. I say we strike now. We have weapons, we have the support of the military. We have a leader in Constantine who can take the throne of Russia and propel us into the nineteenth century of the west. He can be this century's Peter the Great.' This was far bolder than the careful talk at the previous dinner and Nikolay knew where it was leading.

Grigoriev lowered his voice, drawing the men in as he outlined his plan. 'We can force a transition with a palace coup. It wouldn't be the first time, and there's enough dissatisfaction with Tsar Alexander to whip up the dissent in our favour.' He paused, letting his proposal sink in. Nikolay felt Grigoriev's gaze land on him. 'We need a man in place that could rally the troops at a moment's notice. A military man, a man who can lead others, who understands the military and how it works, but also a man who knows court life. A man like yourself, Baklanov.' It didn't get any more point-blank than that. *This* was what Klara had warned him of. They didn't just want him to join them. They wanted him to *lead* their revolution—to be the face of it on the ground. 'Think it over, Baklanov. It's not a decision to be made lightly.' Grigoriev smiled easily, but Nikolay was not fooled.

Every sense was on high alert now. All the doubt came roaring back. Did Klara know the stakes were this high? Had Grigoriev used her to reel him in for this purpose? Had she wittingly accepted her father's dictate and merely done what she was told? Was even her scene at the tea table this afternoon expertly designed to draw him close? Was Grigoriev betting he'd join for the revolution for the sake of pleasing Klara? It wasn't beyond the scope of imagining. What a man wouldn't do for war, he might do for love.

Chapter Sixteen

Oh, what a woman might do for love, for trust, to prove herself to the man she wanted! Klara's hand hesitated a moment before she knocked. The hallway was dark and quiet around her, midnight having sounded half an hour ago on the big clock in the hall. The house was officially asleep. No one would ever know she was standing outside a man's bedroom in her nightgown. Yet what she was doing took real courage, known or not. It was a decision she'd have to live with for the rest of her life. It had to be tonight, before her father got his claws into Nikolay any further, before Nikolay could confuse her offering with stratagem. Before she could be accused of whoring herself to gain his compliance. As if she could do such a thing, give her body indiscriminately to any man for whom she might have a use. What she meant to do tonight was no idle whim. Once given, this gift could not be taken back. No unwed girl of fine birth could consider this action lightly. She wanted Nikolay to be the one, no matter how this turned out in the end. It was the single thing she was sure of. Perhaps it was different for men. A woman carried her lovers with her. They were not shed like a snake's skin. She gathered her resolve.

She drew a breath and knocked. She waited. She tried the handle and slipped inside. The room was dark, the only light coming from the fire, but it was enough to discern the tall figure in the chair. 'You're still up. Why didn't you answer when I knocked?' She moved towards him, taking the chair across from him.

'I wanted to see how badly someone needed to come in.' That was when she noticed the pistol in his lap. She brought her gaze up to meet his, questions warring with comprehension.

'You were expecting the Duke? You believe me then, that he means to do you harm?'

'I think *harm* is too mild of a word. Kill me is more likely, based on the glares he shot me at dinner.' Nikolay shrugged. 'Perhaps I exaggerate the harm to myself.' She would not be so sanguine if it was her in that position.

'Do people come to kill you often?' The fire was comfortingly warm in the wake of Nikolay's cold reception. She could excuse it, of course. He hadn't been expecting her. Nikolay's eyes swept her, taking in her attire, or lack of it. She'd chosen a nightgown of ivory satin that clung to her breasts and curved over her hips. He was still dressed, although not in the clothing he'd worn to dinner. He wore a loose, exotic shirt of blue silk with elaborate embroidery at the neck, and trousers. But his feet were bare.

'Often enough.' Nikolay's answer was oblique. His gaze retreated to the half empty glass in his hand.

Klara offered a smile and tried for levity. 'Do they wear silk robes?' She was acutely aware he had not set the pistol aside.

'Assassins in satin,' Nikolay mused unkindly. 'You might be surprised.' He was not thawing.

He couldn't possibly believe her father would send her to do such a thing. He was trying to drive her away. The idea that she'd come to do him harm was ludicrous in the extreme, but that didn't stop it from hurting. He'd done nothing but hurt her since he'd stepped into the drawing room. He'd accused her of scheming to get him here. He was accusing her still. She tried to reason with him. 'I have no place to hide a weapon, as you can see.' She held her arms out to the sides. Nikolay didn't laugh. She'd thought she'd looked rather alluring. Apparently, she just looked deadly.

'You don't need to *bring* a weapon when you could just use something already in the room. It wouldn't be the first time seduction has proved fatal. Antony and Cleopatra, Romeo and Juliet. Your Henry VIII and Anne Boleyn. History is littered with people who loved unwisely and ended up dead.'

'Romeo and Juliet are fictitious. They don't count.' This was a new level of cynicism, even for Nikolay. Then she understood and her heart sank with the realisation. *This had happened before.* She leaned forward and placed her hand over his where it lay on the butt of his pistol. 'Who was she? The woman who hurt you?' Perhaps more than hurt him. Klara became bold. 'Is this how she tried to kill you? She came to you at night and offered herself?'

Nikolay tensed, she could feel the muscles in his hand bunch beneath her grasp. 'Why would you say such a thing, Klara?'

'Because it's true. Your type of cynicism doesn't come out of thin air.' It made sense. He was a prince, a handsome man with power. He would be sought after for all the right reasons, and the wrong. Klara slipped out of her chair and knelt before him, covering both of his hands with her own, no longer afraid of the gun. 'You have lived a luxurious but lethal life, Prince Nikolay Baklanov.' She whispered her request, looking up into his face. 'Tell me who she was. Tell me what she did. Tonight, your secrets are safe with me.'

How safe was he? She could see the debate behind the screen of his eyes. Could he trust her yet? He was calculating the odds. She'd told him the truth this afternoon, because nothing that had happened up against the stable wall or in the carriage had been a lie. He was deciding if he could live with the consequences if he was wrong.

His eyes held hers, dark and glittering. His words came slowly. 'She was cousin to the Tsar. She was older than I, a woman in her thirties with a reputation for danger, deceit and desire. She made it easy to overlook the first two. She was beautiful and men constantly vied for her favours. I was flattered when I won her attentions—'

'She was probably flattered to have won *yours*,' Klara interrupted. It was hard to believe any woman would overlook Nikolay.

'I had something she wanted: my silence. I'd spoken out against her cousin the Tsar's policies too many times. The Tsar wanted me dead and she owed him a debt. One night she came to me with a knife. When that failed, she went for my cavalry sabre.' His tone was solemn, each word measured. Klara could see the scene playing out in a dimly lit chamber like this one, a gorgeous, enraged woman in dishabille wrestling Nikolay for mastery of a sharp blade. Nikolay would be at a disadvantage, swamped by disbelief and betrayal, grappling with his sense of honour; how did he fight a woman, knowing that not to fight would surely be the death of him?

'It was me or her, Klara. She'd made her intentions clear. She would kill me given a half a chance and she'd been given more than that.' His grip on her hands tightened painfully. 'A sabre is a slicing blade, not a stabbing one. I sliced her. She died in my arms, right there on the floor of my bedchamber.'

In his arms. The three words held potent meaning for Klara. Once the battle rage had passed, he'd gone to her, forgiven her, made the woman's death as peaceful as he could. How many men had died that way, in his arms, on the war field, or in a battle hospital? 'Nikolay, you did all you could.' Klara wanted to absolve him. The story was horrible and yet there was a poignancy to it.

'Did I? I was a skilled warrior, she was not. Perhaps I should have found a way to control myself better. It had all been planned. The Tsar's men were waiting for me, dead or alive. I was taken away fifteen minutes later. Only Stepan's intervention saved me from a prison cell.'

And then he had fled. He didn't say it, but Klara could imagine what happened next; facing trial for the murder of the Tsar's relative, and perhaps even charges of treason for speaking out. Nikolay had chosen exile over execution. Now, he was here, drawn back into the fire once more by her father. No wonder he was sceptical of her father and of her. More than ever, she wanted to convince him she was not part of that world. He could trust her. He could trust what lay between them.

Klara moved her hands to the fastenings of his trousers, a promise on her lips. 'I am not her. Let me show you.'

He should show some restraint. He should not allow this until he had figured out where her loyalties lay and fortified his feelings. But the issue was confused beyond redemption the moment her hands reached for his trousers, the moment her hand found him, hard and ready despite the warnings of his mind. Klara kneeling in front of him with her hair down, her hand on him, was too much. She was honest in her passion, if nothing else.

Klara stroked him, his erection straining to her touch. He had questions, too; what had brought her to his room tonight? Was it truly just him or was it something more? He'd not forgotten the desperation underlying their last interlude, but neither had he forgotten how futile it was to resist what lay between them. Those questions would have to wait a while longer. Her other hand cupped him, gently squeezing him towards oblivion. A mad sound escaped him. He welcomed oblivion tonight, was eager for it after the revelations of today. He felt himself slip down in the chair, his body ready to loosen reality's tether. Klara took advantage, spreading his legs apart fully, her fingernails teasing the tender skin of his inner thigh with a raking stroke that had him groaning. She was no Helena, not in touch or temperament. His body knew it, answered to it.

She stroked him once more and then her mouth was on him, sucking at the tender tip, learning her way as she went, lapping the pearl of his desire at its head, licking the length of him as if he were the most decadent of Gunter's ices. Only he was so much warmer. Burning, in fact, his body entirely alive, entirely aware that it was being driven towards exquisite release. His hands had become talons, digging into the upholstered arms of the chair, his last grip on sanity as she tasted him, teased him, a mewling gasp of reckless pleasure escaping her. It was small consolation to note her control had slipped, that she too was caught up in the pleasure of it. Again.

This pleasure had happened before. Once might be discounted as a novelty, but twice? Twice suggested that the fire between them was unique, something able to be quenched only by the two of them together and no other. That would be a certain hell on earth. He could not have her for ever. His body clenched and gathered for final release, reminding him he could have her for tonight, that indeed she'd come here looking for more than mouth-play.

'Klara!' he rasped in warning, feeling his body change, feeling her mouth give way to her hand once more. She held him as release rushed through him, pulsing against her palm, her eyes alive as if she knew this was not the end. These pleasures of mouth and hand would soon be rendered insignificant compared to what was to come.

Nikolay slipped to his knees on the floor beside her, his hands at the hem of her nightdress, pushing it up and over her head, baring her beautiful, naked breasts to his hands. There was no hurry tonight. Tonight he could linger and feast. Nikolay gave a reverent half-sigh, pressing a kiss to her breast, a man prepared to worship at the altar of his beloved. Beneath his mouth, the goddess quivered and it was more than reward enough.

He slipped his hand low between them where her curls were damp, a reminder that while he'd had some satisfaction she'd had none. How long would she wait for him? He rose from the floor and lifted her, carrying her to his bed, a large baronial affair that would serve him well tonight. He laid her down and turned up the lamp.

'What did you do that for?' Her voice was husky from the sheets.

'The better to see you, my dear.' Nikolay let his gaze roam the length of her.

Her eyes narrowed in a coy glance. 'Perhaps the better to see you, as well. Someone is overdressed for my bed.'

It was his bed, technically, but he wasn't going to quibble over semantics. He was, however, going to oblige the lady.

Chapter Seventeen

His shirt went first, revealing the strength of his torso, all sculpted muscular planes from his shoulders to his waist, a muscled atlas interrupted only by the small disk he wore about his neck on a chain and the occasional thin white line, remnants of a scar. The imperfections only added to the appeal of him. He turned away from her, giving her the smooth expanse of his back as he worked his trousers down past lean hips, gloriously rounded buttocks, horseman's thighs and long legs. His hands went to his hair and he pulled free the leather thong that held it back. The intake of her breath was sharp as she let her eyes feast on this dorsal showcase of masculinity. And then he turned.

She had him full frontal and nothing else compared, nothing else would *ever* compare. He was spectacular. It was hard to breathe as she took him in. His hands were on his hips, a thin white scar line on one hip drawing the eye downwards to the crux of him; that splendid phallus straining upwards already although she'd satisfied it just minutes earlier.

He came to the bed like a conquering warrior of old, possessive and primal. He was more pagan god than prince when his body covered her, one hand manacling her wrists above her head as his body found its way between her thighs. She was more than ready for his siege. He entered her, a steady reconnaissance, a slow withdrawal, and a slow return, easing and teasing his way towards her core, until the slide of him was known to her. Her body picked up the rhythm of him; the surge and ebb of pleasure tides against her shore, the waves breaking faster with each foray, pleasure's tide rising and she let it sweep her away even knowing she would be dashed against the rocks, fracturing into a thousand shards in a tempest. He gave a final thrust and they were at sea, together.

Pleasure was generous. It washed her up on a quiet, peaceful shore when it was done with her. Nikolay drowsed beside her, his arm thrown across her. She might have slept, too. Her mind was just now starting to clear, to make the return to reality. The little things came back first. She was in Nikolay's bed. The fire had died down. The lamp had gone out. Ah, so she had slept. How long?

Nikolay stirred beside her, smiling when he saw that she was awake. 'Have you been up long?' His voice was husky with sleep.

'Just long enough to watch you.' She rolled to her

side to face him, to study him. 'What's this?' She played with the disk on the chain at his neck. His eyes were friendly at the moment. She wanted them to stay like that. She knew too well how quickly they became sceptic's eyes of hard obsidian instead of warm, melted chocolate.

His hand covered hers on the disk. 'It's the medal of St John the Divine. He's the patron saint of loyalty, among other things. He's a good patron for a soldier, a reminder that patriotism is a type of loyalty, that defending one's friends and one's country is the highest loyalty of them all. My father gave it to me when I took command of my own cavalry unit.' A father, a saint's medal. Further signs of how rich and full his former life must have been, how much that woman in Kuban had taken from him. Further signs, too, of how much she didn't know about him, how much she wanted to know and how much she already accepted him without the knowing. But knowing was dangerous. When one knew someone, they became more than pawns on a chessboard. Knowing made one vulnerable. She was certainly that. Falling for Nikolay was pitting her against her father and his game. It was forcing her towards a choice—her father or Nikolay? She didn't want to give her Prince to her father's game. She was a selfish woman, she wanted Nikolay to herself in all ways. Mind and body and soul; no politics, no doubts. The depth of that realisation was shocking.

'You must miss Kuban and yet, except for the night at the bistro, you never talk about it. I thought people talked about the things they loved. Incessantly so.'

He gave a half-smile. 'Like mothers with children, who go on about their sweet prodigies? I think it's the other way around. Perhaps some things are too precious to discuss out loud.' What else did this magnificent man keep bottled up inside him? What other secrets? What other sorrows? She wanted to know them all. Would he trust her with them now?

He sighed, acceding the argument. 'Perhaps the tendency to hold in reserve those things that are important to us comes from our neighbours. There are Muslim Turks on our borders with whom we do battle and business by turns. They keep their women in seraglios, female-only quarters, so that they are not subjected to the gaze of other men. They are jewels to be treasured, not ogled, not trotted out on the marriage mart the moment they turn eighteen, dressed and designed to draw the eye of an eligible *parti* with enough money to buy them.' The cynic was rearing his head again.

Klara pondered the idea for a moment. 'I would not like being hidden away.'

'Of course you wouldn't.' Nikolay laughed softly. 'You're English. It's not the British way, and yet it is a sign of honour and wealth in that part of the world for a woman to be protected thusly.' He paused. 'Not all prisons have four walls, Klara.' He captured her hand and kissed her palm. 'Did you find some freedom tonight, Klara? It's what you were looking for, wasn't it?'

She tried to draw back her hand, but he held fast, his voice hypnotic. 'Don't be ashamed, Klara. You said you did not come for your father. If so, it stands to reason you came for yourself. What did you want, if not freedom? Pleasure?'

If. The most damning two-letter word of all. He still didn't believe her entirely, but here in the warm cocoon of his arms the words stung a little less. She had his body, after all. She ventured the raw truth of her choice. 'I *did* come for myself. But I also came for you, Nikolay. I wanted you to believe me. I couldn't stand the idea of you thinking our relationship has been contrived for ulterior reasons.' She licked her lips. 'Believe me when I say I am my own person, with my own feelings, not a pawn of my father.'

'I wonder if *you* believe that? Perhaps you do for the moment. It is easy right now, here in each other's arms, to believe a great number of things—mainly that the impossible is possible.' Nikolay levered up on arm and rolled to face her, something akin to pity in his eyes. 'What will you choose when you're held to the flame? Will what you believe in this moment matter when you have to choose between your father and a prince?'

'A prince to whom I have given my virginity, a prince on whom I have made no claims and expect no claims in return, but whom I have trusted with this gift none the less. Does that mean nothing to you? Coming here is no small thing!' Klara protested. If this was not a token of the depths of her intentions and affections, what was?

Nikolay shook his head. 'It's not that I don't *want* to trust you, Klara. It's that I *can't*. How will you decide when put to the test? I don't think you know either.' His tone softened, his knuckles skimming the side of jaw in a gentle caress, 'My dear girl, what do you think can be accomplished in this bed? I can give you pleasure tonight, tomorrow night and the next, but beyond that, there can be nothing else. You were right. They asked me to join the revolution. They want me to take the arms to St Petersburg.'

She didn't know what to feel. She should feel elation. Her father had what he wanted. But she felt fear, too. Fear because she didn't want Nikolay caught up in the dangers that would ensue? Fear that he'd say yes, or fear that he'd say no? Most of all, she feared she'd been too late with her offer. Her father had already asked him. Had that already tainted their night together before it had even begun? 'What did you tell them?' Klara ventured, wary of the answer. He was right. How could she win?

'I said nothing. Not yet. They expect me to think about it.' His gaze darkened, not with desire this time. A chill travelled her spine. She had been too late. Her offer could not be viewed out of the context of what had happened behind closed doors after dinner. Nikolay was too astute to overlook the coincidence. He gave a hard chuckle. 'See, the choice comes already. Your father or me, and you don't know how to decide.' He gave cold smile. 'We've had our pleasure, Klara. We've satisfied what it is that might lay between us on a physical plane. Perhaps we might satisfy the truth, now that's out of the way. Did you know what your father intended to ask me? Is that part of why you came to me tonight? Is your father expecting me to say yes tomorrow morning after a night of your charms?'

Klara threw back the covers in anger and climbed out of bed. 'No! After everything I've shown you tonight, *given* you tonight, you still have the audacity to ask that?' Rage coursed through her. How could anyone fake what she'd experienced tonight? How could he be so blind? She wanted to hit him. She grabbed up the nearest item to her, a pillow, and struck out, once, twice, before he got a hold of the pillow, tugging until her rage turned to tears. This was all her fault. Now she was paying for it, spurned by the man she'd unwisely chosen to love.

Her tears were his undoing. Nikolay wrested the pillow from her and gathered her into his arms, regretting his harsh words instantly. She'd given him an extraordinary gift and he'd thrown it in her face. 'Klara, don't cry. Please don't cry.' It was poorly done. The woman who had moaned her pleasure beneath him had been no man's pawn. She'd been real in her passion as he'd been real in his. To depict what they'd done as anything other than genuine was to do it a disservice. He held her to him, rocking her against him.

What the hell was wrong with him? Why did he hurt the women he loved? He squeezed his eyes shut, pushing back the memories Klara's questions had opened tonight; Helena with the knife, coming at him, stabbing him before he could disarm her, before he could dispel his disbelief. And the sabre, dear Lord, the sabre! There'd been only seconds to hold the lightning-quick debate in his mind: do or die? The warrior in him had won, but Helena haunted him and likely would for ever. He would never completely banish the images of her crumpled on his floor, life seeping out of her. Had there been another way? He'd taken her life, held her in his arms as she slipped away. He could rationalise his decision, but he couldn't accept it.

Here he was on the brink of making that same decision again: his survival over another's. He'd hurt Klara. 'Klara, I should not have said it, I should not have…' he murmured the words into the softness of her hair.

'No, it's me who should not have done so many things,' Klara sniffed through her tears. 'I should never have walked into the riding school. I should never have agreed to vet you. I should have walked away after that first dinner. But I was selfish. I thought I could serve my father and myself.'

He could feel the fatigue in the weight of her body against his. He'd not thought of the toll this was taking on her. This whole time he'd thought only of himself, the hunted victim. But Klara was a victim, too, and perhaps less well equipped to handle the consequences than him. 'You were so handsome, so charming, so different, and you knew so much that I wanted to know. I couldn't resist.' She sniffed again. 'You were right all along. I did play a double game; one for myself and one for my father. But I never told him about Soho. I never told him about the stables, or the kill pens. All the best parts I kept to myself. I promise.'

His best parts were starting to rouse, finally recognising that they were both naked and in close proximity. Or perhaps it was his mind registering that this at last was the complete truth, as imperfect as it was. 'Klara, I believe you.' He kissed the top of her head where it rested on his chest. 'It's not all your fault. I gave in when I could have walked away.' He could give her this at least. 'You intrigued me, just you. I didn't want to let you go.' They'd both been selfish and it had led to this untenable situation.

'What would you be doing if you hadn't met me?' Klara's question was like yarn in the dark.

'Giving riding lessons. Tolerating the Four Horsewomen of the Apocalypse.'

'Is that all? I can't imagine that's it. That life is too small for the man I know.' She snuggled up against him. His groin responded. They were past the anger now, past the hurt. 'Is that why you go to the kill pens? Just for the adventure of it?'

He took pity on her. Klara wanted one more small piece of him. Perhaps she was entitled to that much. 'I go when I am called. There are those who know I am a friend to horses. When there's a horse in jeopardy, they get word to me.'

'That sounds nice. Worthy. Far worthier than anything I've done in my life. What do you do with the horses? You can't possibly keep them all.'

'I am building my string, for my riding school.' He laughed. 'Does that satisfy your curiosity, Miss Nosy-Parker? Or does that disappoint you? That your prince is a simple man, after all?'

She wiggled more intentionally now, her tone becoming playful. 'No, it doesn't disappoint me at all. Where do you propose to have this fine school?'

'I haven't decided. I have a few locations in mind.' His hand ran a lazy pattern up her arm. He was starting to be interested in other things besides riding schools. He lifted her on to the bed, his body moving over hers. 'Right now, though, I just want to ride you.'

In affirmation, she reached up for him, her arms about his neck, pulling him down to her and he let her. There would be time later to worry about the revolution. It went unspoken between them that these confessions didn't change anything. She would still face a choice and it was still unclear how she'd answer. And he still faced a choice of his own: assist Grigoriev with his revolt, or risk the ambassador's wrath. Tonight they could have their pleasure, the morning be damned.

Chapter Eighteen

There were blinis for breakfast, the traditional Russian crepe that dominated the Maslenitsa celebration. The buffet table in the morning room was set with every topping imaginable: caviar, sour cream, jams, fruits, even a pot of hot, melted butter to drizzle over them like syrup. Grigoriev and the General must want him badly. Amesbury was already there in the breakfast room, his plate laden with shirred eggs and kippers, very English.

Nikolay gave the Duke a terse nod and set about heaping his plate with blinis still warm from the kitchens, deliberately ignoring the English dishes on offer. He took a seat at the table next to the young man who'd spoken out over drinks last night. His plate, too, showed a hearty serving of the blinis. 'One does not ignore blinis during pancake week, eh?' Nikolay grinned. He could feel the Duke's disgust as the jab hit home. He looked over at Amesbury, his expression bland as if his remark had not been intended to insult. 'No blini for you, Your Grace?'

'No, Your Highness. Sweets are for children, in my opinion. Meat is for men. Keeps up one's strength.' He held up his fork speared with a sausage to emphasise the point.

Nikolay let his accent thicken. 'Ah, perhaps I am mistaken. I thought England celebrated pancake week, too?' He feigned the question. 'Shrovetide, is it not?' He grinned and made a particular effort in taking an overlarge bite of the blini.

'Yes, but not all Englishmen take it seriously. You will find that England is a land of thinking men. We've learned from the past the harms religious zealotry and superstition can bring.' Amesbury took a swallow of his coffee. 'Are you a religious man, Your Highness? I hear so many of your countrymen are. Certainly the Tsar is.' It was not meant as a compliment. In one fell insult, Amesbury managed to denigrate his country and its leader.

Nikolay thought of the St John's medal he wore beneath his shirt. 'I am, Your Grace. Most smart soldiers are. It's an occupation that demands it. And yourself? Do you classify yourself as a religious man?'

'No. I haven't time for superstitious nonsense,' the Duke said baldly, tossing down the verbal gauntlet. Those were fighting words. One could not sit there and insult him, his country and his God. without facing repercussions. Nikolay had no hesitation in dealing out those repercussions, duke or not, but a rustle at the doorway tabled the altercation.

'You don't have time for what?' Klara sailed into

the room, dressed for the outdoors and all smiles; perhaps too many smiles. She looked radiant to him, alive and fresh and *his*. Seeing her sent a straight shot of desire to his gut even though she'd only left him a few hours ago.

Nikolay straightened. It was an easy adjustment since he was already halfway up, or halfway across the table depending on how one looked at it. The Duke rose with a nod in her direction. 'My dear Klara, good morning. You look lovely.' Would the Duke guess? Part of him wanted the man to. Nikolay was already contemplating pistols at twenty paces. Perhaps the south lawn where the grass was flat would be a good place to duel. Nikolay tried to assess her through neutral eyes. Did she look like a woman who'd passed the night in the arms of her lover?

He moved to the sideboard, assembling her a plate while Amesbury was still dawdling over small talk. Was that the best Amesbury could do? *You look lovely?* She did look well in a dark blue riding habit cut with a salute to the military tradition, her hair braided in a neat coronet about her head, but Klara was always lovely. In his experience, actions spoke louder than words.

'Klara dear, do take a seat, shall I get you something to eat?' The Duke pulled out the chair beside him and Klara sat, but Nikolay slid his newly assembled plate in front of her, heaped with blinis and meaning as he tossed the Duke a smug glare.

Klara gave a little laugh, a trifle uneasy with the

attention. 'It seems Prince Baklanov has already taken care of that for me.'

Nikolay boldly took the chair on her other side, abandoning his original seat. 'The blinis are excellent this morning. I've picked out some toppings I think you will enjoy especially.' He gestured to the dark dollop on the side of the plate. 'I recall from dinner how much you enjoy the caviar. Try it first. I think it tastes best before one gets the sour cream on one's palate.'

If circumstances had been different, he would have fixed her a bite and fed it to her as if it were the world's greatest delicacy, but this was not a lady's boudoir in the late of evening. This was an English breakfast room at nine o'clock in the morning and there were onlookers, one onlooker in particular. He wondered what the chances were of selecting swords over pistols? He liked his odds there better.

What he did not like was the Duke. He did not like that the Duke was intimately connected with arms dealers, or that the Duke felt he was entitled to an intimate connection with Klara. The tête-à-tête in the window yesterday had not been a coincidence. Now, Amesbury was calling her 'dear', and the man seemed to revel in doing so, as if he had a claim to her. Was he the Englishman Klara was meant for? The possibility made Nikolay like him even less. He was all wrong for her. Amesbury wasn't a lover, but a dominator. He knew this sort of man. Sex wasn't pleasure to him, but power.

Nikolay watched Klara swallow the blini and caviar, thinking of her mouth savouring other things as it had last night. He could not recall when a woman had affected him so much the morning after. Usually by then his 'perspective' had returned and he found the woman less captivating. Not so this morning. He was feeling surly, protective and wanting Klara all to himself, something he'd be hard pressed to arrange before midnight. He fixed her another bite. 'Caviar from the Caspian Sea is the best in the world. I think it's the water's temperature that does it. Black pearls, we call them.' Nikolay glanced over at the Duke. 'Have you ever been? To the Caspian Sea? Beautiful place. You should go some time.'

He felt a sharp kick to his ankle. Klara was on to him. His possessive male pride wanted to say something entirely childish along the lines of 'She likes me better. I made her shatter against a barn wall and then last night...' But there were dangerous truths that such recognition unlocked. *He* had shattered that night and last night, too, completely undone by her touch, her intensity and what it could mean. Even hours later, the magnitude of what she'd done; she'd come to him as a bride to a groom, offering her body, her maidenhead, a show of her belief in him. Stepan would laugh at this perhaps naïve conclusion. But he was having trouble doubting Klara now. She had managed to separate herself from her father's game, at least momentarily. That separation couldn't last, though, and she would pay the price for it. Would it be worth three nights of passion? Three nights of freedom?

He had until the end of the party before he had
to refuse Grigoriev, and leave Klara. The weekend,
which had loomed ominously at the beginning, now
seemed short indeed. Just two days to go. There
would be consequences if he said no. Grigoriev had
made explicit references to rebellion in front of him
last night. They couldn't let him wander off if he
refused. *If?*

He should say no. He was on the brink of a new
life. His stable was within reach. He was not enam-
oured of doing business with the likes of Cabot Roan.
Yet, the earlier temptation whispered persistently
and with a new refrain. *Do it* for *Klara, do it to* save
Klara. He couldn't help but think this morning how
much it easier it would be on Klara if he said yes.
By saying yes, he could remove the pressure for her
to choose between him and her father, he could as-
suage the restlessness in himself. He was made for
war. It was what he knew. They'd all be on the same
side. These men wanted what he wanted: a Russia
that could compete with western Europe. These ideas
were the very ideas that had forced him from Kuban.
Now he had a chance to march back to Russia and
fight for those ideas. Shouldn't a prince, a soldier, always be ready to protect his country from the enemy,
even when the enemy came from within? Perhaps
there was enough good in Grigoriev's cause to outweigh the bad. It was certainly a convenient argument to make with the beautiful Klara in his bed and
sobbing in his arms. He could hear Stepan's voice of
reason in his head, faint but compelling. *'Perhaps*

it is all still just a trick. Women conjure tears like crocodiles. The risk to yourself is enormous.' Perhaps the risk to Klara was greater, she was far more innocent in all of this than he and she was the one likely to be hurt all the more because of it.

Grigoriev stepped into the room. 'I thought I'd find the rest of you here! The weather is fine and we're ready to head out of doors for a tour of the grounds.' He nodded towards Nikolay. 'We have a riding arena set up for this afternoon. Some of the General's men are going to do a demonstration, if you would like to join them.'

'Absolutely,' Nikolay replied, as if he had a choice. Grigoriev wasn't a man who asked others for permission. Perhaps a display of his prowess would put Grigoriev on alert. It had occurred to him that maybe Grigoriev didn't fear him knowing their plans because a man who refused to participate was a dead man. If so, he'd show them today it might be harder than they expected to kill Nikolay Baklanov. 'Your Grace—' Nikolay couldn't refuse a last bit of prodding. He turned to the Duke '—will you join us for pistols at least?' If there was a duel with Amesbury coming, he'd like to know what he was up against.

If breakfast had been for him, the tour was for the Duke and the other guests, a polite reminder of Grigoriev's own wealth and power and who was really in charge of the revolt. There were gardens to tour with manicured bushes, topiaries and knot gardens. Even in winter, the garden was green and held the promise of spring. There were the stables to see, done in the latest fashion of box stalls and wall feeders for hay instead of troughs taking up space down the centre aisle. The stable was a marvel, built around a square courtyard. There was an indoor riding house as well, constructed with high windows for light. 'For my daughter's hobby.' Grigoriev shrugged, unassumingly proud of both his daughter and the grounds.

Nikolay let himself drop to the back of the group, making it easy for Klara to find him. He was hungry for her, for even the simplest of her touches. She found him as the group moved from the stable to the carriages waiting to drive everyone out to the home farm to see the modern dairy. They took up the seats in a small carriage at the end of the line, most of the group having already moved out.

'You have to stop needling him,' Klara began without preamble the moment the carriage set in motion.

'Him? You mean His Grace, the Duke of Amesbury?' Nikolay watched her fuss with the lap robes, tucking them about her legs to ward off the cold. He smiled. His strong Klara was feeling vulnerable, shy with him after last night's wicked openness.

'Yes. You know exactly who I mean.' She looked up from her tucking, her eyes serious. 'This is not a game, Nikolay.'

He met her gaze with equal seriousness. 'No, it is not. It is a revolution, one whose success is not guaranteed. Not that Amesbury cares. He wants only to sell the arms. He cares not that men will die. The lucky ones will die in battle. The unlucky will be hanged from the ramparts, condemned as traitors for wanting to bring their country forward. For that, they will pay the rather expensive price of patriotism,' Nikolay scoffed. 'The Duke will pay nothing. He will line his pockets.'

'My father needs him. We cannot afford to have him alienated. We need the arms.'

'We?' Nikolay smirked. 'You and your father. You've decided already whose side you're on, even though your father is willing to use corrupt weapons to arm a rebellion.'

'For a good cause, a cause you believe in, too,' Klara argued.

'The ends outweigh the means, then?' Nikolay queried. How very practical of her. He'd do best to remember that when it came to understanding their affair.

'Don't make it sound crass, it's what you're thinking, too. You've been debating the issue all morning, I've seen it in your face.' Klara reached for his hand. 'You don't know what to tell my father,' she said softly.

'No, I don't,' Nikolay admitted. 'I should walk away because my principles will not tolerate doing business with the likes of Amesbury and Roan, men who do corrupt things for corrupt reasons.' He dropped his voice and covered her hand where it lay on his, his eyes steady on her face with its delicate jaw and sharp eyes. God, she was beautiful when she looked at him with green eyes so full of…love. He didn't want her to love him. He was flawed and broken, and there was so little he could offer her. 'Do I support a just cause with materials gained from questionably unethical venues? I am very aware, Klara, if I say yes, I can save you from making a choice.'

He would say yes. *For her.* Was it possible to *feel* oneself turn pale? Klara *felt* white, her body numb with shock and realisation. This was how a warrior loved; not with words but with actions. He was so tactile in the bedroom, all touch and physicality. It stood to reason he'd be the same in life. He showed how he felt with actions. She thought of the foal and the mare he'd rescued because she'd asked him, of the plate he'd fixed for her at breakfast, all thoughtfulness in his selection of toppings for the blini, a very small thing compared to what he shared now. She could not let him do it. 'I don't need to be saved, Nikolay.'

He gave an intimate chuckle that had her wanting to stop the carriage, to stop the world, and make love with him right here in the broad light of day. 'Yes, you do, Klara. You are far too reckless; sneaking off to Soho and into men's bedrooms.' He was teasing her now and it felt good to move away from more serious considerations for just a moment. That moment was gone too soon. He squeezed her hand, his voice private and low. The worst things were said, it seemed, in the quietest of voices, as if to derail the listener from the importance of them.

'I have a father I love very much, too. I had to choose between him and coming here.' He had to stop and collect himself, his grip on her hand noticeably tighter. 'I would not want the same for you. Like you, my mother is gone. The family I know is my father and I.' The father that had given him the St John's medal. Her gaze dropped briefly to his neck, to his chest where she knew the medal lay secret beneath his shirt. No wonder he wore it close to his skin. Not just as a soldier's protection but a reminder of a father's love.

'My father was proud of me. When that woman— Helena…' he hesitated over her name '…cut me, it was he and Stepan who saw that I recovered. He hid me. He denied the Tsar entrance to our home to protect me when the guards came.' He swallowed hard again, his Adam's apple rising in his throat. Klara hung on every word. 'In Kuban, a family has to renounce a traitor among them if they wish to escape a traitor's fate. Failure to do so makes one complicit. He had no choice. I wanted him to do it, but I could see that he'd rather die. The last time I saw him, he'd just come from the palace and it had aged him twenty years. Klara, that is what I'd save you from.'

'And my father, too,' Klara said softly. 'You would save my father, too.' How different he was from Amesbury, who thought only of himself and his money. She leaned into him, her mouth close to his, lips hovering just before a kiss. 'And I *would*

save you.' They were on the same side now. Nikolay and Klara against her father, against the revolution, against the consequences of saying no, against
the consequences of saying yes. Nikolay and Klara,
together against the world.

Chapter Nineteen

'How could you do it?' Klara spoke tersely, barely keeping a rein on her anger as she stood beside her father at the demonstration grounds. It was the first chance they'd had to talk since she'd discovered what he'd asked of Nikolay.

'Do what, Klara?' He kept his eyes forward, gaze on the show, applauding politely when a young captain on the obstacle course sliced the last rope loop with his sabre.

'Use me to send Nikolay to St Petersburg. He told you no at that first dinner and you persisted.'

Her father didn't flinch. Another rider entered the course. 'He's capable of making his own choices. I doubt anyone coerces *Prince Baklanov* to do anything he doesn't wish.' Her father slid her a sideways look. 'Has he told you his decision, then? Are you as close as all that to know his mind before I do?'

'No. He did not say. He said only that you'd asked.' She paused and clapped for the rider. Her father had taught her that nothing was ever as it seemed. Unfortunately, she had not applied that advice to him. She'd assumed there was no need. Of all the people she should be able to trust, her father ought to be on that short list. Apparently he wasn't. 'And Amesbury?' she ventured. 'Have you promised him anything I should know about? He's been proprietary of late.' That was putting it mildly. He'd been violent and threatening.

'He holds you in great esteem, Klara,' her father evaded. 'I promised your mother a marriage to an English peer. He would be a fine choice if it came to that. He cannot be outdone in wealth, stature and social standing. One can never have too many friends.'

The footmen came out to reset the course for the next rider and Klara let her gaze drift to the lists, looking for Nikolay and not finding him. He'd been right. She'd been the bait. Her father had used her. It was so hard to accept that it made denial easy. Nikolay was a cynic at heart. He simply didn't understand. And yet, she very much feared Nikolay's cynical eyes had seen the truth.

Her conscience whispered, *What does that truth mean to you? Is it enough to choose Nikolay over your father?*

There was a rustle in the crowd. The course was reset and another rider was in the lists, drawing the crowd's attention. No, not just any rider. This one wore a brilliant scarlet coat with a placket of dark blue bars trimmed in gold braid across the chest, gold epaulettes on the shoulders. The rider's head was bare despite the cold, his long dark hair braided into a tight queue that hung down his back. It was unmistakably Nikolay. She had not seen him since the tour of the home farm. He'd found time to change into his military uniform and to groom Cossack, who pranced beneath him, looking as sleek as his rider. The warrior Prince was in full glory. It sent a *frisson* of desire through her to think this man had been hers for a night and that he might be hers again if she were bold enough.

Amesbury materialised beside her. 'He still looks a bit rough to me. A uniform is only a piece of clothing after all. I'm surprised you're so taken with him, Klara.'

'I'm not taken with him,' Klara insisted, mortified that the Duke found her so transparent. What else did he see? Information in his hands was always a dangerous commodity.

Amesbury shrugged. 'You've spent a lot of time with him lately when I warned you not to. He will not be careful of your reputation, Klara. He is from a different world. He does not answer to an Englishman's concept of honour.' The Duke nodded towards the course, changing the subject. 'I do think he's attempting a bit much.'

For a moment, Klara thought the Duke was referring to her, that Nikolay had overreached himself, then she followed the Duke's gaze to the course. It had not been only reset, it had been restyled. Where each young captain had run a single lane to exhibit their prowess with a weapon, the course now contained a comprehensive set of obstacles. Her horseman's eye could appreciate the complexity of it: a lane of rope loops to be sliced from horseback with a steady sabre, a line of poles to weave one's horse through, followed by a small flag to pull out of the ground, a dummy to stab while riding at full speed, and a final target to shoot. The course would take concentration and the ability to transition between skills for both horse and rider.

'Shall we wager? I think the Prince shall do handsomely,' Klara offered perversely just to antagonise the Duke.

'I shall pass. I've had poor luck with wagers lately, Klara, dear. I lost one last night. One I did not expect to lose. I misjudged the person in question.'

'I'm sorry to hear that, Your Grace.' Klara kept her eyes fixed on the course, hoping to end the conversation.

Amesbury gave an urbane shrug. 'I did not lose too much,' he went on as if she'd asked. 'Not monetarily any way. It was more of a loss to my pride. You see, I lost a bet with myself. We shall take a walk and I shall tell you about it after the Prince's run.' His voice was at her ear, sending a shiver of fear down her spine. She wanted to go nowhere with him, nowhere away from people, away from Nikolay.

There was no chance to respond. A flag dropped and Cossack surged from the lists, Nikolay balanced in the stirrups, his sabre drawn as he approached the hanging loops of ropes. The trick was to be steady.

The loops were tiny. The slightest jolt would throw a rider off balance, his sabre out of alignment with the loops. She held her breath, worrying Cossack's speed was too fast, that the horse required too much of Nikolay's attention. His sabre sliced the loops without hesitation. He sheathed it and turned towards the poles, Cossack weaving through them effortlessly, changing directions from right to left. They headed towards the flag. It seemed impossibly low, too low to grab. The other men's flags had been higher, coming to the horse's belly. This flag was four inches off the ground. To get it, one would have to lean entirely out of the saddle. To do that required an impossible combination of flexibility and muscle control.

She gasped. Nikolay let the reins drop, then flung his body to one side, the grip of his thighs his only contact with his horse as he swung close to the ground, his hand sweeping up the little flag. The crowd around her applauded wildly. But Nikolay wasn't done. There was a dummy to stab and a target to shoot, but how could he? Klara wondered. He had no weapons.

Nikolay passed the weaving poles. He yanked one out of the ground and twirled it over his head, wielding the pointed end like a lance. He kicked Cossack hard, increasing the horse's speed, his arm drew back and he plunged the tip into the dummy with a force that would have separated most men from their horses. There was just the target left. Nikolay drew his sabre once more and threw as Cossack raced past, the sabre blade vibrating as it found purchase in the bullseye.

'Ingenious!' Klara breathed. He'd done the course with only his sabre when it would have taken other men four different weapons to accomplish it. The whole display had taken less than a minute, but it would be talked about for hours, days even. Klara surged forward with the rest of the crowd to congratulate him, taking perverse delight in knowing the display had rendered Amesbury silent.

Her father and Vasilev reached him first, clapping him on the back in congratulations. 'Splendid, just splendid,' Vasilev was saying. 'You're a credit to Kuban and to the military. Those skills are nonpareil. You must be untouchable in battle. And your troops? Do you teach them to ride like that?'

'Yes.' Nikolay was all politeness, but she could tell he was careful not to be too warm with the General. 'I had my unit train daily on the parade grounds.' Near her, Klara heard some of the women titter and whisper remarks about the crowd that must have drawn, the sight of so many 'talented' men on display.

A drawling voice cut through the exclamations, a reminder that Amesbury was still with her. 'Prince, do all the men in Kuban wear their hair long?'

Nikolay gave him a hard stare. 'Only the real ones.'

Everyone laughed. Even Amesbury pretended to be amused at the response, but he had his hand about her arm again, firmly insistent as he pulled her into the crowd of guests, away from the centre of attention, his tone ominous. 'Come with me, Klara. It's time for our walk, and I'll tell you why I lost the wager.'

Amesbury steered her away from the group. 'I went to your room last night. I wagered myself you'd be glad to see me. You weren't there, much to my surprise.' He chuckled coldly. 'You disobeyed me, Klara.'

'What are you insinuating, Your Grace?' Klara stiffened at the implication, her battle senses on full alert. What did he know? 'Am I not allowed to go to the library and get a book or go down to the kitchen for some warm milk in my own home?'

'Of course not. But that's not where you went, is it?' He accused. 'I know empirically that you went to *him*.' He squeezed, his fingers digging into the flesh of her upper arm. He paused, perhaps to let her become duly frightened by the discovery. It was definitely alarming, but she refused to be cowed by it. There were people nearby. He could not hurt her here. 'I waited for you to come back. You have a very comfortable chair in your room, by the way. Thank goodness, because I sat there for *hours*.'

He'd gone into her room, *unasked*. That frightened her as much as the idea that he'd found her gone. What else would he take from her unasked?

Klara pulled her arm away from his, opting for the high ground. 'I am deeply disturbed that a gentleman would claim he has proof of such a thing when he does not. Sitting in an empty room is *not* empirical proof, Your Grace. For all you know, I fell asleep in the library.' The ice was pretty thin where she was skating. She hoped it held.

The Duke was menacing now, his body rippling with tension. 'Don't play me for a fool like you play your father. I know what my eyes see. You are infatuated with the Prince, Klara, and you've been very foolish,' he hissed in her ear, 'I know the look of a woman who's had a man between her thighs, even if your father does not.'

'How dare you! I will go to my father and tell him all about your dirty mind, how you have laid hands on me twice...' She raised her hand, striking out at his cheek, but he caught her wrist and dragged her behind the wide trunk of an oak.

'You will do no such thing, you little harlot. You will go to your father and you will tell me we have set a date for our wedding. Early June, I think.'

'Our wedding? You haven't even proposed.' This was fast becoming a terrifying situation. The Duke seemed unhinged in his anger.

'Consider this your proposal,' Amesbury growled, his body up against hers, trapping her against the rough bark of the tree. She could feel his arousal against her skirts. 'Unless you need a further display? I am more than capable of compromising you here and now.' She struggled in earnest now, but it only made him angrier. 'You will say yes if you know what is good for the people you love.' His teeth sank into her ear and it was no love bite. 'Marriage to me protects your father and your lover. Your compliance keeps them alive.'

She shoved at him, but couldn't dislodge him. 'My father doesn't need your protection!' His hand closed over her breast.

'One word from me to the Tsar's circles about your father's plans and he's branded a traitor. I could even manage to have him sent home. I *know* I can manage sending the Prince home. His Tsardom is hungry for his head on a spike. Your father will do it for me to save his own hide. He can hardly get away with harbouring a known traitor.' He was rutting against her thigh now in a grotesque simulation of sex, doing it on purpose to humiliate her, to scare her. It was working. She was scared. Her father killed. Nikolay betrayed. Those were very real fears that could come to pass.

'Klara...' His breath was coming hard now. He was enjoying torturing her too much. 'Let me ask you again, will you marry me?'

She could save them both, her father and Nikolay, with a single word. They would not die for her. She gathered her courage. 'Yes.'

'A much better answer, Klara dear. We'll announce it after the dancing on the last night. Until then, it will be our secret. I'd hate for a stray bullet on the pistol range find our Prince because you told him.' The Duke gave her a thin smile, one that was falsely forgiving. 'Pardon my jealousy. Perhaps I may offer my envy of the Prince as a token of my affections for you, a token of my eagerness to have us joined in marriage. An eagerness that I do not think can wait until June, after all, dearest.'

Horror had a way of bringing clarity, mainly the clarity that she was on her own. Klara braced her hands against the windowsill in her room. She fought back tears. Crying would do her no good. Her father could not help her. Nikolay could not help her, especially not Nikolay. He would challenge the Duke to a duel and blood would be spilt, possibly his. She did not trust the Duke to play fair. She'd been so distraught about being her father's pawn, she hadn't seen how she could become Amesbury's pawn. Now, she was all that stood between Nikolay and her father's safety, their very lives. Somehow, she had to go down to dinner and pretend that all was well. Would Nikolay see through her? What would she tell him if he guessed something was wrong? Would he believe her? The terrible mordancy of the situation was not lost on her; now that he believed her, she had to lie to him. For his own good, for his own protection. Perhaps some day he would understand that.

She let Mary come and dress her for dinner in the pewter silk, one of her favourites. She let Mary do her hair in a complicated pile of curls that showed off her neck. She fastened her mother's pearls about her neck. If this was to be her last night of freedom, she would make it count. Not that there would be much of that freedom. Amesbury would be watching. There was no longer a question of going to Nikolay's room or of him coming to hers. Tonight, her door would be locked.

* * *

Dinner featured delicious cold-water salmon and champagne. She barely tasted it. She was too busy plotting how to steal enough time alone with Nikolay. There would be a bonfire and fireworks tonight after the men's brandy. It would have to be then. Beside her, Nikolay was positively charming, laughing at jokes and appearing like a man at ease. She took quiet pride in knowing that she'd been privy to the dilemma that lay beneath his bonhomie. He'd trusted her enough to share his thoughts with her and she'd protected those thoughts when her father had asked. He had his own decisions to make. Tonight they would be together and she would warn him one last time.

She was waiting for him in the hall when the men emerged. She whispered her instructions as she passed him. 'Everyone will go outside to burn Maslenitsa. When they do, come with me.' It was the annual farewell to winter, this bonfire burning of Maslenitsa in effigy. In the dark no one would notice if two people were missing.

As if on cue, her father began directing everyone out of doors to the lawns where a bonfire shot flames into the night sky. She felt Nikolay interlace his fingers with hers, determined not to lose her in the bustle. 'Stay with me, I know a place.' A place to be alone, a place to forget. Klara shivered. If Amesbury discovered them together...well, people duelled over things like that. And for good reason. But there would be no more chances after tonight.

This time tomorrow, her engagement would be announced. Amesbury would have her under proverbial lock and key with his constant attentions and Nikolay would absolutely despise her. She wouldn't think about that now.

She led Nikolay around the corner of the house. 'We're safe here,' she murmured.

He was hungry for her, too. His lips found hers unerringly in the dark, his kiss confident. She tried to answer in kind. He was not afraid of discovery. He was not afraid of the Duke. But he should be. If he knew what she knew…but he couldn't know. If he did, he'd wind up dead. Nikolay pressed her against the wall, his body blocking the bonfire from view and she welcomed the strength and warmth of him. She had not expected it would be so hard to let him go when the time came. But there was so much she hadn't anticipated when she'd begun this gambit. It had morphed from being a mere task for her father, to being an adventure for herself, to something far more than that, something she was afraid to give words to. She had fallen in love with him, this brash Cossack Prince, who had shown her a slice of his world, who had treated her as an equal, taken her on adventures, shown her what true passion was capable of. In return, she'd protect him with her life.

His lips skimmed the column of her neck, lingering at the base of her throat where her pulse beat fast and strong. 'Do you feel what you do to me?' she whispered.

He took her hand and drew it against himself.

'Feel what *you* do to *me*, *lyubov*. Feel how hard I am for you.' His voice was a sexy rasp, hoarse with longing. Heat curled low and damp in her stomach as she stroked him, her hand outlining the length of him beneath his trousers. *This* was her man, this potent, virile warrior. His hand pulled loose the low bodice of her gown, baring her breasts for his mouth. Who knew a mouth could wreak so much havoc on a body without any words?

Desire was rising swift and hot between them, devouring them, sweeping aside practised seduction and replacing it with a riot of kisses and caresses driven more by need than art. They were mad for each other up against the wall while the guests partied below. She fumbled with his trousers as his hands slid up her legs, pushing aside her skirts, baring her to the night air, to him. 'Now, Nikolay, now,' she begged, the moment she had him free. She was hot with want, too hot to wait, too hot to play. Release would be explosive and quick like the fireworks detonating in the sky above Nikolay's shoulder in celebration of the effigy.

'Hurry!' she urged, barely recognising the husk of her own voice. It was a voice that belonged to a wanton, a woman used to making love out of doors with party guests a stone's throw away.

Nikolay lifted her, gathering her legs around him, his hands cupping the rounds of her bottom as he positioned himself. The first thrust took her deep and hard.

He surged into her again, his own language reduced to groans, part desperation to reach the release that would calm them, part desire to be overwhelmed by the pleasure between them. There was no time for thought, no time to consider that this was the last time. There was only time to become part of him, to hold him inside as she buried her hands in his hair and her cries in his shoulder.

Klara arched her neck, lifting her gaze to the night sky, watching the last of the fireworks fade in the sky. She felt entirely complete. She shut her eyes, wanting to commit the moment and the man to memory, something to hold fast inside her against the darkness that would come.

'What are you thinking?' Nikolay murmured against her collarbone, his head on her shoulder.

'That this is the last night of the world.'

'Of a certain world, but not ours.' He kissed her softly and she wanted to weep. He didn't know how wrong he was.

Chapter Twenty

'Shall I come to you tonight when the house is quiet?' Nikolay asked softly as they joined the crowd of guests filing back into the house. He was already planning an enticing evening of lovemaking. The wall had been a potent appetiser, the thrill of sex out of doors, intoxicating, even if there had been a certain urgency to Klara's lovemaking. Perhaps she wasn't comfortable with the risk of discovery just yet. He'd have to show her how to appreciate the risk, how to let it work in her favour.

'No, you must not,' Klara said quickly, too quickly. He halted her with his hand, pulling her aside. Something was wrong. Perhaps the urgency had not been about her inexperience.

'Why not?'

Her gaze darted through the crowd as if she was looking for someone. Her words were rushed. 'Amesbury knows I went to your room last night. He will be watching. He cannot find us together.' Even now she was afraid of Amesbury. It was him she was looking for in the crowd.

'I'm not afraid of him. Let him find us. It will give me an excuse for a duel.' He was heartily sick of the Duke. Then he softened. Those had been warrior's words, a warrior's reaction. Klara was a woman. Those words would alarm her. She would want the words of gentleman, too. 'I will protect you, Klara. I will not allow him to slander you.'

'It isn't about me. He frightens me, it's true. But he would not publicly shame me, not when he covets my father's friendship.' She had her hands fisted in the lapels of his coat, words coming fast. 'Nikolay, listen to me. Put your decision off about the revolution as long as you can, until the very end of the party. As long as they have hope you'll join them, you're safe. Then, tell my father no. This is no place for you. Go and get your riding stable and never look back, no matter what happens. Promise me?'

He took her hands in his—they were cold. 'Klara, what is going on?' Something had happened. Her edicts were driven by more than Amesbury.

'I can't tell you. You just have to believe me. Please?' She took a step away from him before he could reach for her and melted into the guests. The party still had a day and a half to go, yet he knew what she'd done. She'd said goodbye. That was the urgency, only it wasn't urgency at all. It had been desperation. It had been farewell. She'd known the whole time there would be nothing more. Betrayal niggled at him. Klara had left him, after she'd begged for his trust, after she'd given him her body, she'd left him with a warning.

He could not let that lie. Klara would not give him up without reason. He would wager his fortune she was protecting him. From Amesbury most likely. She needed to believe him when he said he could handle the Duke and tonight he would. He wouldn't let Klara out his sight until she'd locked her door.

Nikolay watched her enter her room from a distance, close enough to be of use, far enough not to be noticed. He watched the door close and he stayed in place, his body tense and ready just in case Amesbury had decided to surprise her with another nocturnal visit and was already inside. He stayed at his post another hour *just in case* Amesbury decided to creep up the hallway, because Klara was still his to protect, would always be his to protect. She could decide to leave him, but he hadn't decided to leave her. When it came to women, Cossack honour ran deep and true.

He *loved* her in spite of his efforts not to, in spite of the impossibility of their situation. The realisation was heady and surprisingly *new*. He had never loved a woman. He'd not known his mother. The women he knew were a certain type—more interested in the physicality of being with him than the emotional aspects of a relationship and that had been fine. He knew how to be an entertaining escort for them, something dazzling on their arms, the warrior Prince who could dance the *hopak* like an acrobat, who could amaze on the parade field from the back of a horse and then bed them senseless at the end of the night. He knew how to be good fun, as did they. Whatever he gave those women, he got in return. But that had never been love. It had been easy to be with them. They'd never asked for anything beyond what he was willing to give, never challenged his rule that he would seek nothing permanent.

Now there was Klara Grigorieva, who had challenged his marital promise. It had been done most stealthily. She'd started as many of his women had—bold and outrageous. But she'd got beneath his skin and stayed there with her stubborn streak and her determination. It wasn't just that he loved her; she loved him. Which made tonight even more of a mystery. Who gave up the person they loved?

Footsteps sounded in the hall and Nikolay came alert. His lingering watch had paid off. The bastard had come. Amesbury knocked on her door. 'Klara, open up,' he whispered harshly when the door didn't open immediately. He whispered again. Nikolay put his hand on the hilt of his dagger.

Klara had been afraid tonight and now he saw the reason for it up close. Amesbury meant to force his way into her room, perhaps even on to her person. Amesbury would not hesitate to terrorise her in order to get what he wanted. Klara needed a champion. Nikolay stepped out of the shadows. 'The lady is likely asleep and can't hear you.'

Amesbury turned from the door, a sneer on his face. 'Are you an expert on Miss Grigorieva's sleep patterns now?' His lip curled. 'Or are you hoping to send me away in order to take a try at the door yourself?'

'If you are insinuating that I would make an unwanted visit to a lady's boudoir and attempt to force my way in, then, no. That is not why I am here.'

He would not dignify the Duke's implications with a direct response. His fingers flexed around the dagger hilt. 'I suggest you go back to your room and stay there. She was clearly not expecting you.'

The Duke gave a cold smile as he stepped away from the door. 'I don't need a weapon to bring you down, Baklanov. Remember that the next time you try to play the knight-errant. I know what you are—a murderer of the Tsar's cousin, a member of the Southern Union of Salvation, a man wanted for treason in his own country. I could have you sent back to Kuban in chains with a single word.'

So Amesbury knew. How much had it cost him? That kind of information wasn't cheap. Nikolay played with his dagger point. 'I'd slit your throat before I allowed you to drag me anywhere.' This was how they meant to blackmail him into the joining the revolt. No wonder Klara had warned him. Oh, God, no.

A horrible thought came to him. Perhaps Amesbury hadn't paid anyone at all for the information. Perhaps Klara had told him. Klara knew. He'd told her himself! Had she warned him out of guilt tonight? Was this why she'd said goodbye? Because she had no more use for him? She'd got what she wanted—

what her father wanted—leverage. No wonder she'd told him to wait until the last minute to announce his decision. Had she warned him? Or had she betrayed him? And to think a few moments ago he'd been ready to admit that he loved her. His stomach churned as he faced down Amesbury, his mind replaying the evening through a different filter now.

Amesbury gave him a nod. 'I see my news holds some fascination for you. I'll say goodnight and leave you to ponder it.' Nikolay's eyes tracked him down the corridor and out of view. He waited another half an hour to make sure the Duke didn't return. Klara was safe for now. Surely, he had the wrong of it. Surely, Klara had not given his deepest secret over to Amesbury whom she despised. He would ask her first thing in the morning. He'd been so careful in withholding his trust. Now that she had it, how could he have been so wrong about her? He wasn't. He *couldn't* be. His heart depended on it.

Something was wrong. What had begun as a seed of worry last night was blossoming into full-blown concern. There was no chance to get near Klara in the morning. At first, Nikolay told himself it would have been this way regardless. There was dancing tonight, a mini-ball for the guests and neighbours, all done in a traditional Russian folk theme. She was busy coordinating it all as her father's hostess. But as morning turned to afternoon and there was still no chance to sneak her away, Nikolay began to assume the worst. She had indeed 'left' him. His assumptions about last night's final intimate moments affirmed what he had originally viewed as urgency had been desperation, a farewell. It was the desperation he focused on now as he dressed for the ball. Why had she broken with him? Why had she acted today as if he didn't exist? In his gut, he felt there had to be something driving her decision other than just her fear of Amesbury's threats. But what? If he couldn't get near her, he couldn't ask her.

Nikolay pulled on a silk tunic, a red one this time, with elaborate embroidery on the chest placket. He belted it over his loose black Cossack trousers and stuck his ceremonial dagger in the sash. Everyone would be dressed in folk costume tonight and the dancing would be the dancing of the homeland. If he wasn't so worried about Klara, he'd be looking forward to this. What if he *had* lost her? He'd not allowed himself to think such things today. It had been too soon for that conclusion. But now, with the day behind him, those thoughts crept back. She was *his*. He had made love to her, had confessed his soul to her and he was not ready to let her go or to believe the worst.

The valet came to help with his toilette, but Nikolay sent him away. He would wear his hair loose tonight, over his shoulders. He was well aware that he looked the complete Cossack Prince like this: loose hair, native garb. It was done quite purposefully. Let Grigoriev see, let Amesbury see, let Klara see what he was in truth—a dangerous man who would fight for those he loved. At the last, he reached into the small leather box in the bureau and took out a sapphire ring set in a thick burnished gold band and slipped it on his third finger. Sapphire—the stone of truth and the apocalypse, the stone of protection.

He always wore it into battle. It seemed fitting that he wore it tonight. Amesbury would laugh at such superstition. All the more reason to wear it. There were plenty of battles to fight tonight aside from Klara. He had not forgotten that by tomorrow an answer would be expected of him regarding the revolt. He had not forgotten either that declining the offer to join would not be met with acceptance. He could not be allowed to leave with their secrets. He would deal with that later. First, there was Klara. He would dance with her and in the privacy of the dance floor he would ask his questions and have his answers.

Downstairs in the ballroom, Grigoriev had outdone himself with fiddlers, guitars and balalaika players. The atmosphere was festive from the folk music to the attire. All of the guests were turned out in traditional outfits; the men were in embroidered shirts and trousers like his, cinched in with wide belts, and finished with high boots; the women wore white blouses and colourfully stitched aprons. Some of the women even wore the traditional headdress, while others wore their hair in tight, braided coronets. In the niches lining the ballroom walls, blue Lomonosov vases were filled with red roses and dark blue stems of dendrobium. Out of habit he counted the flowers in each arrangement. All odd numbers of blooms in each vase. Good. No bad luck. Klara had remembered one of their lessons.

Spirits were high as guests crowded on to the dance floor for *khorovods*. Nikolay prowled the perimeter, searching for Klara. He found her on the sidelines, dressed in a red skirt and a pretty, embroidered apron, hair pinned up in a sleek coronet. Even better, she was alone for the moment. He set a stealthy trajectory, careful not to be seen. If she was truly avoiding him, she would run before he could reach her.

He came up behind her, a hand at her back to warn her before he whispered, 'It's not the same as the café, is it?' He let his hand linger. In the press of guests no one would notice the little intimacy, no would notice the brief close of her eyes as if she were savouring this moment.

'No, it's not.' Her voice was wistful. 'This is too…' she groped for the word '…staged?' She sounded tired.

'Shall we show them how it's done?' The musicians were transitioning into a polka, one of his favourite dances; fast and furious, it was for the bold dancer. 'Are you ready to fly one more time?' he murmured, already prepared to lead her on to the dance floor.

'Nikolay, I cannot.'

He'd not anticipated resistance. 'What is it you're not telling me, Klara?'

She wouldn't look at him. She kept her eyes on the dance floor. 'Step away from me. Please. If you ever had any feeling for me at all, you will let me be. I warned you last night. Leave me alone.'

The hell he would. He'd never left a woman in distress and there was distress etched in every cruel word she'd spoken. 'Klara,' he began. The crowd about them shifted and Amesbury stepped to Klara's side, taking proprietary claim of her arm.

'Klara, my dear, is there a problem? Is the Prince bothering you? You seem upset.'

Nikolay fingered the hilt of his dagger. He'd be 'bothering' the Duke in a moment if the man didn't take his hands off Klara.

'We were just having a small disagreement,' Klara managed.

The Duke gave him a brief nod. 'If you'll excuse us then, Prince Baklanov, this is our dance.'

Nikolay shot Klara a final look. If her eyes had pleaded for help, pleaded for intervention, he would have offered it even if he'd had to brawl in the ballroom. But her green gaze, which had sparked so often with mischief and life, was empty. She asked for nothing from him. He watched Amesbury lead her out on to the floor and put his hand at her waist. He felt explosively possessive. That should be him! He should be dancing with Klara. The litany that had sustained him all day returned; there was something wrong. But now he had to wonder—what if the only thing wrong was him? What if Klara had made her choice?

She had made her choice. She had known it would be hard, she had not known how it would feel—like a knife twisting in her gut every time she denied Nikolay and the biggest betrayal of them all was yet to come. Klara tried to lose herself in the speed of the dance, but the Duke held them to a more sedate pace. She could not fly, not really. She was a falcon in jesses, tethered to this man's dictates. *So that two other men might live.* Surely she could make some peace with that, except when she glanced to the sidelines to see Nikolay staring hard at them, his dark eyes hooded while his mind worked. He was sorting through the puzzle of her. She knew the questions he'd be asking himself; why had she left him? What had happened? She prayed he would not guess. Amesbury would see him dead before Nikolay even saw it coming. Amesbury was stealthy like that, tricky. He would send thugs in the city, make it look like a pickpocket robbery gone bad. She was doing this for Nikolay, so that he might be safe from such treachery, so that he might have his riding school and the life he wanted.

'The Prince is displeased, Klara.' Amesbury chuckled coldly. 'I trust you were convincing?' He swept them through a turn, teasing her with the invitation to speed that he would withdraw momentarily. His eyes were steady on her. 'I would sacrifice a great deal, even social pomp, to make you mine, Klara. I am thinking now that June is too long to wait with Baklanov on the loose. I worry that he might try something drastic like taking you away. Perhaps a special licence is in order when we return and a quiet wedding shortly after. If all goes well, we could be married this time next week.'

She said nothing. She was too busy tamping down the fear that threatened to break loose inside of her. He was giving her no quarter. His eyes glittered dark and dangerous. 'A wife obeys her husband, Klara, in all things. I am prepared to be grateful for that obedience in return. I am prepared to harbour your father should his revolt fail. But if I am disobeyed, Klara, punishment will be harsh.' Amesbury leaned close. 'Let me remind you what is at stake. One word from me and your father could be ruined. An ambassador who plots revolution is no small matter to the British or the Russians.'

She saw the full hell of the bargain she'd struck. Amesbury would be a stone about her neck for the rest of her life, her marriage a constant source of leverage. 'My father has made you a fortune already,' Klara protested. 'Surely those earnings pay for his protection.'

'Yes, they have. That's why I haven't said a word. Yet.' Amesbury chuckled. 'You're so naïve, Klara. It's called hush money for a reason. I would think you'd be interested in keeping it that way. Don't forget what I can do to the Prince, too. Your marriage saves them both, Klara.' The music stopped and he bowed to her, reaching out his hand. 'Come, my dear, it's time to make your deal with the devil official.'

This was how it must feel to mount a scaffold, to see the noose and know that your life was very nearly over, Klara thought as Amesbury led her on to the musicians' dais. Her father was already there, tapping a fork against a glass for attention. She'd heard accounts of the nearly departed looking out over the crowd for a friendly face, someone to focus their eyes on as the end came. Her eyes did the same. Against her better judgement, she let her gaze seek out Nikolay. She did this for love. She did this so he might live even if he hated her. She would see the moment that hate took up residence in his soul. She would take strength from that, knowing that she'd been compelling in her performance and that would keep him alive. It would be the first of many performances she would give to keep him and her father alive. She didn't dare look at her father, who was so happy, so proud of her decision, believing he'd kept his promise to her mother, never thinking at what cost that promise had come.

'Everyone, attention, please!' her father began. 'As our Maslenitsa party comes to a close, I want to celebrate with all of you the engagement of my daughter to Frederick Bixley, His Grace the Duke of Amesbury.' He gave a chuckle. 'I have it on the Duke's good authority they will be married as soon as possible. Tonight, join me in wishing them all happiness.'

Nikolay's face was a study in disbelief. She forced herself to hold his gaze, to see every message of his eyes as her heart crumbled. *Do you need me?* was the instant message in his eyes, his immediate concern for her. He could not believe what he was seeing, what he was hearing. He wanted to believe his senses had failed him. She showed him nothing, careful to keep her expression blank. It would be too easy to plead for the help he offered. She couldn't even give him an apology with her eyes. If she said she was sorry, he would know something was wrong, that this was a sacrifice. If he charged the stage, he endangered her father as well as himself. She couldn't allow that to happen, never mind the hurt that grew in his gaze. She knew his thoughts in those moments; she was Helena all over again. He was thinking of all he'd told her and believing that she'd shared that with Amesbury and her father, that she'd used him most foully. Then, she let Amesbury take her mouth in a kiss to please the crowd and her betrayal was complete. When she looked out over the crowd again, Nikolay was gone and he'd taken her heart with him.

Chapter Twenty-One

Klara had betrayed him! Nikolay reached his room. Somehow. He didn't remember the walk, only the anger, the burning in his gut, which was not that different from being stabbed. She'd stood up on that dais beside corrupt Amesbury and denounced him! With her eyes, with her words! As much as he hated her, he hated himself more. He'd warned himself, he'd taken precautions, he'd been alert to every scheme and in the end he'd taken those precautions and cast them aside, telling himself this time it would be different because *she* was different. Klara was real. But she hadn't been real, she'd simply been very good at her job: baiting a prince by making him believe she was in love with him. The only difference between her and Helena was that he hadn't ended up near death. Not yet.

That was to come though, wasn't it? He still had to decide about the revolution. *No* meant death. *Yes* was unappealing. His motive for joining, the idea that he could fight for Klara, taking away the horrors of deciding between him and her father, was no longer there. Perhaps that motivation had been an illusion all along. She'd never truly seen that as a dilemma. She'd already decided to support her father, already decided to side with the crooked Duke.

The engagement announcement had been masterfully planned. Doing it at midnight ensured it was too dark to leave. He was trapped here until morning. By then leaving would no longer be an option. The men were spending the morning at the Duke's munitions factory to take the next steps forward with the revolt. Grigoriev would want a decision then.

Nikolay's eyes fell on his dagger. He was going to have to fight his way out. Not with weapons, but with words—not his first choice, but his only choice. He couldn't commit and he couldn't decline, but that assumed there was going to be a revolt. He couldn't be pressed for a decision if there wasn't anything to decide.

A plan started to form. Revenge burned hot in his veins. He couldn't bring down Klara. Even as wounded as he was, he couldn't bring himself to deliberately strike out at her. But he could bring down the Duke. Ruin him, in fact. If Klara needed to be free of the Duke, ruining Amesbury, exposing him, would free her. *Free her. Save her.* What nonsense! Nikolay pulled at his hair, a moan escaping him. What an idiot he was! Even now after being betrayed by this woman, he still harboured a tiny kernel of hope that she'd been forced to it somehow. By St John! When would he accept that she'd used him and left him? Why did he keep pretending it wasn't over? Good Lord, she was to be another man's wife. She was beyond his reach now. It couldn't get much more finished than that. Klara was gone. For ever.

The pain of loss swept him again. How could she have done this to him? Made him trust, made him feel, only to take it all away? This was why he had his code! He was on the eve of battle and his thoughts were distracted by emotions and hurt when they should all be focused on bringing down Amesbury. But he could not control his thoughts. They were with Klara. The sickening agony of her betrayal ripped through him once more. He tore open the windows and howled at the moon like a wolf of Kuban who had lost his mate.

Klara was gone in the morning. Already back in London to make wedding preparations, a beaming Grigoriev told departing guests. Many of the women left early as well without their husbands so the men were free to set out on horseback for the munitions factory. This was the last official party duty, the last barrier protecting him from announcing his decision. Nikolay was ready. He'd had all night to prepare. He'd ruin the Duke, whatever else happened.

At the factory, they were shown the impressive machinations that turned out the standardised bullets and artillery shells at an unimaginable rate. 'Russia has nothing like this,' Vasilev breathed in awe next to him. 'This is the kind of progress we need to bring to our country.'

'Think of the money you could make selling such a machine to the army.' Amesbury stood to Vasilev's other side. 'Invest early, get in on the ground floor where you can control the contracts, and you'll have a fortune in no time. There's always a war, always a need for an army to fight. If Russia wants to move forward, this is a good way to start building an empire.'

'Progress is more than mass-producing weapons, I hope,' Nikolay corrected him, earning a steely gaze. 'The progress we need is much larger than weapons factories. It's the whole philosophy we need, an entirely new way of thinking.' Machines were just some results of that thinking. 'War for profit is hardly a noble philosophy to franchise.'

'Precisely.' A warm hand came down on Nikolay's shoulder as Grigoriev joined them. 'Well said, Your Highness. War should always be a last resort. We are planning a revolt, not a civil war. There is a difference.' There was, to him and other men of principle. But not to men like Amesbury. War was business, a commodity to be traded. He had to help Grigoriev see that.

'Come with me, gentlemen. We are going to try out the bullets with some of the firearms in the shooting gallery. I am told there's champagne as well.' Grigoriev smiled and nodded to the Duke. 'Your

Grace certainly knows how to entertain. This is quite the arrangement you have here, Amesbury.'

The Duke owned large shares in the factory. Nikolay didn't let that slip by him. The man had a rather *large* financial stake in it if he was allowed to give tours and serve champagne with firearm demonstrations. No wonder the Duke was eager to contract for the arms. As the middle man he had commissions from Cabot Roan and the ambassador for facilitating the deal, plus the profits his factory made.

Nikolay let himself fall to the back of the group in order to give his brain time to think, the pieces he'd laid out last night falling into place. The Duke was pushing for the rebellion because he made money. He let his mind stop on that fact. Amesbury was waiting for him at the door to the shooting gallery. 'Figuring it out, are you? It's supply and demand at its most basic root,' he sneered. 'I'll be able to keep Klara in all the silks and satins she wants. As my wife, she'll want for nothing. It's no wonder she chose me over you.'

'What did you threaten her with?' Nikolay growled. Even in the morning light, he couldn't come to grips with the idea Klara had left him wilfully.

Amesbury crowed. 'You poor man! You can't accept the fact that she chose my money over your cock. Women are practical creatures, Prince Baklanov. Besides, why would she ever want to hook her name to a murderer's? A man wanted for treason?' He lowered his voice. 'I know you've had her, but after a couple nights with me, she'll forget all about you. Don't worry, your secrets are safe as long as she behaves. The question is, knowing Klara as I do, will she behave? What do you think, Baklanov?'

'I think you've just declared war.' Nikolay strode past the Duke, to a vacant shooting station. It was taking a considerable amount of his self-restraint to keep his temper under control. Dear God, the man was vile. The only reason he didn't give in to rage and shoot the Duke right there was that was what the Duke wanted; Amesbury wanted him mad, wanted him to act rashly. Perhaps Amesbury even wanted him to take a shot. That would be quite the black-mail indeed: lead the revolt and we won't tell any-one you fired at a duke. Of course, Amesbury would have to dodge the bullet. That might be harder to do than Amesbury realised. He wasn't in the habit of missing.

Temper under control, Nikolay picked up the gun at his station, one of Collier's new revolvers, impres-sive and expensive. The beauty of a revolver was that it had multiple chambers and could fire multi-ple times before having to be reloaded. He'd heard of these, but had not had the privilege of firing one. He extended his arm, testing the weapon's weight and balance. The soldier who wielded this gun would have the element of speed on his side.

'These are the guns we'll give our officers,' Grig-oriev said, loading for another round. 'It will give them an advantage. I don't think the palace guard will have widespread access to such things.'

'Not yet, anyway.' Nikolay eyed the target and took careful aim at the end of his lane. 'That would be true, if the arms dealers didn't catch wind of your plans and sell to the other side.' Nothing prevented the Duke from playing the other side as well.

Grigoriev shot him a strong look. 'That would be most unfortunate indeed. That is why we do business with our friends.'

Nikolay fired his first shot, hitting near the target, impressed with the revolver's accuracy. 'You count Amesbury as your friend?'

'He is to be my son in-law.' Grigoriev's hackles were up. Nikolay relented in his interrogation. He had to proceed carefully here. Perhaps he'd planted enough seeds to make Grigoriev think.

Nikolay concentrated on shooting. He fired again and again. His fifth shot went wide for no apparent reason. He reloaded and fired. Ten shots later, he missed again. In the next round, his fourth shot went wide. Then nothing for another ten. Forty shots in all, with four going wide. Odd, considering he wasn't doing anything noticeably different and he was usually a good shot. He laid the gun down and studied the others, especially Vasilev's young officers, who should be reliable shots. They, too, missed sporadically. Not enough to comment. No one was perfect all the time and the guns were new. Any soldier could tell you that his own weapons fit him a certain way, that other weapons felt different until one grew accustomed.

Nikolay began looking at the pyramid of bullets

stacked before him, feeling the lead balls in his hand, rolling them in his palm. Most were smooth lead spheres. Every so often, there was one with a twist on the end the way one would tie off an inflated pig's bladder, as if it hadn't been clipped and sanded down. That would explain the deviation. The deformation and the added weight would skew the ball's trajectory. Nikolay pocketed two balls as the shooting wound down and Grigoriev gathered everyone into a conference room next to the gallery.

The officers talked excitedly about the new guns. They compared the flintlock-style Collier revolver to the percussion-cap revolver lately out of Paris in eager debate until Grigoriev silenced them. 'We can get the Collier revolver in mass production, although it's expensive because they're still considered new and there's not many factories producing them.' He shook his head. 'But we cannot get near enough of the percussion cap. They're too new, not widespread.' He looked at the Duke. 'How long will it take to get the arms and munitions of the scope we're talking about?'

'Four months if we push,' the Duke answered.

Nikolay watched the by-play, looking for his opening. The General was ecstatic. 'Four months and we can attack.'

Grigoriev was more reserved. 'We don't have to go the minute the guns are ready.' Other heads nodded. The group was split. It became apparent as they pored over maps and time lines in the conference room, no one knew when it would occur. It might be a year from now, or two years, or it could be in the next six months.

'Your Highness, what do you think?' Vasilev asked.

This was his chance. He marshalled his arguments. 'I think you'll need help from the south.' He was aware of Amesbury's gaze on him. 'For this to succeed, and by that I mean for the rebellion to last, we need this to be more than a palace revolt limited to St Petersburg. We've already seen how the lack of widespread coordination is the reason we can't overturn the Ottomans. Sporadic village revolts can't hold off the Ottoman Empire. We need time to get everything in place.' His best hope was in arguing for more time while sounding committed. Heads nodded and the Duke shot him a scathing look.

'Do not delay. Take the arms you have and focus on St Petersburg. It is the political hub,' Amesbury said. 'Capture its attention and the rest of the nation will follow. You have limited resources. You should focus them where they can do the most good. If you get spread out trying to do too much in too many places, you'll accomplish nothing.' *You*. Not *we*. Did Grigoriev notice? 'Specifics can be decided at a later date.' Amesbury looked at the group. 'You can't necessarily decide when the rebellion will be, but you can decide how to prepare for it. What needs to happen today is signing the contract for the Collier revolvers and the munitions.'

Vasilev nodded, his assent encouraging others,

many who were desperate for any type of progress. Nikolay was losing them. Having the guns made the chances of revolt more likely.

Nikolay spoke up. 'Is there an exclusivity clause?'

Amesbury glared across the table, doing murder with his eyes. 'There doesn't need to be. We are gentlemen. Such clauses are for businessmen who cannot be trusted to keep their word.'

'True, but this is not your factory alone, is it?' Nikolay pressed. He began to explain, looking each man in the eye to make his point. 'Perhaps your word is good, Your Grace...' he doubted it but he'd give the Duke the benefit '...but your partners may learn of this venture and seek to sell arms to the other side, to the palace guard loyal to Alexander. Our advantage would be lost. I would wager your board of directors already knows about us.'

'The board of directors must discuss everything,' the Duke answered sharply, 'otherwise we'd have no accountability between us.'

'Of course. But what about your accountability to us?' Nikolay argued, watching the impact settle on the men's faces, watching it register with them that their secrecy was shattered and had been for a while. There were men outside this room who now knew they planned a palace revolt in St Petersburg, men who could exploit that information for their financial gain.

'How many people know?' Grigoriev's jaw was tight. 'I had no idea you were not keeping this quiet.'

'The board is discreet, we don't tell anyone who

we do business with,' Amesbury began. His eyes were narrow. He was nervous.

'Except each other.' Grigoriev put in sharply.

'It hardly matters. What does matter, Your Excellency, is that you're harbouring a man wanted in his own country for treason. His own Tsar can't trust him and you are taking his word over mine.' Gazes shifted around the table, people exchanging anxious whispers. The ironclad circle of secrecy was ironclad no longer. This was how rebellions failed.

'I'm not the one making faulty bullets.' Nikolay produced the two balls from his pocket and set them on the table side by side. 'Did any of you notice the shots you missed? This would explain why. My guess is that the machines error at regular intervals. The Duke is interested in mass production and money, regardless of quality. We are putting our lives on the line with faulty products backing us up.' The table murmured, each man imagining facing down an opponent thinking they had a shot left in their chambers only to have that shot go wide and the enemy have another chance at them.

'This is ridiculous!' the Duke growled. 'You are deliberately attempting to blacken me because you are jealous. You wanted Klara for yourself.'

'What I want is for men fighting for good principles to be safe.'

Vasilev looked from him to the Duke. 'I will not encourage men to fight, knowing I cannot give them the protection of their arms.' He fixed his gaze on Grigoriev, a silent message passing between them.

Nikolay braced himself. This was it; this was when they'd decide. Vasilev spoke. 'It is my recommendation, Your Excellency, that the rebellion be set aside.'

Nikolay stood, wary of the Duke's malevolence even as elation poured through him. Perhaps some day he would be part of a rebellion, if it was about the cause as Grigoriev intended. 'Reforming Russia is worth believing in. But a rebellion that is built for the sake of generating profit, for the sake of creating war, is something I want no part of. Greed betrays men as certainly as men betray each other. Gentlemen, I think I have said enough for one day. Please consider my opinion as you see fit. If you will excuse me?'

A few minutes later, he swung up on Cossack and let the horse eat up the miles to London. He tried to focus on the victory: he had no doubts that between his and the General's appeal the revolt would be put on hold indefinitely. He'd managed to escape without committing. He'd taken his revenge on the Duke.

Those victories came with a tremendous price. He felt like the General who'd won the war but sacrificed his troops to do it. His history was not a secret any longer. He was a man in exile with charges hanging over him. If the Duke had his way, that news might be spread across the *ton* when the Season opened. He could hear the mamas whispering already. *Rumour has it he murdered the Tsar's cousin in his bedroom, but he's rich as Croesus and easy on the eyes.* Most of all, he'd lost Klara, if she'd ever been his to begin with. Stepan had been right there.

The ache he felt when he thought of her was no better this morning. The wound she'd dealt him would be a long time in healing, if ever. But he knew how to deal with pain. He'd deal with this the way he had with Helena, with losing his father, with losing his country; by looking forward, not behind. It was time to get on with his new life. He would stop at Number Four Leicester Square before he went home.

Chapter Twenty-Two

The Kubanian Prince had ruined him, in front of people that mattered. With a few sentences, the upstart Cossack had exposed him and destroyed him. Amesbury gave himself a sharp appraisal in the long glass as his valet finished brushing his coat. He still had one card left and he would play it. Desperate times called for desperate measures. After Baklanov had walked out, the munitions deal had metaphorically followed him. Vasilev had backed down from his eagerness and Grigoriev wouldn't sign on the basis of his damn principles. Grigoriev had been polite. Perhaps another time, when things were more certain. In fifteen minutes, the Prince had destroyed everything the Duke had worked two years to achieve. Did Baklanov have any idea how much money he'd cost him?

Amesbury dismissed his valet and took a pistol from his bureau drawer. He would have recompense in a pound of flesh if that was what it took. He understood it was not realistic to restore the rebellion.

But he could make Baklanov pay and Grigoriev pay where it would hurt them the most—through Klara.

From another bureau drawer he took a folded paper, the special licence he'd managed to procure yesterday. He'd been busy after the meeting. He'd gone straight to Lambeth Palace understanding that time was of the essence. Grigoriev had looked upon him in distaste yesterday, his high-minded principles taking precedence, making it clear the engagement was potentially in danger.

Amesbury weighed his assets. With the rebellion called off, there was little chance he could prove a plot and implicate Grigoriev in a treasonous scheme. Without that leverage, he had less to hang over Klara's head. She no longer had to worry about keeping her father safe. There was only Nikolay to protect now. Still, her father wanted a noble marriage for her. He had that going for him. There was no one more noble, more eligible than he. Perhaps that would be enough in the end. But why risk it? Why not turn this whirlwind marriage into an elopement? Grigoriev had already laid the grounds for that last night. They were expected to marry in haste and Society would forgive a duke anything.

He stuffed the pistol into the waistband of his trousers, the special licence into a pocket and headed downstairs to his carriage. He was prepared for all eventualities. Klara could do this the hard way or the easy way, but either way, she would be his. 'Has the note been sent to Baklanov?' he asked in low tones as a footman lowered the steps to his vehicle.

'Yes, Your Grace. He will receive it at half past two, as you said.' Amesbury smiled, pleased with his machinations. He would steal her away in the broad light of day and the Prince would know the price to mess with the Duke of Amesbury. Klara would know it, too. He would not be made a fool. When he was done with Baklanov, she would be more than happy to have the Duke of Amesbury for her husband.

'*Samogon* can't make you happy.' Stepan threw back the library curtains, flooding the room with bright light.

'It can try,' Nikolay growled, wincing. 'Damn it, shut the curtains!'

'It's been two days and you've done nothing but sign the Leicester Square deed and drink yourself into oblivion.' Stepan slouched down into the winged chair across from him. 'You'd better start talking. I assume things went poorly in Richmond?'

Nikolay managed a stare through one eye and groaned. He ran a hand over his mouth and sat up very slowly. He felt awful and smelled worse. Stepan wasn't going anywhere. He might as well get it over with. 'She's going to marry the Duke. It was announced during the last night. Out of the blue. I never saw it coming.' It hurt just to think about it. 'But in retrospect, I should have.' That hurt even worse. 'The last time we were together, she all but begged me to let her go. The whole time she was saying goodbye and I didn't understand.'

Stepan's posture became more alert. 'The last time you were together? Together how?'

'How do you think?' Nikolay pushed a hand through his hair. He was not spelling that last bit out for Stepan.

Stepan expelled a breath. 'I thought you weren't going to seduce her until we were sure?'

'I *was* sure, damn it!' Shouting hurt but not as much as the next words. 'I thought I loved her and I thought she loved me. I thought it was safe.' He cradled his head in his hands. 'I told her about Helena and Kuban, and my father.' He'd told her everything that was important to him. Would this rage never go away? Howling, drinking, riding like the devil, none of it ate up the rage. He looked at Stepan. 'Are you satisfied now? You were right.'

'No, I am not satisfied,' Stepan said sternly. 'I never wanted to be right and I never wanted to see my friend in so much pain he has to drink himself into a stupor to find peace.' He waited a moment before continuing. 'Sometimes it helps to know why. Do you have any ideas? If you were sure of her, perhaps something happened? I can't believe your instincts were entirely wrong.'

'That's the problem,' Nikolay said wryly. 'I can't believe I was wrong either. She begged me to believe her, she gave herself to me and then she left me, with no real warning. I keep searching for an answer.' The pain was starting to hurt again.

'Walk me through it,' Stepan interjected patiently.

Nikolay let all spill out; the warning at the fireworks to reject the revolt, to walk away without looking back. 'She said there was nothing there for me, and the next night in the ballroom she denounced me. Oh, not in words—how could she, up on that stage in front of everyone?—but with her eyes. They looked right at me as if I was just another face in the crowd, as if everything we'd had together was nothing. I was nothing. Then at the factory the next day, the Duke said she'd chosen his money over my— well, never mind. It was quite a crass comparison.' He still burned when he thought about those comments. 'He intimated Klara would forget all about me after a few nights in his bed.'

'The bastard needs to be shot,' Stepan mused.

'I thought about it. Munition factories make those fantasies quite plausible.' Nikolay's voice trailed off, his mind replaying that conversation with the Duke. *Don't worry, your secrets are safe as long as she behaves. The question is, knowing Klara as I do, will she behave? What do you think, Baklanov?* His eyes came up to meet Stepan's as he repeated the words slowly, meaning coming to him. He'd been angry the first time, in the throes of new rage and desperate to control that rage with rational thought. He knew the Duke had wanted to provoke him. He'd not looked further than that. Now, he saw the Duke had given himself away, given Klara away. 'The Duke knew about my situation in Kuban. He'd confronted me with it earlier, thinking to blackmail me for the revolution. If he threatened Klara with that...' Klara would have sought to protect him. His Klara, who jumped into pens with wild stallions and helpless foals to save them; his Klara, who sold her jewellery to buy a mare scheduled for slaughter. His Klara, who had risked herself to come to the stable and warn him about the house party, and who had cautioned him again. *'Don't look back, there is nothing for you here.'* Nothing except the bravest, most courageous woman he'd ever met. 'Stepan, she didn't betray me. She was trying to save me.'

Stepan nodded. 'I do believe you're right, old friend.' He smiled broadly and Nikolay felt the weight he'd carried lifted from his shoulders. Klara loved him still.

The butler entered with a note. 'Sorry to interrupt, but this just came for you, my lord.' Nikolay took the note, expecting a horse rescue or paperwork for the Leicester Square property. His elation faded as he read.

'What is it, Nik?' Stepan leaned forward to take the paper.

'It's a wedding invitation.' Dear God, not now when he'd just got her back. 'Stepan, Amesbury has her. What time is it?'

'Half past two.' Stepan rose and held out a hand to stay him. 'Nikolay, we have to think. You can't rush off without a plan.'

'I *have* a plan. It's called "Stop Amesbury".' He knew Stepan meant well, but he had only half an hour to reach Klara and that assumed Amesbury was waiting for him. It was entirely possible Amesbury had the note delivered too late and they were already underway.

'Nik!' Stepan called after him, but he didn't listen. He had a wedding to stop.

She had to stop being maudlin. She had to find a way to be happy again. She'd saved Nikolay and her father. Surely that was enough? Klara looked down at her needlepoint and her eyes blurred with tears. She was stitching St Basil's Cathedral, the multicoloured one with domes in Moscow for the receiving room at the embassy. Even her needlework reminded her of Nikolay. Everything reminded her of him. He haunted her sleep. She dreamed of his face, the way it had looked when she'd turned away from him and allowed Amesbury to kiss her, the utter grief she'd seen there. She worried for him—had he been able to extricate himself from the revolution? She hoped for him—had he returned to the city and purchased his riding school? How were the horses? Would she ever see the foal and the mare again? Oh, how she'd have loved to have seen the stallion come into his potential, and the thoroughbred. He would make an amazing addition to Nikolay's schooling string. Klara swiped at her eyes. She was missing so much. She'd not counted on this when she'd given him up.

'Miss, there's a gentleman to see you.' The butler announced. She glanced at the clock. A quarter to three. For a moment her heart thumped with the thought it could be Nikolay, then realised how foolish that would be. He would never come to her now after what she'd done. 'Send him in.' She wiped at her face, smoothed her skirts and sat on the edge of the chair, posed demurely. Footsteps sounded in the hall. She pasted on a smile and prepared for the worst. Only one gentleman would call.

'Hello, my dear Klara.'

Amesbury stood in the doorway, impeccably dressed in riding gear appropriate for an afternoon call. He bowed and offered her the flowers he carried, expensive yellow and white roses, an even dozen. Nikolay would never have brought an even number.

'In Russia, yellow flowers are often considered bad luck,' she said with crisp aloofness. 'I am sorry my father is not here to see you. He is not back from Richmond yet.'

'I didn't come to see him. I came to see you.' Amesbury grinned. Her hands were clammy where she clutched the bouquet. Who knew what he'd try if he thought they were alone? He gestured to the window. 'I brought the carriage and the greys so we could go for a drive. The weather is quite fine.'

She didn't want to go anywhere with him. But how did she refuse? She gestured to the needlepoint in her lap. 'I cannot go out. I have to finish this.'

'Come with me, Klara.' He drew back his coat to reveal the ivory butt of a pistol.

It took a moment to digest the sight of it. 'Are you threatening me?' The gun flustered her. A gun in her hand was one thing, she was quite comfortable with them. A gun in the hand of a man who'd threatened her, her father and the man she loved in order to coerce her to the altar was something else altogether—something frightening. Incredulity marked her tone as she tried to fathom the Duke's thoughts. 'You can't shoot me in my drawing room.'

'I hope not.' Amesbury's hand drummed on the pistol butt. 'If you do what you're told, there is no threat.' He shrugged. 'At any rate, the threat isn't to you directly. Surely you don't think I mean to shoot you, my bride? I might, however, shoot Prince Baklanov if we're still here when he arrives. I sent him a note. I told him to be here by three.' He withdrew the pistol and sighted it through the window. 'He must have abandoned stalking you. It's indecent, the attention he shows another man's fiancée. Don't worry, I should have a perfect shot through the window. He won't even know what hit him.' Amesbury laughed, sounding entirely unhinged. 'What am I saying, my dear? Of course he'll know what hit him. He'll figure it out before he bleeds to death on the pavement. I hope he doesn't leave a stain.'

Klara felt cold, immobile. But she had to move and she had to think. Fast. It was nearly three now. Did she stay and wait for Nikolay in the hopes he would rescue her? That she could warn him before the Duke fired? Nikolay was twenty times the warrior Amesbury would ever be, but that would be of no use if Amesbury took him by surprise. Or did she save him and leave with the Duke now? Would Nikolay come after her? Would he see through the layers of ruses, both the Duke's and hers, and conclude the truth that lay at the bottom?

'Klara,' the Duke warned, 'time is passing. I will ask you once more to get in the carriage. Do I need to cross the room for you? I assure you, it won't be as pleasant as walking over to me. I have long thought a nice hard spanking would do you a world of good.'

'All right. Let me put the flowers in some water and we'll go.' She spotted two vases and separated the flowers into bundles of white and yellow, six white in one vase, six yellow in another, and set them on the centre table where Nikolay couldn't fail to notice them.

Amesbury gloated. 'I thought you might see it that way. This way, my dear.' His hand skimmed her back as he ushered her out the door. She fought the urge to cringe at his touch as he handed her into the curricle. How amazing that a man's touch could be so different. This was nothing like being touched by Nikolay, where every touch sent tremors of pleasure through her, where every touch created *frissons* of expectation. She scanned the street for Nikolay as the Duke merged into traffic, but there was no sign. The desperate, frightened part of her knew she was going to miss him by mere minutes. The brave part of her knew relief. She had kept him safe.

They turned past the entrance to Hyde Park, eschewing the common driving area and headed towards the Thames and Parliament. 'Where are we going?'

He drew his pistol and laid it across his lap on the

driving rug. 'We are going to a little church I know on the Strand. Very quaint and very much in need of stained-glass windows.' A tremor ran through her. Why would they go there? 'You and I will be married this afternoon, and then we will take ship for a honeymoon in Paris. It will be the surprise of the Season and the Season hasn't even started. Can you imagine the parties you'll be able to host as the Duchess of Amesbury?' He smiled as if he'd bestowed a great gift. 'And the townhouse needs redecorating. You can spend whatever you need.'

Married? Had Amesbury lost his mind? 'But what about guests, and flowers?' Klara sputtered. What about all the pomp that mattered to an arrogant man like himself? He married to be seen, to make a spectacle about himself.

He flashed a cool grin. 'I find that I simply want to bind you to me more than anything.' His gaze travelled over her. 'I can hardly wait for our wedding night, when I can erase every trace of the Cossack from you and show you what an Englishman can do.

'Do you think he'll come after you?' His eyes glinted with malevolence and madness. 'He's welcome to, although I doubt he'll be successful.' His gaze went to the pistol in his lap. 'I'll shoot first and seek your forgiveness later if you do anything untoward.' He turned into a narrow street. 'Let me be clear as to what that means: it means no crying out, no protesting, no stalling with the vicar. You will say your vows without complaint and I'll let him live. But one misstep from you and I will shoot him. Do you understand? Ah, here we are, my dear.' He picked up the pistol as he jumped down. 'Stay where you are and I'll help you down.'

'Perhaps he won't come,' she challenged, sensing Amesbury hoped that he would, so that he could settle this feud once and for all. Amesbury presented her with a horrible dilemma. Hope for rescue and risk Nikolay's life? Or hope she'd been abandoned to her fate?

'He'll come, my dear. Now the question is whether or not he'll come in time? I've asked for the short version of service. Wouldn't it be delicious if he came too late for his effort to make a difference? To see us already enjoying our marital bliss, our for ever after.' Dear Lord, Amesbury *was* mad. Diabolically so. His grip on her hand was tight as he led her into the church.

'What makes you so sure?' Klara probed. Information was power and she needed all she could get. Amesbury was a showman. Perhaps if he were bereft of an audience, he'd be inclined to wait.

'I saw what you did to the flowers, my dear.' Amesbury whispered at her ear. 'Even numbers and the colour yellow. The worst sort of luck for a superstitious Russian.' Amesbury was sure Nikolay would come. So was she. That was what had her worried. How did she save both of them now?

Chapter Twenty-Three

Klara was gone. Nikolay knew it the moment he saw the flowers. He counted the buds. Twelve. Six in each vase. Even numbers. And the yellow, bad luck as well. Amesbury had taken her. The butler protested she'd left amicably enough with the Duke to drive. But he knew better. She was with the Duke, that was all that mattered. He knew, as the butler did not, that the Duke had threatened her, that this was the Duke's revenge against him for exposing his treachery. This was to be the ultimate revenge and the clock was ticking.

Nikolay began to pace, trying to keep his eyes off the clock, trying not to think about the time passing. The clock would only distract his thoughts. Klara was the perfect piece of revenge, the only tool the Duke had left. Would he want her dead or alive? He put a hand on the back of the sofa to steady himself, the thought nearly inconceivable. Klara dead, perhaps even now floating in the Thames. Or perhaps, Klara was not dead yet. Perhaps she hovered among the living yet, while life drained out of her and he dallied in her drawing room wondering. It was terrible to contemplate. Amesbury was angry enough to do it. In the Duke's mind, Klara had cuckolded him and Nikolay had shamed him, destroyed him.

What would he want in retribution for those crimes? Something more enduring than death, Nikolay thought. Amesbury would want the two of them to pay for as long as possible. He'd want a lingering retribution. Perhaps he wouldn't kill Klara immediately. Amesbury would marry her first, take her dowry as financial recompense for what he'd lost in the arms deal that hadn't happened. Amesbury could make Grigoriev suffer that way. And it was obvious how he meant to make him suffer—Nikolay gritted his teeth—by keeping Klara out of his reach through matrimony.

The marriage scenario seemed most likely. But where? There were over a hundred churches in London. He could eliminate a few. Amesbury wouldn't take her to the big places, he wouldn't be able to. It would be small and it would have to be at least moderately close. He'd want to hurry.

'Get me a map of the city and paper, something to write with,' he barked, and the butler jumped into action. Within minutes, a map had been spread out on a table, weighted down with porcelain statues of dogs. Nikolay put his finger on the Mayfair street where the ambassador lived and traced a circle around it. His mind needed to settle, to stop focusing on the improbability of finding her. He could do this. This was no different than being on campaign and scouting out where the enemy would be hiding.

He took the pen and began crossing out unlikely choices: St Martin-in-the-Fields, St George's, the Grosvenor Square chapel. They were all too well known. He needed little and desperate. The Duke would not drag her to St Giles or Whitechapel, of that he was fairly sure. The Duke wouldn't risk being mugged. Some place in between. Nicolay's finger tapped on the Strand. Not overly shabby, but certainly not uptown. He would start there. He scribbled a hasty note. 'Send this to Kuban House, give it to Stepan Shevchenko. Tell him what's happened. Tell him to bring help.' Then he was off, bolting down the front steps and swinging up on to Cossack. It would be faster to navigate a horse than a carriage through London streets, perhaps that advantage would help. He'd already lost twenty minutes. He would lose forty-five by the time he reached the Strand.

The first church he checked was empty. So was the second. A clock chimed four in the distance. Had he missed them? Had he guessed wrong? Were they even now at some other church in some other neighbourhood? London seemed suddenly immense and Klara was counting on him.

He was a street from the third church when its weathered wooden doors burst open, a well-dressed man and woman emerging—too well dressed for the Strand. The man was tugging, the woman pulling. They did not look happy.

'It's not legal until it's consummated!' The woman tugged at the man's grip on her hand and spat in his face, cursing loudly…in Russian. Then her face turned towards him as she scanned the street, looking for something, for someone. Klara!

She saw him and screamed. 'Nikolay!' But Amesbury had seen him, too. Amesbury held her bodily now, dragging her, carrying her to the curricle. He saw Amesbury dump her on to the seat and climb over her to pick up the reins and turn his team into traffic. No, he wouldn't let them get away! Nikolay urged Cossack to a quicker pace, as quick as he could manage in the crowded street. Damn it! He was losing them. They had a head start and traffic in their favour, carters with their last deliveries of the day filling up the narrow streets.

They turned and he followed, forcing Cossack to a fast trot, weaving in and out between wagons, earning a vivid vocabulary from the drivers. He was closing on them when Amesbury turned and raised the pistol, shooting into the crowd between him and the curricle. Klara screamed and Nikolay ducked reflexively. If he'd meant to scare the horse, he'd misjudged. Cossack, well trained for battle and bullets, kept going, dodging the ensuing chaos. But not every horse was as well trained. Nikolay swore, pulling Cossack hard to the right as a wagon overturned in front of him, spilling barrels everywhere. He kicked Cossack and rose up into the two-point position over the horse's neck. There was no choice but to jump them. Cossack soared, one barrel, then two, three, and they were clear.

Nikolay's blood was pounding now, as the curricle headed towards the river. This was battle and he was trained for it, if only he had some speed. There was no room to manoeuvre. Traffic boxed him in. He couldn't go around, couldn't go under. Through! He could go through it. Without hesitation, Nikolay leaped from Cossack's back to the nearest wagon. Cossack would follow as he could. Nikolay began to climb, to leap from one wagon to the next, going through and over the traffic, always making movement towards Amesbury's curricle.

He could see Klara clearly now, pale-faced and furious, fighting Amesbury for the pistol, and it drove fear into him. Didn't she know the dangers? That pistol could go off. He bit back his panic at the thought of Klara's danger. This was what he'd feared the most—being unable to save the person he loved and now that fear was playing out in front of him. All the skill in the world couldn't help him move London traffic. He pushed his worry away and focused on the task at hand. One more wagon and he'd be there. The river was on his left now, the river road narrow. He balanced himself and leapt for the curricle, landing on the tiger's seat at the back.

Amesbury whipped his head around, his pistol arm back, but Nikolay was ready for him. He grabbed Amesbury's arm, twisting until there was a sickening crack. Amesbury screamed his pain as his arm broke, the pistol clattered to the dashboard, the horses spooking into a gallop. 'Klara, the reins!' Nikolay yelled. But a quick glance told him it was useless, the reins had fallen between the traces. They were on a runaway curricle and their situation had just got infinitely more dangerous. He got an arm around Amesbury's neck in a stranglehold, dodging punches from Amesbury's good arm and trying to stay on the carriage. If he lost his hold, he'd never catch up and if Amesbury fought any harder, he'd throw Klara from the carriage. There wasn't room for all three of them.

A flash of chestnut caught his periphery. Cossack! The blessed horse, loyal to the end, was running beside the carriage. 'Klara, jump, get off the carriage! Take Cossack!' If he could get Klara to safety, he could finish off Amesbury. He saw a flurry of skirts out of the corner of his eye and knew she was safe. Relatively speaking.

'I've married her. You're too late,' Amesbury gasped as a bump in the road loosened his grip. Nikolay struggled to hold on to the racing curricle. If he fell, he'd be in the river or crushed under the wheels.

'Not if she's a widow,' Nikolay snarled, ducking swiftly. Amesbury swiped backwards with a knife from nowhere. It missed his face just barely.

'Let me go, or she'll get neither of us.' Amesbury was grunting now, worn down by the pain of his arm. 'Road's run out.' Nikolay chanced a glance ahead. The road indeed ended, in a pier-like embankment. There was nothing beyond but water. He had six hundred feet to make a decision.

* * *

He would not die for her! Klara saw the road give out into the river, dark and treacherous. A man would never kick free of the debris of wrecked carriage and horse. She'd managed to get astride Cossack and now she whipped him up with a saddle leather. Faster, faster, they had to pull alongside! Cossack had lost ground when she'd leapt.

It was risky drawing up next to the curricle as it veered on the narrow road. She risked being forced into the river or being tripped up by the wheels. A less steady horse would have not survived, but Cossack was as steady as they came. He held even.

'Nikolay! Let him go!' she screamed, panic rising at the disappearing ground. She had to be in time! The carriage veered and she gave up ground and had to try again. 'Nikolay!' She reached for him and failed, falling back. The end of the road neared. Cossack was tiring. She had one more chance. She pulled near, nearer than she'd yet dared, the curricle wheels dangerously near Cossack's hooves. If the vehicle veered now it would be disastrous. She couldn't reach out for him, she needed both hands for the reins. She gauged the distance. Five seconds and she'd have to cry off, four, three, two, at the last, Nikolay leapt. She felt Cossack's back take his weight and knew a moment's joy. Nikolay was safe. She was safe. And then the terror of watching Amesbury's body flying in the air with an eerie ragdoll likeness as the curricle crashed into the Thames. She turned away, her head buried against Nikolay's chest as Cossack came to a stop at the water's edge.

Riders passed them, led by Stepan. She heard Nikolay bark an order. 'Get the horses, they're trying to swim. Get them free!' The next few minutes were all action as the three men dived into the river, cutting horses free from harnesses. She jumped down with Nikolay, running to the water's edge to help the horses up on the muddy bank. Thank goodness for action. She didn't have to think about what had just happened and what had just about *not* happened. A second later, Nikolay would have been in the water, dead, too.

Nikolay led her away from the banks, back to Cossack. 'Are you all right?' He was wet and muddy, his hair loose, his clothes splattered as he settled his hands, strong and assuring, on her shoulders. 'Did he hurt you?'

'I'm all right now. You came. That's all that matters.' She breathed in slowly and out. She wouldn't give in to hysteria, not now when it was over and she was safe. He was safe. 'He wanted to kill you. I had to get him out of the house.' She was starting to babble.

'And you did.' Nikolay settled a kiss on her forehead. 'I never want to feel the way I did today when I discovered you were gone, or when I saw you with him, the pistol between you, or when you nearly came off the carriage.' He sighed, a deep, cleansing breath. 'But knowing you, I probably will. I'll have to get used to it.'

She melted into him then, wrapping her arms around his body, assuring herself he was whole and hers.

His arm tightened around her. 'This might not be the best time to ask, but I was wondering if you could find room in your schedule for a second wedding this week?'

'I could.' She looked up at him with a smile. 'I had something I wanted to ask you, too. I have hopes you might be looking for a riding instructor. I hear you have a new mare who might be a steeplechaser.'

He grinned. 'I do have a mare and I am looking for an instructor. Do you know any good ones?'

'I hear your wife is a pretty fair rider.'

He stole a kiss. '*My* wife. I like the sound of that.'

'Do you know what I like the sound of? For ever.' She'd almost lost him tonight. She wasn't ready to give him up again to anyone or anything. She wanted for ever to start right now.

Epilogue

They did wait. Two months, to be exact. Nikolay insisted on it, saying that when they looked back they would be glad they did it right. A man and a woman only married once. He wanted the day to be perfect and each day after. That meant there was a home to prepare and a riding school to ready. He and Klara had thrown their energies into furnishing the house and repairing the neglected stables. The horses were already there, the mare and foal thriving in their new home at Number Four Leicester Square. Tonight, Klara would join them. His pride as bridegroom demanded he not bring his bride home to a borrowed townhouse for her wedding night, but to her own house, her own bed. Their bed where, God willing, they would make a family over the years.

Nikolay drew a deep breath, trying to calm his nerves as he stood at the front of the church waiting for her, Stepan beside him, acting as his *koumbaros*, or best man, the friend who would lead him through the ceremony and into married life. His friends were all here in the front row, including Dimitri and Evie. Evie's hand rested on the belly protruding beneath her gown, her other hand holding her husband's. He'd never been as nervous before battle as he was right now staring out over the crowd gathered at London's Russian Orthodox house church of Dormition of the Mother of God and the Royal Martyrs. The place was packed with Grigoriev's connections, who were eager to get to know Grigoriev's new son-in-law. There would be time for that later. Nikolay's gaze was fixed on the tall doors in the back, his heart waiting for them to open. And then they did.

His breath caught. His throat tightened at the sight of Klara in her mother's wedding gown, Russian lace veiling her face, gliding towards him on her father's arm. These months had been emotional for her as well. Her father had not been in favour of a Russian wedding. He'd wanted St George's on Hanover Square, something English. But he had relented, coming to grips at last with his past, opening up a future where Klara was free to embrace all parts of her heritage. At the front, her father placed her hand in his and Nikolay lifted the veil to see the green eyes he loved so well already wet with tears of joy.

The priest, James Smirnov, intoned the opening and service started. Although he'd never thought the ceremony would be applied to him, Nikolay knew the stages by heart: the blessing of the rings, the candles, the crowns with their white ribbons binding he and Klara together for ever. They sipped from the chalice and circled the altar, Stepan and the priest holding the ribbons of the crowns behind them. The priest began the final benediction, 'Be thou o magnified… walk in peace…work in righteousness… *Na zisete*. May you live.'

He would live. *They* would live. Together. Every day a blessing in this new world. He bent to kiss her, his mouth hovering just above hers as he whispered his own benediction, 'Klara, I love you.' The old world had gone. Everything had become fresh and new, a world where a warrior could be saved by love, proving anything was possible. That was a world and a woman worth fighting for.

* * * * *

*If you enjoyed this story
why not explore the critically acclaimed
WALLFLOWERS TO WIVES quartet,
also by Bronwyn Scott?*

Read:

*UNBUTTONING THE INNOCENT MISS
AWAKENING THE SHY MISS
CLAIMING HIS DEFIANT MISS
MARRYING THE REBELLIOUS MISS*